MW01279787

A Daughter's Doubt

by Richard Audry

The Third Mary MacDougall Mystery

Conger Road Press
Minneapolis

A Daughter's Doubt
By Richard Audry
Copyright © 2016 D. R. Martin

The Unfortunate and Mysterious Disappearance
of Jeanette Harrison
Copyright © 2016 D. R. Martin

Published by Conger Road Press
Minneapolis, Minnesota

ISBN: 978-0-9850196-6-2

Cover design © 2016 Steve Thomas

Cover art:
"Strolling along the Seashore"
by Joaquin Sorolla, from Dover Pictura

For more information, visit drmartinbooks.com.
Contact the author at drmartin120@gmail.com.

Chapter I

Perched on a bluff above downtown Duluth, Cascade Park was awash with ladies attired in white and cream and the pastel colors of summer. Wide-brimmed hats decorated with silk flowers nodded this way and that. Gentlemen stood in clumps, talking and smoking cigars. Children dashed here and there. Off in a corner of the park, a small brass band tootled away on a medley of patriotic tunes.

Mary MacDougall walked around the freestanding stage in the center of the park for one final inspection. She had paid for it to be built. And in a few minutes it would become the focus of attention for all those who had come to enjoy the Ladies' Guild 1902 Decoration Day festivities. Glancing out into the crowd, Mary was trying to make a rough count of the gathering audience when a baritone voice interrupted her tally.

"Miss MacDougall, good morning. Lovely day for a celebration."

She turned to regard the ruggedly attractive, brown-haired, brown-eyed gentleman standing there, in his brown suit and brown fedora.

"Detective Sauer!" She beamed at him. "So nice to see

you. And it is indeed a lovely day."

Mary hadn't talked with the detective for a number of weeks, not since her last visit to police headquarters. After helping him recover a stolen sapphire six months ago, she had occasionally imposed upon him to answer her questions about the craft of detecting. He had even entrusted her with a small assignment earlier in the spring. She had sat for stretches of several hours in a restaurant, watching out the window and writing down the comings and goings from a certain address across the street.

"Are you here on business?" she asked eagerly. "Is some malefactor on the loose?"

The detective gave her a wry look. "I hate to disappoint you, but I'm not on the hunt for any villains. And this crowd," he said, nodding at several white-bearded veterans in wheelchairs, "doesn't look to be very troublesome."

"Have you been working on any interesting cases? Anything I could help with?" It was Mary's improbable dream to become a consulting detective. She didn't want to be a pest, but she was ever hopeful that the detective would have something for her.

"Nothing, I think, that requires an inquisitive young lady. How about you? Have you done any sleuthing lately?"

"None at all." She frowned. "Everyone I know is perfectly well behaved. It's all very boring. The only thing I've been working on is the construction of this new stage for the *tableaux vivants*."

"Been up there hammering and nailing, have you?"

2

Mary laughed. "My carpentry skills leave much to be desired. But I was in charge of building it and you can be quite sure that stage is solid as a rock. We wouldn't want any accidents, with all those people up there posing for our scenes."

"As a matter of fact, that's the very reason I've stopped by. I enjoy seeing the *tableaux vivants* each year. They're quite a spectacle."

The *tableaux vivants*—exact reproductions of famous historical scenes, portrayed by real people—were the highlight of the Decoration Day celebration. And this year Mary had a special interest in these living images.

"Be sure to pay particular attention to Lady Justice," she said proudly. "She's my Aunt Christena, filling in for the first Lady Justice, who took ill at the last moment."

"I will indeed do that. After all, in a sense, I work for Lady Justice, don't I?" Detective Sauer paused as a troop of jabbering school children marched by, each with a little version of Old Glory in hand. "Does your aunt live in Duluth?" he said, turning his attention back to Mary.

"No, she's visiting from Pittsburgh. She and I are heading off to Mackinac Island soon, for a few weeks at the Grand Hotel. We'll be hiking and biking and playing tennis and going to parties—all the usual stuff one does on summer holiday."

"Not the usual stuff of *my* summer holiday," the detective sniffed. "I go fishing with my brother. Our accommodations are an army tent pitched on the dirt."

Mary smiled at his reply. Over the last half year, she

had come to enjoy the detective's company and found his droll observations quite amusing.

Detective Sauer went silent for a moment, then cocked his head. "You say you're going to Mackinac Island? You'll be taking the train through the eastern part of Upper Michigan, I'd imagine."

"It cannot be avoided," Mary noted, "if one means to travel to the island."

The detective appeared to be mulling something over. Finally he spoke. "If you have some time during your journey, Miss MacDougall, I may have a lead for you on a case there."

A thrill of anticipation coursed through Mary's body. A case! What did Detective Sauer have in mind?

He started to explain. "A young lady stopped by my rooming house recently and—"

"Ladies and gentlemen, your attention, please," bellowed a rather large and formidable lady from the stage above them. "The time has arrived for the sixth edition of the Ladies' Guild Decoration Day *tableaux vivants*. Please do take your seats."

It was Mrs. Mason, president of the Ladies' Guild, who had come out and stood in front of the stage's curtain.

"Better go grab a chair," Detective Sauer said. "We can talk about the matter after the show."

Mary didn't have a chance to say another word before the detective scooted off. But her head was spinning.

A real investigation! And Detective Sauer thought she was capable enough to look into it.

She dashed off to join her father and their housekeeper, Emma Beach, in the third row of seats back from the stage. Up front, Mrs. Mason droned on about the good works being done by the Guild.

"And how is Detective Sauer?" asked John MacDougall in his mild Scotch burr. "You and he seemed to be having a lively conversation."

"Quite well," Mary whispered. "We were just exchanging pleasantries."

It wouldn't do to say anything about a potential case in Michigan. Mary's widowed father frowned upon her unorthodox aspiration to become a detective. It was simply not an appropriate choice, he had told her, for a young lady of her class. Mary knew he hoped that marriage to a sensible young businessman would be in her immediate future.

Mary, however, had no desire to see "Mrs." affixed to her name. She had no desire to cede her rights to any man, even a good and well-intentioned one. She had no desire to cloud her mind with the narcotic effects of infatuation. She wanted first and foremost to have her independence.

But then there was Edmond Roy.

Mary couldn't quite decide how to describe her association with him. The word "friendship" just seemed inadequate. But anything stronger than that carried a hint of commitment. Still, she knew her connection with Edmond was something special, and she was determined to carry it forward. But to what end? It was so hard for her to say.

From the stage, Mrs. Mason's stentorian oration crescendoed. "Now, my friends, watch as history comes alive right before your eyes."

A teenaged girl with straw-colored hair cascading down her back marched out from between the curtains, carrying a large cardboard placard. She held it up to the audience and loudly repeated the words inscribed on it.

"Abraham Lincoln and the Signing of the Emancipation Proclamation."

The girl darted back out of sight and the fancy brocade fabric began to divide. The audience erupted in *ooohs* and *aaahs* as the scene was revealed.

There, seated at a small oak desk, was a lanky, bearded gentleman in an old-fashioned black frock coat. He was the spitting image of Honest Abe. Frozen in place, he peered down at the document on his desk, a steel pen held in his hand, poised above the paper, ready to inscribe his signature. Arrayed behind him stood half a dozen men in old-fashioned coats, regarding the "president" with studied soberness. They, too, held perfectly motionless. They may as well have been caught in amber.

After about thirty seconds, the curtain trundled shut. The audience burst into exuberant applause.

"Superb!" John MacDougall exclaimed to his daughter. "How do they hold so still?"

"They've been rehearsing for weeks," Mary answered. "It's just a matter of practice and good breath control. Now it's Tena's turn."

"That girl was always one to help out in a pinch," her father said approvingly. "My very favorite sister."

"Your *only* sister," Emma Beach pointed out. It was an old and tired joke, but Mary's father enjoyed repeating it.

A terrific good sport, Christena MacDougall had agreed at the last minute to fill in for the ailing Mrs. Halliwell, who was to have portrayed Lady Justice, the Roman goddess. It was presumed that, as a sometime actress upon the amateur stage, Christena would project a vivid presence.

Several minutes later the blonde girl reappeared. She held up a new placard, and turned it around so everyone could see.

"Lady Justice," she announced, then quickly retreated.

The curtains parted again and there, center stage, stood Christena, tall and regal, in her green Roman gown and wig, with a green blindfold across her eyes. Every inch of her skin was green, as well. The effect was supposed to be that of a weathered, copper-clad statue. In her right hand she held a sword by its grip, pointed down. In her left was a scale. She seemed the very embodiment of the goddess.

Mary thought she could detect a hint of a tremor in her aunt's right arm. And who could blame Christena? That sword looked awfully heavy.

"Lady Justice," though, stood proudly and, for the most part, firmly in her half minute in the spotlight.

The curtain closed and the crowd clapped its approval.

Following Christena came Rembrandt's "Aristotle Contemplating the Bust of Homer" and "Betsy Ross Sewing the First American Flag." Both elicited much applause and robust shouts of approbation. But Mary hardly noticed

Aristotle and Mrs. Ross, her mind being on her upcoming holiday off in Michigan.

The prospect of a real case to work on en route was quite delightfully unexpected. She was dying to know the details. What was the client's problem? Was it a domestic matter? Or something to do with a business? Why would a woman in Duluth need to find out about some doings hundreds of miles to the east?

Even more exciting, the train Mary and Christena would be traveling on went right through the town of Ishpeming. And in Ishpeming, the handsome Edmond Roy was busily painting a large mural in a bank. Edmond, with whom she had corresponded since January, was expecting Mary and her aunt for a brief stay.

With any luck, Mary and Edmond would find themselves alone. And he would pull her close and kiss her again, as he had back in December. It was a memory that she had savored countless times since.

The rousing applause for Mrs. Ross and her flag brought Mary back to the here and now, just in time for the afternoon's final and most dramatic *tableau*.

The blonde girl came out front and lifted up her placard. "In honor of Decoration Day and our brave men of the Grand Army of the Republic," she announced, "we present 'The Charge of the First Minnesota Regiment at Gettysburg.'"

The crowd went silent and serious at the gravity of the event they were about to witness. The curtains parted.

When she saw the dozen or so men in blue uniforms,

arrayed in an arrowhead formation with their bayonet-tipped muskets and sabers, Mary's eyes teared up. The power of the scene was incredible.

The men's faces were dappled with gun soot, their expressions grim, their postures suggestive of headlong movement. Old Glory was held high among them.

Then it was over, almost before it began. The curtains rolled shut and the audience erupted once again in applause.

As the band struck up a Sousa march, the crowd began to disperse. John MacDougall and Emma Beach left for the big house on Superior Street, where they would be hosting a Decoration Day dinner. While Mary waited for her aunt to reappear from backstage, she scanned the crowd for Detective Sauer's distinctive brown fedora. He seemed to have vanished, but her disappointment was short-lived, as he emerged from a scrum of men at the far end of the park, making his way toward her through the now-empty folding chairs.

"I don't have much time to chat, Miss MacDougall," the detective said. "But I can tell you that the young lady has the idea her mother died in unusual circumstances when she was traveling in Upper Michigan. Personally, I don't give her suspicions much credence. I think the daughter is overwrought. She just needs someone to set her mind at rest. Someone to go ask a few tactful questions on her behalf. And I thought that perhaps you could..."

"Oh, yes!" Mary exclaimed, clapping her hands together. "I would love to help her."

"Well, don't get too excited. This is undoubtedly some innocent matter that merely requires reassuring the client. Now, if you'll drop in at headquarters Monday afternoon at, say, about two, I'll tell you what I know about the mother's death. And you can decide then whether you're interested."

"Is there any chance at all that it might have been foul play?" Mary blurted. She couldn't help herself.

The detective shot her an exasperated look.

"I get the impression that you hope so," he said. "Well, you can get that idea out of your head, Miss MacDougall. Really, now, do you think I'd send a young lady of nineteen off to investigate a possible murder?"

Chapter II

As always, Mary found the main office of Duluth's police headquarters a beehive of activity. Uniformed and plain-clothes officers bustled about, shuffling papers, consulting with one another, fetching cups of coffee and tea. In the far corner of the room, a lone drunk slumped in a holding cell, snoring loudly.

The officer at the front desk had told her that Detective Sauer was upstairs, talking to the chief, and would be down presently. Mary didn't mind waiting in the straight chair by the detective's desk. She enjoyed taking in the atmosphere of the place and watching the professionals as they went about their work.

She finally saw the detective come into the broad office from the lobby and stood to greet him. He was a robust and good-looking fellow, but unmarried and unattached, as far as she knew. Mary, on occasion, had tried to imagine the kind of woman who might be right for him, but came up empty. He was such a taciturn, self-contained person. The thought of him whispering sweet nothings into some lady's ear almost made her giggle.

"Miss MacDougall," he said, taking his chair. "Thanks

for coming."

Mary sat down again in the chair next to his desk. Judging from the detective's preoccupied expression, this was no time for chitchat.

"Detective Sauer, I've been on pins and needles all weekend, wondering about this affair over in the Upper Peninsula. Tell me all about it."

The detective swiveled his chair to face her. "My landlady had a cousin who recently died over there in a town called Dillmont, about midway between Sault St. Marie and St. Ignace—where, I imagine, you'll be catching the ferry to Mackinac. Her name was Agnes Olcott. Her daughter's name is Clara McColley, and the young lady came to visit me a week or so ago for some discreet advice. It seems she has suspicions about her mother's passing."

"And why is that?"

"I'll get to that. But first, a bit of background. Clara McColley's late father was the sole owner of Garlock & Larson Furniture. Oscar Larson."

Mary nodded in recognition. "The firm that supplies schools and businesses with desks and chairs and the like."

"The very same. As you may recall, Mr. Larson died about two years ago. Mrs. Larson, Agnes Larson, wore the widow's weeds for a while. Then she made the acquaintance of a man called Merton Olcott, who had found employment at the company she now owned. A bookkeeper and a kind of efficiency expert."

"Let me guess," Mary said, narrowing her eyes. "He was a charming, younger fellow and swept the lonely widow right off her feet."

Sauer shrugged. "Something like that. Apparently, she found a kind of solace in him and married him toward the end of 1900, five or six months after Mr. Larson's passing. It was thought unseemly at the time by her only child, as well as by people at the company. She passed the reins of management to Olcott, though she remained the sole own-er. Not an unintelligent woman, apparently, but with little interest in business."

"The daughter had no say in all this?"

"As laid out in her father's will, Clara McColley re-ceives a stipend in the amount of one hundred dollars per month. A nice sum, to be sure, but hardly a fortune. All else was the mother's."

"And why does Mrs. McColley think her mother's passing was suspicious?"

"For a start, Agnes Larson—now Agnes Olcott—was a healthy woman of about fifty. She became ill quite sudden-ly in Dillmont this April. She and her husband had stopped there to view a scenic waterfall near the town, on a belated honeymoon trip to New York."

"And what was the cause of death?"

"Cholera. The course of the disease was rapid appar-ently, and she died within a day or two. She had to be isolated in an infirmary near the town."

Mary was puzzled. "I thought that cholera wasn't all that common these days, what with modern sanitation and hygiene."

"That's as may be. But the local physician determined

it was cholera. And that is what it said on her death certificate."

"And the woman's daughter doesn't believe it?"

Sauer shook his head. "And what really rankles her is that, upon Mrs. Olcott's death, under the terms of her newest will, ownership of Garlock & Larson went to Mr. Olcott, with the stipend to his stepdaughter continuing. So after being married just a year and a half, he now owns quite a valuable business here in Duluth."

Mary sighed. "It does seem unfair. But these things do happen, you know. The lady drank tainted water or took a bite of the wrong piece of chicken. Just an accident of fate."

"True enough, Miss MacDougall. But the odd thing is, instead of bringing the body home, the new widower had his late wife buried in Dillmont."

"Now that *is* quite irregular," Mary said, raising her eyebrows. "How could he possibly justify not bringing Mrs. Olcott back?"

"He told his stepdaughter that's what the doctor recommended. He thought it best to play it safe, and to not expose others to the remains and the infective agent."

"That makes sense, I guess, though I don't know anything about cholera. But it seems to me that the daughter really hasn't made much of a case against her stepfather. What does she hope to gain by having a detective look into the matter?"

"Peace of mind, I suppose. And assurances from the doctor that everything possible was done to ease her mother's suffering."

"Then why doesn't she just go out to Dillmont herself? She might even arrange to have the casket brought home. Certainly the risk of contagion must be over by now."

"She would like to, Miss MacDougall. But she has two small children, one of them chronically ill. Her husband doesn't support such a trip. Thinks she's being overemotional. Moreover, she has no legal claim to the body. That devolves to Mr. Olcott."

Mary furrowed her brow. "All right. Then why doesn't the lady simply send a note to the police in Dillmont?"

"It would be the county sheriff," the detective corrected.

"The sheriff, then," Mary continued. "And just relay her concerns. Have him or a deputy look into the matter."

"I made the same suggestion, but she said that it wouldn't do."

"Why in the world not?"

"If her suspicions should happen to be incorrect, and Mr. Olcott is quite innocent... Well, there could be a scandal come down on Mrs. McColley's head. In that case, she's on record as accusing her stepfather of murder. She does not care to risk putting her young family through that."

The detective knitted his hands together. "She simply needs to know that her stepfather did nothing to hasten the demise of Agnes Olcott. And she wants to keep this business confidential. So I would suggest that you play the role of her friend, as you make your inquiries. I figure you'll be well up to the job."

"You figure right, Detective Sauer," Mary replied, gratified by the compliment. "*If* she hires me. Now where does Mrs. McColley live?"

Still walking on air, Mary arrived home later that afternoon after a nice long amble from downtown along Superior Street. She checked through the late post on the table in the front vestibule for an envelope from Ishpeming, but none had arrived. Back in the kitchen, she said hello to the cook, Mrs. Erdahl, and grabbed a sugar cookie from the counter. It was still warm from the oven.

"Have you seen my aunt recently?" she asked, taking a bite.

"I believe she's in the garden," the cook replied, "visiting with Signor Morelli."

Mary went out the back door and saw her aunt chatting with the MacDougalls' gardener by the lilacs—now splendidly in bloom, in their shades of purple, white, and lavender. Christena seemed to be doing most of the talking, with Signor Morelli peering up at her and nodding vigorously in agreement.

Christena MacDougall was John MacDougall's much younger sister, fourteen years his junior. The millionaire liked to joke that it was hard to say who had been more surprised by her arrival—his parents or himself. Unlike her brother, she was born in the United States, in Pittsburgh, where the MacDougalls had settled after emigrating from Scotland. The business empire that John MacDougall built from next to nothing provided his sister with a comfortable income from stock dividends. He had left Pittsburgh as a young man, but she had remained to care for their widowed mother.

Christena was tall, redheaded, and, if not exactly pretty, striking. John MacDougall had always expressed disappointment that his sister had never found the man of her dreams. But he put it down to her stubborn independent streak, not unlike his own.

Mary admired Christena's ability to make conversation anywhere, anytime, with anyone—and do so knowledgably and amiably. She had seen her aunt charm her way across Europe during their tour there in 1898, even when Christena didn't know the language. And here she was chatting with Signor Morelli like they were the oldest of friends.

Coming down the stairs onto the lawn, Mary strode toward her aunt and the gardener, passing by beds of delphiniums, phlox, coral bells, irises, and lilies, awaiting their days in the spotlight.

"I would highly commend Madame Alfred to you, Signor," Christena was saying, as Mary joined them. "One of my favorite roses. It's classed as a Noisette, but the full blooms are more of a Bourbon or hybrid tea in shape. They're very fragrant, you know, and the color goes from the palest pink to a creamy white."

"A fantastic idea, Miss MacDougall." The gardener, a stubby little man with a fiercely waxed black mustache, turned and smiled at Mary. "Now your niece only needs to persuade Mrs. Beach to allow me to order them. If you don't mind, I will excuse myself and get back to work."

The two women watched him march back to his shed, then faced each other.

"Well, how did it go?" asked Christena.

Mary had taken her aunt into her confidence about the possible case, and they had agreed to keep it strictly between the two of them. There was no reason to bother John MacDougall with it just yet.

Mary quickly related the details, most notably that Clara McColley suspected her stepfather may have had a hand in her mother's death.

"Detective Sauer is convinced otherwise. He believes Mrs. McColley is simply overwrought, letting her deep dislike of her stepfather cloud her good judgment. But he thinks it would be a simple enough matter for me to visit Dillmont and ask a few questions. To put the daughter's doubts to rest."

"You could pretend to be Mrs. McColley's friend. Come to pay your respects."

"That's exactly what the detective suggested. And he said he was sure I was up to the job."

Mary studied the profusions of lilacs for a moment, then frowned. "Now all I have to do is convince Clara McColley that I am."

Chapter III

Clara McColley's expression on Tuesday morning, when she answered the door of her little house on East Second Street, was at first one of relief, then puzzlement.

"You're not the new visiting nurse, are you?"

Mary attempted to answer, but Mr. Olcott's stepdaughter kept talking.

"You're a bit too young. And you have no medical kit. And your jacket and skirt are…"

"Are what?" Mary asked.

In the house, a baby started to mewl. The young mother looked back for a few seconds, then focused her attention on Mary again.

"Well, I've never seen a nurse come in something so stylish. Nurses tend to wear brown and gray things a baby can spit up on. Or uniforms. I wouldn't think you'd want to soil that lovely jacket."

Mary smiled at the woman's astute assessment. "You're very perceptive, Mrs. McColley. I'm no nurse. My name is Miss Mary MacDougall and I'm a detective."

The woman's eyes widened with surprise. "You? A detective?"

Just then, the baby's wails grew louder.

"Would you excuse me, miss?"

And without another word, Clara McColley retreated back into the house. When she reappeared, it was with a pink-faced infant in her arms. The child looked to be six or seven months old. It had stopped fussing and appeared to be sleeping.

Clara McColley was a comely woman, with her ebony hair and light brown eyes. But Mary wondered about the circles beneath those pretty eyes. Were they because of her young child's illness? Or due to despondency over her mother's fate?

"Mrs. McColley, I do apologize for arriving unannounced," Mary began, anxious to get to the point. "But Detective Robert Sauer thought that I might be able to help you. I'll be visiting Upper Michigan, you see, and will be near Dillmont, where, as I was told, your mother passed away. I am eager to make inquiries on your behalf."

Far from wearing the expression of happiness and relief that Mary expected, the woman looked baffled.

"I don't mean any offense, miss," she said, "but I was hoping Mr. Sauer had found some gentleman detective whom I might be able to afford. I wasn't expecting a young lady. Why, you look like you're just fresh from high school."

For a few seconds, Mary *was* offended. Then she realized that she might have had the same reaction in Mrs. McColley's place. She imagined what she must sound like to this grieving woman. *You say you suspect your stepfather of being a nefarious no-good, ma'am? Well, I'm a teenaged girl and I'm here to help.*

"I know that I may not look the part," Mary said, "but I do have *some* experience in rooting out villains. And my rates are very reasonable." She actually had no idea what she should charge. "May we at least talk a bit about your mother and stepfather? If you decide I can't be of assistance, well…"

Clara McColley pursed her lips, then nodded.

"Yes, of course. A cordial young lady comes to call and I treat her like a bothersome door-to-door salesman. That won't do, will it? Please come in."

She ushered Mary into the tidy living room, holding the sleeping infant in her arms. The furniture was quite handsome, if severe. Chairs and tables that looked as if they belonged in a school—which, in fact, they probably did. But why shouldn't the daughter of a furniture maker have some of her father's wares? There was, though, a green brocade davenport that looked quite plush and comfortable. Mary sat there.

"Might I offer you some tea or coffee?" Mrs. McColley asked.

"A cup of tea would be nice."

"Do you mind?" The young mother handed her infant to Mary. "I don't think there's any danger to your jacket."

Enough babies had been thrust at Mary over the years so that she was not taken aback. In fact, this one was rather sweet, as she, or he, slept peacefully. But Mary gladly handed the little creature back to its mother a moment later.

"May I speak frankly, Miss MacDougall?" asked Clara McColley, sitting next to her and gently rocking the infant.

"Please."

"I mean no disrespect, but you seem rather an unusual person to be a detective. Can you tell me about your experience?"

Mary was tempted to embellish her achievements, but she decided against it. Best to keep it simple and factual.

"I've worked on two cases, both with satisfactory results."

"What kind of cases?"

"In my first, I helped to spare an innocent man from jail, while identifying the members of a kidnapping gang. They were all apprehended, tried, and convicted."

"My heavens!"

"In my second, I helped to recover a rather valuable object. Sadly, the thief died while attempting to flee the police. Without my timely insight, though, the item might never have been recovered."

By then, the teakettle began to whistle and Mrs. McColley excused herself, handing the baby over again. She returned a few minutes later with a strongly brewed cup of tea for Mary.

"I've thought it over, " she said. "I trust Mr. Sauer's judgment, and if he sent you here, that's good enough for me. Now let me tell you what I think happened."

Mary nodded in return, her heart beginning to race. *This is how it begins*, she thought. *This is the best feeling in the world.*

"Miss MacDougall, I believe… No, I am quite sure that Merton Olcott murdered my mother. He poisoned her."

Mary was shocked at the certainty of the accusation. Clara McColley *really* believed it. Her words almost brought a chill into the room.

"Please tell me what you know," Mary said evenly, trying to tamp down the excitement she was feeling. "And tell me what you suspect."

Clara McColley recounted how, after her father's sudden death, her mother was not only desolated, but thrown into a deep depression. An ordinary widow might have had the time to mend and pull herself together.

But the Garlock & Larson Furniture Company, which she now owned, was in the midst of fulfilling several large contracts that would have challenged even the late Mr. Larson. His widowed wife sat stone quiet in meetings, only to burst into tears when she was pressed for comment or decision. The company manager, Jack Tilson, a good man, kept things together. But certain documents needed Agnes Larson's signature, and she was frozen.

"I urged her to give Jack leave to run things while she recovered," Mrs. McColley recalled. "But she would never respond. The bank, well aware of the situation, became reluctant to provide the customary operating loans. Then something of a miracle occurred. The recently hired bookkeeper took Mother aside, and *him* she responded to. He and Jack Tilson together walked her through the things that needed doing, and the crisis was averted."

"The bookkeeper was Merton Olcott?"

Clara McColley nodded. "At first, after the hard months of Mother's depression, it was wonderful to see her come back to life. For many women, right or wrong, a man gives them meaning. Merton, my stepfather, is handsome, confident, charming, and a good ten years younger than Mother. I can understand how having an admirer like him might turn one's head. He certainly turned Mother's. None of us, though, expected them to visit a justice of the peace and get married—less than half a year after my father died."

"A bit unseemly, perhaps," Mary agreed. "But not unheard of. I presume she gave over management of the company to your stepfather."

"Yes, and I suppose that's to be expected. But I was surprised when Mother allowed Merton to dismiss Jack Tilson. Jack was as loyal and capable as they come, Papa's right-hand man."

"Not a good sign," Mary noted darkly.

"Indeed. Then Merton quickly began to cut corners at the factory. I have this on good authority from men I've known since I was a child. He started to use cheaper grades of wood. He let people go—real craftsmen who had worked for Papa for decades. Garlock & Larson, for the first time ever, has been overdue on payments it owes. Furniture has been returned for defects. That never happened before. I tell you, Miss MacDougall, Merton Olcott is slowly starving the company. And there are rumors he may even be trying to sell it."

"But surely you spoke to your mother about what was happening."

Clara McColley's face showed deep frustration. "Of course I did. She simply tut-tutted me. 'Merton is an expert in efficiency,' she said. 'Merton knows what he's doing.'"

She stood and went over to a crib in the corner of the living room. She gently laid her sleeping baby in it.

"Poor little Agnes has been colicky for months," she said, coming back to the sofa.

So, it's a little girl, Mary thought. How sad that she'll grow up without knowing the grandmother she was named after.

"Doctor Burns says the baby's problems could be my fault. My distress might be affecting my milk, and causing pain for the little one."

Poor woman. It was bad enough to lose her mother. But to feel guilt about her infant was just too much.

"I'm sure that's not the case," Mary said reassuringly. "But all the more reason to uncover the facts and put your worries to rest. Tell me, what leads you to believe your stepfather poisoned your mother?"

Clara McColley looked distraught. "In the end, I suppose it's because I despise the man and don't believe a thing he says." Then her back stiffened and her expression turned resolute. "I realize, Miss MacDougall, that anyone can catch an illness such as cholera, given bad luck. But once infected, many sufferers do pull through. And I cannot believe that Mother couldn't."

At that, the woman rose and disappeared down the

hallway, returning a moment later with a framed picture. She handed it to Mary. The photograph showed Clara McColley and her older child with what must have been her father and mother.

"Just look at her. She was strong and stout and healthy, apart from her depression after Papa passed. If anyone could have survived a bout of cholera, it would have been Mother. That's why I believe that her death was due to some kind of foul play. I think it's no coincidence that the tragedy occurred only a month after she wrote up that new will, giving everything to Merton."

Mary was as keen as anyone to uncover a nice, juicy conspiracy. But what she heard here was a woman grasping at straws, searching for some reason to not believe that her mother had fallen prey to very bad luck.

"But would it be possible to poison your mother," she asked, "and produce symptoms that could be mistaken for cholera?"

"I have no idea," Clara McColley said dejectedly. "I asked Dr. Burns, when I took my little boy to him some weeks ago, and he said he didn't think so. But if I could only talk to the physician in Dillmont, who cared for Mother. He might be able to provide the details that would reveal a poison. Perhaps he could even be persuaded to perform an autopsy."

"Do you know the name of the doctor?"

"That's about all I do know. Merton showed me the death certificate. It was signed by a physician called Applegate and it said Mother died at the Westerholm infirmary in Dillmont."

"I heard," Mary said, "that your stepfather did not bring your mother home for burial."

"Yes, supposedly because of concerns about the infectiousness of the germ." The young woman sniffed. "Well, Dr. Burns tells me that deceased cholera victims can be transported, if precautions are taken. Since then Merton has changed his mind. He says he'll have her brought home later this summer. But I don't believe him. It wouldn't surprise me if he has sold the company and left town by then." She shook her head. "Miss MacDougall, I simply do not trust the man. I want to find out the true facts of my mother's death."

"Of course," Mary said. "That's entirely reasonable."

"I would have gone myself, but as you can see, I've got my hands full." Mrs. McColley nodded in the direction of the crib. "We have a four-year-old boy, as well, and he's sickly. And I can't afford much."

For a brief instant, Mary thought the woman might burst into tears. But then she appeared to pull herself together.

"My husband thinks I'm being a typical hysterical female. He says I just ought to accept that Mother is gone and be done with it." She gave a long, deep sigh. "It's two months since she passed and I miss her so much. We were such good friends."

Mary reached over and patted her hand. "I know what it's like to miss your mother."

Clara McColley looked her in the eye. "If you could go

to Dillmont and make inquiries about my mother's death, maybe I'll be able to get on with my life. All I want is to hear that it really was the cholera that took Mother. Then Merton Olcott can run my father's company into the ground, to his heart's content. Sell it. I don't care."

Mary was about to speak, when Mrs. McColley put up her hand. "But may I ask what your fee is?"

Mary panicked for a second, then pulled a figure from her head. She wanted to be cheap enough so Clara McColley could afford her, but not so cheap that she might look like an amateur. "Does five dollars a day sound practicable? Perhaps for two or three days?"

Mrs. McColley thought a second, then nodded. "Yes, it does, Miss MacDougall. Consider yourself hired."

The two women shook hands, and that was that.

Out on the sidewalk Mary almost jumped for joy. As of this moment, she finally was a professional detective!

Chapter IV

Mary's head was spinning.

In just a week, she and Christena would be leaving for their holiday on Mackinac Island. Now that she had been hired to do her first real investigation, it was imperative that she devise a plan of action for her limited time in Dillmont. Thinking it over, she realized that, despite all her reading and questioning of Detective Sauer, she wasn't nearly prepared to do what the case required.

She had already walked a block east of the McColley house, heading for home, when she decided that home wasn't where she needed to go. She turned around and made for downtown. Her first stop was Gustafsson's Café on Second Street, for a quick lunch of chicken salad and coffee.

At a little table in the far corner of the bustling restaurant, Mary reflected on everything that had happened in the last year. She had solved two cases, including the one that freed Edmond Roy from jail and brought him into her life. Mary was absolutely certain that she had the innate talent, the intuition, the doggedness needed to untangle the gnarly knots of mysteries large and small. But she still lacked skills. She lacked knowledge and experience. In the last six months, she had been trying to rectify that deficit.

She had obtained a Smith & Wesson Model 10 revolver for her purse. Joe Morrison, the caretaker at the MacDougalls' lake cabin up the shore of Lake Superior, had taught her and her brother Jim how to shoot rifles and pistols during summer holidays. So Mary felt quite comfortable with the weapon, though she had never yet shot at a living thing.

She had informally taken up the study of crime detection with Detective Sauer. Many men in his position would have brushed off Mary MacDougall. But he patiently answered her questions and suggested material she ought to read.

Mary had also found another mentor. She had heard about a Chinese woman who owned a laundry down on Michigan Avenue, in the Bowery. Mrs. Chin was known to teach ladies, quite discreetly, how to defend themselves by means of an ancient method of hand fighting called Fujian White Crane. After a number of weekly lessons—and bruises here and there that no one, fortunately, could see—Mary was finally getting an inkling of how it worked. She had gained enough confidence to believe that she might be able to physically discourage any unfriendly advances, should the situation arise.

It had been hard, at first. Getting the postures right. Understanding when to kick and when to snap the fists and when to block. Mrs. Chin, even after months of tutoring, made it very clear that Mary was only a raw beginner, and that mastery of Fujian White Crane would take a lifetime. But Mary thought the technique perfect for herself. After all, the legend of White Crane said that a woman had invented it back in the mists of history.

Still, Mrs. Chin had warned, "Do not try to stand, fight big man. Hurt him, surprise him. Then *run*."

Mary had also spent many an hour volunteering in Dr. Burns's office, where Mrs. McColley had taken her colicky baby. Mary helped at the front desk, and learned a bit about anatomy and medicine on the side—feeling it would be useful knowledge for her career in detection. But she volunteered there as much to be with Dr. Burns's daughter Lillian as to further her understanding of the human body and all its frailties. Lillian, her best friend, was heading off to college in the fall and Mary already felt sad that their years of constant companionship would soon just be golden memories.

After finishing her lunch, Mary strode downhill to First Street and walked two blocks west to Salter's Saloon—well loved by working men for its cheap beer and generous sandwiches. Detective Sauer usually took his lunch there.

Who better to help her hone her strategy than the very capable police officer? Surely he would not mind her stopping by to ask a few more questions.

Mary entered Salter's through a fog of cigar smoke and noisy conversation. She wended her way past a group of men standing near the bar, collecting a few surprised looks. The only other women in the place were three harried waitresses scurrying about with plates of food and glasses of beer. Mary knew she stuck out like a sore thumb.

But she was in luck.

At a table off to the side of the bar sat Detective Sauer, reading a newspaper. He was just about to finish his last bite of pie when she plopped down in the chair across from him. The expression on his face as he held his fork in midair was one of only mild annoyance. Mary took this as a good sign.

He put the fork down. "Miss MacDougall. I suppose you just happened to be passing by."

She smiled brightly. "Right you are, Detective Sauer. And I wondered if I might trouble you for a few moments. You see," she continued, not giving him a chance to reply, "I'm leaving for Michigan in a few days and I wanted just a little more idea of what I should do there. By way of investigation, that is."

"So you've reached an arrangement with Mrs. McColley?"

"I have. I agreed to spend a couple of days in Dillmont, where her mother died."

The detective's piercing eyes glanced around the room behind Mary, and she realized her appearance had made their table a focus of attention. Detective Sauer might be in for some ribbing later on. She felt sorry putting him on the spot, but it simply could not be helped. She wanted his advice on how to approach the Olcott inquiry, and she wanted it now.

The detective folded up his newspaper and leaned back in his chair. "I suggest, to begin, that before you leave, you find some pretext for meeting Mr. Olcott and letting him know you plan to visit his wife's grave."

Mary was surprised. "Why take that risk?"

"Because you want to see how he reacts," the detective answered. "Make up a story about how you happen to know his stepdaughter."

"She goes to the doctor's office where I volunteer," Mary said. "I could say I know her from there."

"That's good, that'll work. He'll never suspect a thing. You're simply doing his stepdaughter a kindness. Meanwhile, watch his face, his movements. Look for nervousness, dissembling, any other signs of dishonesty. Doesn't prove anything, of course. But if Olcott did play a role in his wife's death, you might detect some uneasiness in his demeanor. Sizing up potential suspects is part of the job. A good detective must develop that skill.

"Once you get to Dillmont, it should be simple. Mostly, you just need to visit the physician who treated the woman. Was there any chance at all that she was poisoned? Is there an agent that could mimic the symptoms of cholera? If you come up with anything suspicious—anything that can be backed up—you could go to the county sheriff. That's apt to be a bit tricky, though."

Mary looked up from the little notebook she was scribbling in. "Why is that?"

"Miss MacDougall, if you were a lawman in his thirties or forties, how would you regard an eighteen-year-old…"

"*Nineteen*-year-old," Mary corrected.

"…nineteen-year-old young lady who comes to you with wild claims of dark doings in Dillmont?"

"Ah, I see." Mary understood perfectly.

"I've observed you in action and know you have some talent in this area. But to that fellow out in Michigan, you're just a pushy, presumptuous girl. Even worse, a pushy, presumptuous *rich* girl."

That stung Mary a little, but she took his point.

"My advice is to be as quick about it as you can in Dillmont. It's not your job to right any wrongs. Uncover the facts as best you're able, then write up your findings for Mrs. McColley."

Mary nodded. Detective Sauer was right. She wasn't a police officer. Her job was to investigate and report.

"I'm still quite sure there's no crime here," the detective continued. "So you shouldn't encounter any difficulty." Then he leveled that intense gaze at her. "You *have* told your father that you're doing this, haven't you?"

Truth be told, Mary had decided to not tell John MacDougall until the case was concluded. He was in the midst of an important business negotiation, and she didn't want to bother him. Christena had concurred, since the simplicity and safety of the inquiry seemed beyond doubt. Mary understood, of course, that there would be hell to pay, should she get hurt or become the subject of notoriety. But she was positive that nothing like that would happen.

She managed to meet the policeman's gaze without flinching.

"Detective Sauer, can you imagine the trouble I would be in if I didn't tell him?"

Chapter V

The cramped lobby of the Garlock & Larson Furniture Company smelled of varnish and sawdust when Mary and Christena entered it the following day. From the factory floor came the screeching sound of machinery sawing through wood. A workman in denim overalls directed them through a door to the left, behind which was a small suite of offices. They thanked him and went in.

"We're here to see Mr. Olcott," Mary told the dour-looking secretary whose desk blocked any further advance. "I telephoned this morning."

From behind her typewriter, the unsmiling woman inspected Mary through her small, gold-rimmed spectacles. "You're Miss MacDougall?"

"Both of us are, actually. But I am the Miss MacDougall who made the appointment. My aunt just happens to have accompanied me this afternoon."

The secretary stood up. She wore a severe black dress and was as thin as a rail. She had the manner of a person whose entire diet consisted of lemons and vinegar. "Just a moment, please," she said, opening the windowed door to a private office and speaking a few words. She turned back to Mary and Christena. "Mr. Olcott will see you now."

As they walked into the private office, a tall, handsome man came around from behind a well-made oak desk, a product, no doubt, of Garlock & Larson. He was wearing a gray suit with a blue patterned tie. His thick, dark-blond hair was parted decisively in the middle. Around his left arm he had a black band of mourning.

"Miss MacDougall," he said offering his hand. "I'm Merton Olcott. So pleased to meet you."

"Thank you for seeing us," Mary said, shaking his hand.

"Are you any relation to John MacDougall?"

Mary nodded. "Yes. He's my father."

"I've been an admirer of his for some years," Olcott said unctuously. "And this lovely lady must be your aunt."

"Indeed," said the older woman. "Miss Christena Mac-Dougall. John's sister."

Mary thought she detected a glint of interest in Olcott's eyes when her aunt's unmarried status was made known to him.

"Please, make yourselves comfortable." The man gestured to two oak office chairs before his desk. Then he sat back down, tenting his fingers beneath his chin. "Mr. MacDougall wouldn't be interested in buying a furniture company, would he?"

Mary was surprised at his boldness. The rumor Clara McColley had cited—that Olcott wanted to sell the company—appeared to be true.

"I'm sure it's a very fine firm," Christena answered

with a charming smile. "We'll mention your proposal to my brother."

"Thank you so much," Olcott said. "Now, my secretary told me about your phone call this morning. You are generously donating new chairs and desks for the several classrooms at your church. For Sunday school. Is that right?"

Mary nodded. "Correct, Mr. Olcott. There's such a mongrel mix of battered old things in the classrooms now, it's a miracle some of them don't collapse under the children. I would want thirty new chairs in three different sizes. Also, little desks to match. What would be the most economical wood for them?"

"Nothing is sturdier than oak." Olcott rapped his knuckles on his own desk. "Maple's cheaper, but I'd go for oak. It'll take more punishment. And the wee little mites do batter the things in the classroom, don't they?"

Christena laughed, tilting her head coquettishly. "I taught third grade for a few years in Pittsburgh, and I quite agree. But I'm sure your chairs and tables will stand up to the punishment."

"Oh, you can be assured that they will," Olcott boasted, hooking his thumbs into his vest pockets. "They will indeed."

Mary could see how Clara McColley's mother, a lonely widow, might find someone like Merton Olcott attractive. His face was nicely formed, if a little fleshy in the cheeks and beneath the chin. He had a ready smile and a pleasant laugh. His voice had the deep and honeyed tone of an actor. But those pale gray eyes could not disguise a certain cold calculation behind them, she thought.

Nor could they disguise his obvious fascination with Christena.

As Olcott and Mary spoke, his eyes continually darted to the left, where the older woman sat. Christena seemed to be purposely playing the flirt, and he appeared to have found her rather appealing. He wouldn't have minded, Mary suspected, a chance to court the wealthy old maid.

"May I show you our catalog?" Olcott asked. "We have several different styles of classroom furniture on offer."

Mary and Christena spent the next few minutes looking through catalog pages at etchings of school desks and chairs. Consulting with her aunt, Mary picked a style that she liked and asked Olcott for a written bid.

"I plan to talk to a couple of other manufacturers, as well," she explained. And she did intend to, after the trip to Mackinac. Loch Lomond Presbyterian Church's Sunday school chairs and desks actually were in need of replacement, and Mary would fund the purchase herself. It had already been arranged with Reverend Fraser.

The man's face betrayed no disappointment. "Of course. I understand perfectly. I am confident that I can earn your business with a very reasonable price. And," he added in an obsequious tone, "may I say how fine a thing it is you're doing for the little lads and lasses."

"Well, when one has the means to do good, one ought to, don't you think?" Mary shot him a fawning smile.

Olcott bowed his head in agreement. "Oh, indeed. Good deeds come 'round back to us, don't they?"

"I think so, too," Mary said. "Don't you, Tena?"

"Oh, absolutely," Christena agreed. "The Orientals call it karma. You are ultimately rewarded by your own good deeds. Or punished by the evil you've done. The world will give you what you have given the world."

Mary thought she saw a little flinch in Olcott's left eye, as if he had felt a small sting of something. Guilt perhaps? Of course, it may merely have been a nervous tic.

She leaned forward in her chair, and rested her clasped hands on his desk. "Mr. Olcott, there is another good deed that I wish to perform," she said with studied gravity. "But I want to make sure that you approve."

Olcott looked a bit at sea. "I'm not certain what you mean, Miss MacDougall."

"I am acquainted with your stepdaughter, Clara McColley…"

Mary spied another twitch of the eye.

"…through my volunteer work at Dr. Burns's practice. She and her children are patients there. And I heard about her mother's tragic death from cholera." Mary summoned up her best mournful look. "Please accept my sympathy for your loss."

The man's features turned melancholy and seemed quite sincere. "Much appreciated, Miss MacDougall," he said, casting his eyes down. "It was a dreadful thing, a dreadful thing. I miss my wife terribly." He looked back up at her and Mary could actually see a bit of moisture in his eyes. "It broke my heart that I was not able to kiss her one last time. But the doctor forbade it."

If the man was lying, Mary thought, he was putting on an excellent performance. That last comment almost brought a tear to *her* eye.

"How horrible for you. And for your stepdaughter. Mrs. McColley told me that as much as she wished to visit her mother's plot, she was unable to do so with two small children to care for."

The widower nodded solemnly. "Yes, Clara is quite upset about her mother's passing. But what involvement, may I ask, could you have in the matter?"

"As it turns out, Christena and I are soon to travel to Mackinac Island for a nice holiday. And as the town of Dillmont is right along the way, I thought to bring some flowers to the late Mrs. Olcott's grave, on behalf of her daughter. Do I have your permission?"

Mary had hoped to see a reaction on the man's face that signified an emotion of some kind—fear, anger, annoyance, gratitude, sadness—anything that might provide a clue. But his expression was blank. Nothing at all. That, in itself, seemed notable.

"You don't need my permission, Miss MacDougall," he replied with a shrug. "Anyone may visit the cemetery in Dillmont. It's a kindly thing you're proposing, if quite unnecessary."

"What do you mean, 'quite unnecessary'?" Mary asked.

"On the doctor's recommendation, I had my late wife

interred in Dillmont to spare any danger to those who might handle the coffin on its journey to Duluth, not to mention possible danger to loved ones here. But since it is so important to Clara to be able to visit her mother, I'm having the casket disinterred and brought here in the near future. With proper precautions, I am told, it should be safe. I had planned to replace the wooden cross with a permanent monument in Dillmont, but now there's no need."

"Ah then," Mary said, "perhaps we can forgo the visit, after all."

He gave her a warm smile. "Quite so. You can forge on straight to Mackinac. I've heard it's a lovely spot for a holiday."

Mary and Christena thanked him and made their way out of the office and back onto Grand Avenue. "So, what do you think of Merton Olcott?" Mary asked, as the two women stood before the three-story brick furniture factory.

Her aunt ruminated over the question. "He has charm aplenty, in the superficial way that businessmen do. But he kept shooting me the eye."

"Not that you discouraged him."

"So you noticed." Chistena looked rather pleased with herself. "I was trying to take the measure of the man, make him relax. And it worked quite well, I must say. But flirting with a middle-aged woman doesn't necessarily mean he's a wife murderer, now does it?"

Mary still had much to do before their departure for Mackinac the following Tuesday.

Thursday was entirely taken up helping Lillian Burns at her father's clinic. There was filing to be done and letters to be typed. And Dr. Burns found a few minutes to talk to Mary about cholera and its terrible effects, though he was puzzled by her interest in the disease.

"It often begins with diarrhea and vomiting," he explained. "Dangerous dehydration may occur literally within hours of onset. The patient needs to drink quite a lot and must be isolated, for the disease is highly communicable through the emissions. That's why sanitary practices on the part of the physician and nurses have to be absolutely up to snuff. A person with cholera will find himself on a dreadfully arduous road. Dying of it is not a serene thing. In my opinion, hydration is the key to survival."

"How do you handle and transport the dead victim?" Mary asked, a bit concerned at posing such a peculiar question.

But Dr. Burns answered matter-of-factly. "Sometimes folks go to extremes, and cremate the remains immediately. Certainly, one must be masked and gloved and take care that no secretions are spread from the body. But I believe, with great care and rigorous method, the victim can be handled and moved. It would be up to the medical man in charge, I would say."

Mary left the doctor's office feeling a little queasy. Cholera was nothing she ever wanted to encounter firsthand.

On Friday she went to pick up the bicycling outfit that Zoya Kuznetsov, her seamstress, had made her—with its very practical short, divided skirt. Mary planned to make good use of it, cycling the paths around Mackinac Island. She already had a trio of lovely new evening dresses created by Madame Zoya for the trip.

When she arrived back home, Mary saw the afternoon mail sitting in a pile on the side table in the vestibule. As she did every day but Sunday, she started to riffle through the various envelopes.

"Nothing from Ishpeming today."

Mary nearly jumped out of her skin. Emma Beach had glided up by behind her. It wasn't the first time the housekeeper had teased her about Edmond. Of course, the woman knew every blessed thing that went on in the house, including what came in the mail. And it didn't take much to figure out who might be sending Mary missives from Ishpeming. It annoyed Mary to have it jested about. But Emma was more than a mere housekeeper. After Alice MacDougall had died, she became something like a second mother both to Mary and her brother Jim. And Mary loved her dearly, no matter what.

It became even clearer at dinner the following Monday that Mary's correspondence with Edmond Roy had become an item of interest in the household.

"So," John MacDougall said, piling mashed potatoes next to his roast beef, "are you two excited about your holiday?"

"Oh, Johnny," Christena said, "it's going to be just

splendid. I wish you'd take a week off and join us." She gave Mary a sly, quick wink.

Mary smiled back, knowing that her father would no more take a weeklong holiday than swear an oath of poverty and give up all earthly wealth.

But despite his millions, John MacDougall was a down-to-earth businessman who had no time for the airs and pretensions of some of his peers off in New York and Boston. No one would guess his wealth by looking at him or talking with him. Though he lived in a fine big house on Superior Street, he had no valet or butler, and only a small domestic staff. He had no particular ostentations. He was a simple, practical Midwesterner who just happened to enjoy making money.

Mary's father wrinkled his nose at his sister's suggestion. "Can't imagine there's enough to do on the island to keep a fellow from dying of boredom. Sheer torture."

"So terribly tedious," Mary put in. "You'd have to golf. Go fishing. Go sailing. Read good books. Go sightseeing. Meet new people. Eat three wonderful meals every day." She gave her father a pitying look. "You'd *hate* it. It would be just too arduous and awful."

"And I hear," her father continued, ignoring her tease, "that Ishpeming is particularly pleasant this time of year, too."

The subject of Edmond Roy was a touchy one for Mary, when it came to her father. She knew he thought she had become infatuated with an unsuitable man. And she had to agree that he was right—about the infatuation. But since Mary had no intention of marrying anyone—neither a struggling artist nor a young businessman—she felt her father should have no worries on her behalf. And thankfully, he had not forbidden her absolutely from contacting Edmond. This was a great relief, but she understood all too well that she needed to tread carefully.

"You know, Father, that we're only stopping there to see Mr. Roy's bank mural," she said evenly. "If I'm to be his... Patroness..."

John MacDougall's thick eyebrows shot up. "Oh, a *patroness* are you?"

"Well, I did get him that lucrative commission from Mrs. Ensign." Edmond was, in fact, scheduled to come to Duluth at the end of July to begin on portraits of the wealthy old lady and her granddaughter.

"I trust 'patroness' is all you're planning to be," John MacDougall grumbled.

Mary tried to look outraged. "I'm sure I have no idea what you're talking about, Father."

"I shall watch her like a hawk, Johnny," said Christena, making a crisp salute. "There will be no mischief in Ishpeming while I'm on duty."

A younger, less mature Mary might have sputtered some retort and stomped out of the dining room. But this older, wiser Mary bore up and presented a composed expression. She would not allow herself to be flustered.

"So, Father," she said sweetly, "how in the world are you and Emma going to get along without me for *three* whole weeks? Whatever will you two have to fuss about?"

Chapter VI

As they crossed over the water into Wisconsin, Mary took in the panoramic view of the docks and towering grain elevators on St. Louis Bay. She and Christena were riding in the observation car of the Duluth South Shore and Atlantic 7:50 to Ashland, Marquette, and points east, and had just come onto the Soo Line bridge across the bay.

Mary always enjoyed the beginning of a journey—however brief or long the trip. It held so much potential. New things to be seen and experienced. People to meet. Food to be eaten and savored. But this particular journey might well prove to be the most exciting ever for the neophyte detective. Not only did it promise a much-anticipated reunion with Edmond Roy and a busy stay on Mackinac Island with Christena, but also her first actual paying job as a detective. Mary could hardly believe her good luck.

It was Tuesday, June 10, about a week since she and her aunt had visited Merton Olcott in his office. They would spend tonight and tomorrow night in Ishpeming, west of Marquette, where Edmond was now working. She was anxious to see his bank mural and meet his little band of artistic friends, whom he had so entertainingly described in his letters. On Thursday, she and Christena were to spend the day in Dillmont, overnighting there, so that Mary might make her inquiries. Then Friday, they would arrive at the glorious Grand Hotel on Mackinac.

The shops and factories and little houses of Superior, Wisconsin, rolled past them, under a light drizzle of rain. Holding umbrellas above their heads, people on the streets rushed along to drier places.

"Now you haven't told me much about your Mr. Roy," Christena finally said, turning to regard her. "Or should I call him your protégé?"

Mary rolled her eyes at that word. She had, in fact, written her aunt about her involvement in the case that had Edmond Roy at its center as chief suspect. And she had told Christena about his artistic talent and her hopes to help him obtain the success he richly deserved.

What Christena didn't know about was the emotional roller-coaster ride that her niece had experienced in the year since she had met Edmond. Mary had studied painting with the man, then saved him from unjust imprisonment. She had assumed her affection for him was reciprocal. But he had vanished from her life for months, only to reappear unexpectedly at her door last December. By then, Mary was in such a state, she didn't know which way was up.

But she wasn't about to share all that with her aunt. "We've exchanged a few letters since I last saw him in December," she said off-handedly. Her mind went back to the train station and the kiss. She would never forget the sensation of Edmond pulling her tightly to him. The warmth and sweetness of his lips. The sudden pounding of her heart at the emotions set loose. She hoped that the pleasure of the memory did not show on her face.

"So when I got the idea for this trip, and inviting you along," she continued, "I naturally thought that Ishpeming is right on the DSSA line. Why not stop and say hello to my friend Edmond? Truth be told, I'm very eager to see his new project. After all, if I'm going to help promote his career, I must stay current on his work."

"You really do fancy yourself a patroness of the arts, don't you?" Christena nodded approvingly. "Well, why not? You have the means. A person in your position can do a lot of good, helping worthy artists and scholars. After all, where would we be without the pope who hired Michelangelo and the noblemen who supported Beethoven?"

Christena shifted her gaze to view the landscape rushing by outside. "Johnny seems to think you're besotted with the man." Then she looked back with a tiny, teasing smile on her face.

Mary frowned. "Yes, well, Father may know everything there is to know about buying and selling commodities, but he *does not* know anything about the modern woman." She crossed her arms in a huff. "He can't imagine a woman being content not to marry. He can't imagine a woman enjoying the companionship of a man who will never be her husband." She peered at her aunt in frustration. "You of all people should understand. Have you ever regretted *your* choice to stay unmarried?"

Christena shrugged. "One always wonders about the path not taken, Mary. I had a proposal or two that I turned down. But I can't say that I would have been any happier as a missus, rather than a miss."

The train trundled on through the pines and maples and birches at a slow pace, stopping for five or ten minutes at towns along the way—Ashland, Ironwood, Nestoria. People and goods came onto the carriages and off. Eventually, the train emerged out of the drizzle into a summer day of blue sky and puffy white clouds.

The two vacationers visited the dining car for a lunch of sandwiches and coffee. Between bites, Christena queried Mary about Jeanette Harrison. Jeanette, Mary's cousin in St. Louis, had stopped writing last year, not even sending a Christmas card. Mary explained that as the winter wore on and no word came from St. Louis, she had wanted to go south to find Jeanette. But her father forbade her. Instead, he promised to hire a detective to track down the woman. To date, Jeanette had not been located.

For Mary, her cousin's fate had been a nagging concern these last months. She prayed that nothing awful had happened. But she understood that nothing good could have caused Jeanette to vanish so thoroughly.

Back in their seats, Mary read the new mystery by Conan Doyle—the pages ripped from her issues of the *Strand* magazine, mailed all the way from England. She did not for a moment believe the hound loose upon the moor was a supernatural creature. But the story was gripping, nonetheless.

Christena concentrated her efforts on a novel by Constance Fenimore Woolson that was set, in part, on Mackinac Island. She intended to make a list of places mentioned in the book, and then visit them.

By now, the train had rolled into the biggest town they had seen since Ironwood, and their interim destination—Ishpeming. Edmond would be waiting for them at the depot.

It had been six months since Mary had last laid eyes on him. Funny, she thought, how she had met him in Minneapolis, reconnected with him in Duluth, and now would have a reunion with him in Ishpeming. It wasn't exactly Paris, Venice, and Rome, but it would have to do.

Would he still have that heavy beard, she wondered. And does he still use that same pomade with the faint floral aroma? And would looking into those deep brown eyes make her feel warm and breathless once again?

She smiled at her silly ruminations. Heavens, she sounded like some infatuated schoolgirl. But she was *very much* looking forward to spending a couple of days with the man. And she devoted a few extra minutes to tidying up her wavy chestnut hair and pinning on her straw hat before the lavatory mirror.

The train slowed and lurched to a halt. Mary and Christena packed their reading materials away, gathered up their coats and umbrellas, and descended onto the platform. Mary anxiously looked this way and that, but saw nothing of Edmond.

By and by the porter brought them their two valises—

their trunks having been sent on to the Grand Hotel. But still no Edmond Roy materialized. The train pulled away eastward, on to Marquette. Finally, with the porter carrying the bags, Mary and Christena headed out through the station's now-empty waiting room and onto the street. Just as Christena was about to send the porter for a cab, a man's shout echoed from across the muddy road.

"Miss MacDougall! Mary!"

And there he came, dashing along at full speed—just barely dodging a baker's wagon—and skidding to a stop right in front of Mary and Christena.

"I am so sorry," Edmond panted. "Horse threw a shoe. So, *so* sorry. Keeping you waiting that long."

Mary felt her heart race and her cheeks flush. Their farewell at the station in Duluth last December had been quite emotional, sealed with that lingering and exquisite kiss. But she was determined to not be demonstrative in front of her aunt. Edmond, though, seemed to have no such compunction. Having caught his breath, he grinned broadly and gave her an exuberant hug, then a quick kiss on the cheek. He still had his beard and it tickled Mary's face.

"Well, you needn't suffer too much guilt, Mr. Roy," said Christena. "We were ourselves a bit late. A spot of bother with a coupling rod back in Nestoria."

Edmond turned his attention to Christena and beamed at her. "And you must be Aunt Christena." He looked as though he was ready to administer another bear hug, but thought better of it. He offered his hand and shook hers exuberantly.

"I'm so looking forward to hearing about your travels," he said. "Mary writes that you're contemplating a trip to Yosemite."

Christena smiled and gently extracted her hand from his grip. "Yes, indeed. And I'm hoping to persuade my niece to come along. But right now, Mr. Roy, I must say that a little nap sounds heavenly."

Edmond looked suddenly abashed. "Of course, forgive me. You both must be exhausted. I've booked you rooms at the hotel for two nights. It's just a few blocks away. Let me trot over there, and I'll fetch their wagon and bellman."

Thirty minutes later, still flushed and giddy, Mary sat cozily ensconced in her hotel room—spartan, but clean and comfortable. Next door, Christena was enjoying a lie-down. They had two hours to rest before going with Edmond to a friend's house for a welcome dinner party. At last, Mary would have a chance to meet his new circle of chums, of whom he'd written so much.

She didn't know what to expect at the gathering. The host, Edmond had explained, was a furniture-maker—coincidentally, her second furniture-maker in about a week. She had never even met one before Mr. Olcott. Other artist friends of Edmond would be there, as well. Mary was flattered that he wanted to show her off to them. She had to admit, though, that she was a bit nervous about making a good impression.

But what impression was it she wanted to make?

Did she want to merely be Edmond's young lady friend and nothing more? Did she want to make it clear that she was an independent woman and had no intention of becoming the appendage of a man, even one so appealing as Edmond? Did she want his friends to hear about her two adventures in detecting? Did she want anything said about being the daughter of a millionaire?

In the end, she figured all she could do was just try to sound halfway intelligent and be herself, without being too pushy. She did tend to espouse strong opinions, but usually among those she knew best and trusted most.

Mary had intended to tell Edmond about her new case at the first opportunity, but was now having second thoughts. In his letters, he had seemed somewhat relieved that no new matters had come her way. And he had made subtle noises that perhaps she could find different avenues to satisfy her sense of adventure. He had been quite circumspect about it, commenting that he was hardly one to tell anyone what to do, but that "the people who love you might worry." There was both good news and bad news packed into that sentiment.

Upon reflection, she decided it would be best to not tell him about the matter of the late Mrs. Olcott until the investigation was concluded. That way, she could weave it into an entertaining tale, not unlike Conan Doyle had done for his readers.

Out the window, Mary could see a bustling, thriving little town, which was supported by nearby iron mines. On the ride from the station, she had counted a number of shops, cafes, and offices. There was money here. She wondered if her father had any business interests in the area. It wouldn't surprise her if he did.

Mary felt a bit of regret about having sent her trunk along to Mackinac. Her evening dresses were in it. All she had for the brief stay in Ishpeming were her traveling clothes. She suspected, though, that they would do adequately for this evening's gathering of artists and working folks. It would probably be better, in fact, to not overdress.

Not wanting to get caught napping by Edmond when he arrived, Mary pulled the final pages of *The Hound of the Baskervilles* out of her purse, sat by the window, and started to read.

But her mind was far less on the newest adventure of Mr. Holmes and Dr. Watson than on the evening she would be spending with Edmond Roy and his friends.

Chapter VII

Edmond fetched them promptly at six-thirty that evening, in the buggy borrowed from his landlady—the horse's shoe having been restored. They rolled out of Ishpeming's downtown district and into a somewhat hilly neighborhood of modest dwellings. A few minutes later, the buggy pulled up in front of a white clapboard house. Mary had been to many parties, some of them quite fancy affairs, but this one had her feeling a little more nervous than usual.

"Here we are," Edmond said, hopping down from the driver's seat and tying the animal to a post. He helped Mary, then Christena, from their seat, and led them up the board-covered walk. Before they even reached the porch steps, the front door swung open and a big, bearded bear of a man stepped out, grinning broadly. Behind him came a rosy-cheeked girl of about nine or ten.

"Edmond, hello," the man boomed. "And I'm guessing these lovely ladies are the MacDougall girls. Welcome to my humble abode. I'm Dan Gilroy. And this is my daughter Ellen."

"Mr. Gilroy," Christena said, climbing the steps. Her

hand disappeared into his giant paw. "Hello, Ellen. I'm Christena MacDougall. Thank you so much for inviting us."

"The pleasure is all ours," the big man said. "Just call me Dan."

"And I'm Mary MacDougall." Mary, following behind her aunt, felt immediately comfortable with him.

"Nice to meet you at long last," Dan said, enthusiastically shaking her hand. "Edmond speaks highly of you. *Very* highly." He gave her a wink.

Mary didn't know how to respond to that. She avoided looking at Christena, but gave Edmond a quick glance. He was busy listening to Ellen talking animatedly about something. Apparently he hadn't heard Dan's remark.

"And he's told me all about your little band of artistic compatriots," she said to her host. "There's quite a collection of talent here in Ishpeming, I understand."

"And many of them are waiting inside to meet you. So, ladies, after you." The burly furniture maker gestured that they should step inside.

Mary took a deep breath and went into the house. She knew she would be on display this evening. What would Edmond's friends think of her? Normally she wasn't concerned about the impressions she made. But right now she had a bit of stage fright.

The front parlor was packed with people, like sardines in a can. There were pairs and trios and clumps of them, jabbering away. About what, Mary couldn't discern, given the din made by all those voices. Many were holding glasses of beer and whiskey and wine, and smoke from cigarettes and pipes filled the air.

The other female guests, for the most part, were attired in shirtwaists and skirts. Some of the men wore suits, but others had on dungarees. All of which made Mary very glad that she had on her rather plain traveling clothes—far more appropriate than one of Madame Zoya's evening dresses. It pleased her to think that she fit right into this bohemian crowd. She hoped that no one could guess, by simply looking at her, that she was an heiress with tens of thousands in the bank.

Edmond guided Mary and Christena around the room, making introductions. Mary was not surprised to meet artists and writers and musicians, but a banker and a Methodist minister were also in attendance. Within minutes, Christena was engaged in an intense discussion about Rookwood, a type of pottery that she collected, with an impassioned female potter.

Mary found herself standing in a corner with Edmond and a painter named Mrs. Rosiland Lehmann, or Rosie, as she insisted Mary call her. Edmond was drinking a beer, while Mary and Rosie sipped on little jelly jars of the elderberry wine that Mrs. Gilroy had made.

Rosie was a petite but voluptuous woman with raven hair piled atop her head, lively green eyes, and strikingly pretty features. Mary guessed her age at about thirty and she found her an intriguing person—a woman with an improbable dream, much like Mary MacDougall. There weren't, as far as Mary knew, very many successful women painters, just as there were very few women detectives.

But the evidence of Rosie's skill with a brush hung on the wall right behind them, a canvas of medium size depicting a fierce dark thunderstorm, wracked with lightning, advancing across the open prairie. It was really quite evocative—vivid and wild. The painter made modest mumblings when Edmond compared her landscape style to Turner and Courbet. It was a work Mary would have considered buying.

Someone shouted for Edmond to come over for a moment, to settle a bet, and he excused himself, leaving the two women alone.

"Where did you learn to paint so well?" Mary asked.

"I studied in New York," Rosie replied. "For about three years. And before that in Chicago."

"Is the art world very difficult for a woman painter to succeed in?"

Rosie shrugged. "In some respects, I suppose so. But if you have talent and the tenacity to keep going, you can make something of it. And you have to take advantage of every connection you have. I was good at that."

"How so?"

"I worked as a model, you see. It's how I supported myself. I don't mean to sound immodest, but I was in high demand among artists. So a number of painters and teachers and photographers knew me. And knew I was serious about my craft."

Mary was not surprised that this woman had been in demand as a model, considering how attractive and shapely she was. She wondered how Rosie's husband viewed the work that his wife did. Perhaps he was a painter, too, and they had met when she posed for him. Mary glanced around the room, wondering which of the gentlemen was Mr. Lehmann.

"It's not fair," Rosie continued, "but one's appearance sometimes does help one get ahead. But still, to be taken seriously as an artist, you have to produce work of a certain caliber. Good looks and an empty head will only get you into one place."

Mary knew perfectly well what Rosie meant. She imagined that many women shown in famous artworks had arrived on the canvas by way of the painter's mattress. And who was Mary to judge them? They were women with ambition, not unlike herself. The only difference was that Mary had no intention of achieving her goals through flirtation and flattery—or worse.

"Well, after looking at this canvas of yours, no one would dare question your talent as a landscape painter."

Rosie smiled. "I'm quite proud of that one. But I want to expand my skills. Fortunately, Edmond has taken me under his wing, teaching me the craft of still-life work. And in return, I've been posing for him."

Mary couldn't stop the hot flare of jealousy that suddenly surged up inside her. But it was quite unreasonable. After all, she knew Edmond had enlisted lots of his friends as models to portray the pioneers and miners and loggers that populated his bank mural. He had probably sketched everyone standing in this room for his project, even little Ellen and her parents. Perhaps Mr. Lehmann, too.

Still, Mary didn't like the image in her head of Edmond and this woman working together—talking, touching, laughing. But now it was there. And she couldn't remove it.

She forced herself to smile. "He is quite an excellent teacher. In fact, we met in a class of his a year ago. He owes me a few private lessons."

"And you shall have them when I'm in Duluth for the Ensign portraits," Edmond said, rejoining them. "You'll have oils coming out your ears."

Mary gave a quick laugh. "I'm not quite sure I'd like that. It sounds rather messy and uncomfortable. Still, I aim to soak up as many painting pointers as I can."

Just then, Dan Gilroy hollered for Edmond to help him move a table. Rosie gave Mary a friendly nod and wandered off to talk to someone else. Christena stood across the room, chatting with Paul Forbes, a photographer Mary had met earlier. The guest of honor was left standing all alone.

She didn't mind, as it gave her a chance to observe the other guests and attempt to deduce what they were like. Those deductions were interrupted when a thin, sallow young man sidled up to her. He wore an ill-fitting black suit, white shirt, black tie, and black beret. There was a wisp of something spidery beneath his narrow, crooked nose that apparently was a mustache. He had a monocle tucked into his right eye socket. He was clearly trying to look like a bohemian artist, but to Mary he came across as a skinny boy playing dress-up in front of the mirror.

Mary smiled at him. He didn't smile back.

"So you are Edmond's special friend," he said, almost accusingly. "Miss Mary MacDougall."

Mary found his manner puzzling, but she kept smiling. "That would be me. And you are?"

He offered a pale hand stained with ink, almost as if he expected her to kiss it. "Simon Skelton. I'm a typesetter by day at the *Iron Ore* newspaper, a poet by night. Free verse only. No blasted rhyming for me." He scowled, then regarded her for a few seconds. "You know, I've never met a millionaire before."

Ah, Mary thought, a *critic of the moneyed classes*. That explained the cold, scornful attitude.

"I can assure you, Mr. Skelton, that I do not have a million dollars."

He sniffed. "Well, then, your father does. As I understand it, he is among our great oligarchs. One of those who connives to control everything and keep ordinary working folk oppressed."

Mary felt a bit defensive and peeved at this fellow who was judging her father. "Well, he *is* a successful businessman and a millionaire. And he has several companies. But my father employs many hundreds of people and is considered a fair and generous boss. And," she said, leveling her eyes at him, "he started with nothing."

Mr. Skelton gave his head a toss. "It just so happens that my friend Erno Ritala works in one of your father's mines. And he's among those trying to bring in a union." He crossed his arms defiantly. "Once the workers unite, the robber barons like your father might end up having to do their own laundry." He gave a high-pitched laugh at his clever remark.

At the mention of Erno Ritala's name, Mary remembered the first time she had met him, back in December when he and his pretty wife Annika had visited Duluth with Edmond. The Ritalas were both accomplished jewelry makers. Mary had bought several of their pieces for herself and to give as Christmas gifts. When the couple found out about their impending parenthood, they decided to leave Ishpeming and move to the town of Eveleth on Minnesota's Iron Range, to be nearer to their families.

Edmond had written Mary that Erno, an unrepentant socialist, had reluctantly taken a job in a nearby mine to provide the necessary income their growing family would require. But she hadn't known it was her father's mine. Mary understood that it must have been a heart-wrenching decision to give up his craft. Still, she also knew, from what her father had told her many times, that unions were only going to make life more difficult for their members, not improve it.

She was just about to respond to Mr. Skelton's juvenile taunt when, out of nowhere, Dan Gilroy's piercing whistle filled the parlor. "The food is on the table, everyone," the big man bellowed out. "Get yourselves plates and cutlery, find yourselves perches, and dig in. There's plenty more wine and beer, too."

Mary gave Simon Skelton a curt nod and went to join Christena. The two of them loaded up their plates with roasted chicken, boiled potatoes, and bread, then found spots on a handsome mahogany bench in the parlor. They sat on one end, balancing their plates on their laps. As they started to eat, Christena's new friend plopped down next to her.

"Mary," she said, "have you met Paul Forbes? Paul is a photographer. He has a portrait studio downtown, but also strives to make photographs in the style of Alfred Stieglitz."

Paul had a rugged, weatherworn face with kind hazel eyes. And he actually seemed to have captivated Christena, who had focused most of her attentions on him that evening.

"Paul and I met earlier," Mary said, nodding at the man. "But we didn't have a chance to talk. I've heard of Mr. Steiglitz, but don't know much about him."

Paul told her about his efforts in Stieglitz's pictorialist style—photo visions of real life, but with a gauzy impress-sionism to them. The negatives required a great deal of manipulation in the darkroom, he explained, to achieve the characteristic look.

"It sounds quite beautiful," Mary said. "Before we leave town I should like to see some of your work."

The man beamed. "Well, you don't have to go very far. Dan has several of my prints." He pointed. "Over there and there. And another around the corner in the dining room."

Mary had noticed the photos, but hadn't paid them

much attention. She hopped up, set her plate down on the bench, and went over to the first picture, a still life of irises in a vase. Very nice, very pretty. The second showed a fisherman by a lovely bubbling brook, with an ephemeral mist rising into the air. Then Mary went into the dining room, squeezing between several other partygoers.

She stepped up to the framed photo on the wall and blinked at it, leaning in close. It showed a grove of young birch trees, sunlight twinkling among the leaves.

Leaning languidly against one of the trees was a curvaceous woman with flowing, dark hair. In a state of total undress. Looking demurely over her left shoulder.

Mary instantly recognized her. It was Rosie Lehmann.

Edmond's good friend, pupil, and unabashed model.

Chapter VIII

Mary didn't sleep well on her lumpy hotel mattress. She had probably sipped too much of Mrs. Gilroy's home-made wine, making for a somewhat uncomfortable night. Snatches of conversation from the party kept running through her head. And that image of the naked Mrs. Lehmann, Edmond's friend and model, stubbornly resisted expunging. It was something she wished she could un-see. Nonetheless, she was up bright and early, excited about spending the entire day with Edmond and finally having a good look at the mural he had been working on for nearly a year.

Mary had enjoyed the party, though she hadn't been able to spend a single minute alone with Edmond. Even when he dropped her off at the hotel around midnight, Christena had waited by the entrance for Mary. So there was no repeat of the parting kiss she and Edmond enjoyed in the train station last December.

But he would be in Duluth in six weeks, for the Ensign commission, and Mary was determined that the two of them would explore the city quite unchaperoned. She was already making plans for what they might do together, though she would need to be sensible about how often she saw him. Gossip had ways of reaching her father's ear faster than a horse could gallop.

Ishpeming was bustling with activity that morning, as people crowded its sidewalks and muddy streets for their errands and their work. It was a short stroll through warm, muggy air from the hotel to the Pioneer Bank. The brick building was austere and modern-looking, designed somewhat in the style of Louis Sullivan.

Edmond met Mary and Christena outside the bank at ten and ushered them in through its fancy rotating door. Mary's eyes took a few seconds to get used to the dimmer illumination inside. To her left, bankers sat at desks, consulting with depositors and clients. To her right were tall brass counters, where customers scribbled away on deposit slips and what not. And straight ahead stood a rank of ornate brass teller windows.

Behind and above the tellers, the story of Ishpeming and Michigan's Upper Peninsula unfolded across an expanse of wall that was framed by a wide, grand, gilded arch. Mary's jaw dropped at the sight of it.

"Oh, Edmond. It's glorious! Just glorious!"

He made a modest shrug, but couldn't hide how pleased he was with her reaction.

The trio stood there silently and took in the mural. It closely resembled the drawing Edmond had shown Mary six months earlier. But to see it at full scale and in vivid color nearly took her breath away.

On the far left, the tale began with the natives and

settlers, making their peace. Moving rightward, the vast wilderness was tamed by the forces of commerce. Loggers sent fallen trees down a rushing river. Great machines ripped metal ore from the earth. A railroad wove through the wilds, carrying the ore. And, on the far side of the mural, a town, presumably Ishpeming, rose in bright splendor, radiant from the luminous sun above.

Fully twenty-five feet in breadth, the mural seemed alive to Mary—as if the people depicted in it might leap down and greet the tellers standing before them. But for a few bare spots along the top and bottom, it looked complete.

"Remember when I told you people would come from all over to see your magnum opus?" Mary said, beaming at Edmond. "Now I'm sure of it."

"Well, they haven't shown up yet," he laughed.

"Because they don't know about it yet. But they will. They will."

"I have seen many murals in my travels," Christena said, her voice full of admiration. "And I must say that this is right up there with the best of them. Now when will you finish it?"

"A few weeks at most," the painter replied. "Plenty of time to keep my appointment with Mrs. Ensign in Duluth at the end of July."

"Hello, Mr. Roy."

The three of them turned to see a short, young woman looking up at them with almond-shaped blue eyes. She held an envelope and wore the plain, tidy attire of an office girl.

"Oh, hello, Miss Jursik," Edmond answered. "How are you this fine morning?"

"Very well, thank you. I see you've brought some visitors to view your masterpiece."

"Indeed I have. Miss Jursik, this is Miss Christena MacDougall and her niece, Miss Mary MacDougall." He turned to Mary and her aunt. "Miss Jursik is the vice-president's secretary and one of my greatest supporters here."

Edmond had admirers all over the place, or so it seemed to Mary. In addition to being a talented artist, he was, after all, quite handsome, with an effortless charm about him. It was self-deluding, she realized, to think that no other unmarried female had ever noticed him. And why shouldn't he, in turn, be attracted to one of them? And perhaps strike up an alliance? The answer, she knew in her heart, was that no one else could conceivably do as much good for Edmond Roy as Mary MacDougall could.

"Well, welcome to Ishpeming," said Miss Jursik. "I hope you're enjoying our fine little town."

"Oh, we are, we are," Christena replied. "Now tell me, Miss Jursik, what do you think of Mr. Roy's creation?"

After a pleasant lunch at a nearby café, Edmond took Mary and Christena on an extended walking tour of the town. In the short time he had been there, he had clearly made a lot of new friends. It seemed to Mary that every other person said hello to him and called him by name. She enjoyed seeing him so at ease and happy in this place where he had sought refuge after that dreadful business in Minneapolis.

There was no party that evening, but Christena had offered to treat Edmond and the photographer Paul Forbes to dinner at the nicest restaurant in town. As the four of them waited for their orders to be taken, Mary noticed that Christena still seemed quite taken with Paul. The two had been inseparable at Dan Gilroy's gathering the night before.

Edmond and Paul both ordered the baked pickerel, for which the place was famous. Christena selected roast beef pie with potato crust, while Mary chose the Irish stew of mutton. The gentlemen had ales and the ladies shared a demi-bottle of red wine.

"Now tell me," Paul said, taking a break from his pickerel, "how do you two plan to occupy yourselves for nearly three weeks on Mackinac?"

"I'm hoping there might be a lecture or two to attend," Christena answered. "I understand that Mark Twain himself gave a talk at the Grand Hotel a few years ago."

"Funniest man on earth," Paul opined as he buttered a biscuit.

"Oh, I do agree," said Christena. "I love his books. And of course there'll be long walks to take and dances to attend and tennis matches to play. Not to mention lots of delicious food to eat. I heard there's a candy store on the island that makes heavenly fudge."

"Then *I* shall probably spend some of the time at the seamstress, having my dresses let out," Mary observed.

They all burst into laughter.

"You know, I've always wanted to visit Mackinac and do a photographic essay," Paul said. "But it seems that time and money for such an expedition never quite align."

Mary took a long sip of the excellent wine. She was about to ask her aunt what she thought of it, but Christena seemed to be mulling something over.

"I have a little idea," she finally said. "As you two gentlemen are fairly close to Mackinac, just a few hours by rail..." She shot a furtive glance at Mary. "Why don't you come and join us for a week or so. It would be my treat."

Mary let out a gasp under her breath. Her aunt's invitation caught her quite off guard. As much as she wanted to spend more time with Edmond, she had it set out in her head how she was going to manage her Mackinac sojourn.

For a start, she wanted to take care of the Agnes Olcott case and do as thorough a job as possible for her very first client. Even though she would be conducting her interviews in Dillmont, she would be preparing her report and dispatching it from Mackinac.

She had several books in her trunk that she aimed to plow through. Then she planned to spend lots of time bicycling and playing tennis and hiking—activities she sorely missed during the long, indolent winter. There would be social functions to attend. She had no idea if Edmond even enjoyed those sorts of diversions.

Besides, he would be in Duluth later in the summer. They would have plenty of time together then.

But she realized that what it came down to was that she had organized this whole expedition, down to a T, and Christena had just thrown her plans into disarray. Mary was fine with spontaneity, so long as it was *her* spontaneity.

Still, it was hardly her place to veto her aunt's proposal. She could only hope that Edmond or Paul would politely decline, and that would be that.

And indeed, Edmond tried to.

"That's very kind of you," he said. "But I've heard how much the Grand Hotel costs and I, for one, could not accept having you pay for me."

"We could camp out," Paul suggested.

"Nonsense," Christena objected. "If your pride prevents you from enjoying free lodging in the Grand, I'm sure we could find something more modest down the hill from there. Please think of it as a little artistic stipend. When you're not with Mary and me, you can be off painting and photographing."

"Miss MacDougall, I, for one gladly accept your invitation," Paul said, bowing toward Christena from his seated position, "and offer my deepest thanks."

Edmond looked at Mary, who tried to psychically convey to him her opinion on the subject. But the painter apparently did not receive her message. "Well, why not?" he said with a smile. "I won't look a gift horse in the mouth. Thank you so much."

"Then it's all settled!" Christena exclaimed. "You two can wire us at the Grand Hotel and let us know when you're coming, and we'll book your rooms. Oh, we'll all have a splendid time."

The decision having been made, there was nothing Mary could do about it. So she forced a smile and decided to change the subject.

"I was most impressed with Rosie Lehmann's painting of the thunderstorm. She certainly has been well trained. As you said, Edmond, a bit of Turner and a bit of Courbet."

"Indeed," he agreed. "I believe she could have stayed in New York and made a good career. But after her divorce…"

A divorcée. So Mrs. Lehmann was a single woman. Mary had liked her better as someone's wife. A lot better.

"…she wanted to get far away from her ex-husband. So she took her settlement and decided to flee Manhattan. She knew Paul from her modeling work in Chicago."

Mary figured Paul must have gotten to know Rosie very well—every inch of her—after that nude study he did of her. What must Christena have thought when she saw the gauzy photograph on Dan Gilroy's wall? Surely she was now aware of who took the photo and who took off her clothes to pose for it.

"I lured her out here for a visit and she decided to stay on," Paul recounted. "And I must say, she fits in beautifully. Her work is quite fine. I believe she could have a great future ahead of her as an artist. And she's a wonderful model."

"I'm working with her on her still lifes," Edmond said.

Mary took a deep breath. "Has she posed for you, Edmond?"

"Oh, yes. For one of the figures in my mural," he answered, seemingly oblivious to what Mary really wanted to know—*has she taken her clothes off for you?*

They stopped talking when the waitress came to clear their plates and offer dessert of cake or pie. Paul and Christena both ordered the chocolate cake, Mary and Edmond nothing more.

"I saw you chatting with Simon Skelton last evening," Edmond noted. "I hope he behaved himself." He gave her an apologetic look. "We didn't invite him. He just showed up. He's not a bad sort, but can be a bit peevish at times. He wasn't rude, was he?"

"A little," Mary admitted. "He did rather lecture me about having a wealthy businessman for a father."

Paul laughed. "Apparently his father, a printer, is a student of the teachings of Karl Marx. So in that sense, the fruit hasn't fallen too far from the old tree. Until last September, Simon liked to call himself an anarchist."

"And though I hate to say it," said Edmond, "he was not all that saddened when President McKinley died. Actually, quite gratified. But since the president had been murdered by an anarchist, I strongly advised him to hold that political viewpoint close to his vest. On the order of: 'Keep your blasted mouth shut!' He might have gotten beaten into a pulp."

"Or killed," added Paul darkly.

"Then why do you put up with the man?" Christena wondered.

"I think we all feel a bit sorry for him," Paul said. "With that chip on his shoulder, he's his own worst enemy. Anyway, we joke that as long as we keep him under our wing, and get him a free drink now and again, he won't be inclined to go out and assassinate President Roosevelt."

"Buying the security of the nation with an occasional beer," Edmond added, "seems cheap at the price."

"I think what Simon needs is for some solid young lady to take him in hand," Paul contended. "To civilize him."

"To civilize a man like that? That's quite a burden to put on any woman," Christena said. "Though I do agree— the fairer sex has often coaxed the male of the species onto a more enlightened path."

"Precisely," Paul concurred. "I have known more than a few rough, rude fellows who became the epitome of re-spectability once they wed." He shook his head. "It's a pity though. They used to be such good company."

Mary observed her aunt giving Paul a look of amusement.

"Very sad," Mary put in. "Those wives do rather domesticate a fellow. All the color and interest in life, suddenly gone. It's a tragedy, really."

She met Edmond's grin with an innocent smile. Then she looked up at the clock above the entrance and realized the hour was getting late.

She hated for the evening to end. She was having so

much fun, sitting there with three witty, intelligent adults, two for whom she felt a great deal of affection. And they all treated her as an equal. Mary had never felt quite so grown-up, so far removed from that unsophisticated girl who had graduated from high school just a year ago.

But tomorrow there would be real work to do. And she needed a clear mind and a good night's sleep.

"Well, much as Christena and I are enjoying the delightful company of you two *very* civilized gentlemen," she said, "I think we'd best get back to the hotel. We have to get up bright and early to catch the train."

As pleasant as the stay in Ishpeming had been, she was looking forward to finally arriving in Dillmont and starting her investigation. What would she find out? Had the seemingly civilized Merton Olcott played a role in his wife's untimely death? Or would it be, as Detective Sauer had predicted, a simple case of a daughter not wanting to believe that her mother had died by a tragic quirk of fate?

Tomorrow might tell the tale.

Chapter IX

Mary and Christena arrived in Dillmont later the next morning, disembarking from the train with their hand luggage. They asked the station manager where they might stay that evening and he recommended the guesthouse operated by the wife of his late brother. Much nicer than the hotel, was his unbiased opinion.

It was a handsome brick home in the colonial style, set on a narrow street shaded with large maples. For an extra charge, Mrs. Wingate, the proprietress, agreed to prepare them lunch, dinner, and breakfast, and take them by carriage to the station the next forenoon.

During the train ride eastward, Mary had been preparing herself for the task at hand. As much as she would not have minded uncovering some criminal intent in the case, she couldn't imagine what it would be like to tell Clara McColley that her mother had indeed been murdered. The poor woman was already dealing with the crushing grief of her mother's death. Would it do her any good to have the additional burden of knowing that Mrs. Olcott's death was completely malicious and entirely premature?

The closer the train got to Dillmont, the more Mary

hoped that her findings would be simple and straightforward, and would give Clara McColley the peace of mind she desperately desired. The only way to do that would be to give her details about her mother's final days and hours. And the person who could authoritatively tell Mary those details was the doctor who had treated Mrs. Olcott. Mary's first order of business would be to pay him a visit.

It was her intention, after she interviewed the doctor, to find Mrs. Olcott's grave, take a picture of it with her Kodak, and leave some flowers. It would give Clara McColley comfort, Mary thought, to know that someone had gone to the plot to pay their respects, even if Merton Olcott intended to bring the body home to Duluth at a later date.

"If the doctor is available, I shouldn't need more than twenty minutes of his time," Mary told Christena before she left the guesthouse. "Then I'll come back to get you and we can stroll to the cemetery together. If everything is in order, as Detective Sauer suspects it will be, I'll send Mrs. McColley a letter from Mackinac. Our business here will be concluded."

Christena looked perfectly happy to have a quiet spell in the comfortable room after their light lunch. As Mary stepped out, her aunt had put her feet up and was beginning to page through a *Collier's Weekly* magazine she had bought in Ishpeming.

Mrs. Wingate gave Mary directions to the doctor's office at the north end of Main Street, a five-minute stroll from the guesthouse. She arrived at a little yellow bungalow with a black slate roof. On a post behind the white picket fence a sign announced: *Joseph Applegate, M.D.* The air was redolent with the wonderful scent of damp earth and the perfume of tiny flowers tucked in behind the fence.

Standing before the place, Mary gathered up her courage. She had rehearsed in her mind how to approach the physician. He needed to see her as a friend of Clara McColley, come to find out more about her mother's tragic death. Mary merely wanted to gather information, as a newspaper reporter might. In a cordial manner. Nothing to arouse the man's suspicion of a hidden agenda.

With one final deep breath, she opened the gate, marched up the narrow brick walk, and knocked on the doctor's door.

After about half a minute, it swung open and a slender man in his fifties—in shirt and striped vest, sleeves held up with garters—stood before her. His eyes were slightly magnified by the lenses in his spectacles. Mary felt herself relax a bit, now that she was finally face to face with him.

"Good morning," he said. "How may I help you?"

"Doctor Applegate?" Mary asked, smiling at him.

"Yes, that's me."

"My name is Mary MacDougall and I am a friend of Mrs. Clara McColley."

He blinked at her, revealing no recognition of the

name.

"Is it *Miss* MacDougall?"

"Correct," Mary replied.

"Should I know this Mrs. McColley?" he asked, his head cocked slightly sideways.

"She is the daughter of Mrs. Agnes Olcott."

The doctor's face finally showed a sign of recognition. He nodded sadly.

"Ah, yes, Mrs. Olcott. But, if I may ask, what is your visit here in regard to?"

"As you can well imagine, Dr. Applegate, Mrs. McColley was devastated by the news of her mother's death."

Mary felt a slight shift in his demeanor, a trace of suspicion showing on his face. He made no response, so she continued.

"Devastated doubly so because she cannot come all this way from Duluth to visit her grave. She has a sick child to care for."

The doctor regarded her with an inscrutable expression, then said, "I am sorry to hear your friend has such troubles. Please, come in." He held the door open for her.

It appeared that the front of the house had been converted into a waiting room and office. The examination room must have been behind a door down the hallway.

"Do you work alone, then?" Mary asked congenially.

"Not usually," he replied. "But today my nurse happens to be ill with a mild case of the grip. Normally, she would have welcomed you."

He walked behind his desk and sat, gesturing that Mary

should take the straight chair facing him. He clasped his hands on the oak desktop and scrutinized her.

"Do you happen to know Dr. Burns of Duluth?" she asked, as a way to break the ice.

The doctor shook his head. "Alas, I have never had that pleasure."

"Well," she chatted on, "the doctor's daughter is my best friend and I sometimes help out at the clinic."

"Very good of you," observed Dr. Applegate.

"And before I left on my trip I asked him about death by cholera." She frowned and gave a shudder. "He did not make it sound like a very pleasant way to go."

Dr. Applegate nodded. "Your Dr. Burns knows whereof he speaks. Requires intensive care fairly quickly. Highly contagious, so treatment's no walk in the park. Quite unpleasant for everyone involved."

"The thing is this, Dr. Applegate. Mr. Olcott would not share any details of his wife's death with my friend Clara, save for showing her the death certificate that you filled out after her death at the Westerholm infirmary. He claimed the account would just be too upsetting and he wished to spare his stepdaughter any more grief."

The physician took off his glasses and rubbed the bridge of his nose. He seemed to be thinking hard about how to respond.

"A serious illness typically imposes great stress upon the family of the patient. But I'm still not certain why you are here and what it is that you want from me."

Mary gave him her sweetest smile.

"How silly of me. Of course you're confused, as I haven't made myself very clear. You see, Clara, knowing that I was going to the Grand Hotel on Mackinac Island, asked me to stop in Dillmont and see if I could glean a few more details about her mother's passing. And who would know more about it than you? For example, was her death as awful as Dr. Burns described? I sincerely hope not."

Dr. Applegate looked uncomfortable at being put on the spot. Mary didn't want her probing to provoke his reticence. It might be best to move on to the one crucial question that could most ease Clara McColley's mind.

She leaned forward in her chair. "Dr. Applegate, might it have been something other than cholera that caused Mrs. Olcott's death? Perhaps food poisoning or another toxin?"

The doctor stared at her for an uncomfortably long moment, and Mary thought she saw a flash of anger.

"You know, Miss MacDougall," he finally said, "I understand you are trying to do a kindness for a troubled friend. But I do not believe it is my place to share the clinical details pertaining to any of my patients with a person I do not know. I hope you don't take offense."

Mary tried to say something about Clara McColley having no other recourse, but the doctor put up his hand and stopped her in mid-sentence.

"If Mr. Olcott didn't think it right to tell his step-daughter about the particulars of her mother's illness, far be it for me to go against his wishes. That is a matter for the two of them to resolve. And it's nothing that you and I should be discussing." He looked at his pocket watch and stood up.

"Now, if you will excuse me, Miss McDougall, I'm expecting a patient in a few minutes. Thank you for stopping and please give my regards to Mrs. McColley. And tell her that if she should ever be able to make the journey to Dillmont, I would be glad to accommodate her."

Well, thought Mary as she tramped out onto Main Street, scowling, *that went poorly*.

She had found out nothing that would lead her forward in the investigation or reassure her client that no foul play had taken place. She was no better off than she had been when she first knocked on Dr. Applegate's door.

It was a delicate situation, she understood—a doctor inserting himself into a matter involving stepfather and stepdaughter. Still, she felt that Dr. Applegate could have at least confirmed that Mrs. Olcott did not die of poisoning. Doing so would certainly not have violated any oath of privacy between him and his patient's husband.

Since her interview had been cut so short, she decided on an amble through the heart of Dillmont. Christena wouldn't be expecting her for a little while, and it would give Mary time to consider other approaches to the case.

She went down one side of the little business district and up the other on the plank sidewalk. There was a post office, a bank, a dry goods store, an office of the Sheriff of Chippewa County, a blacksmith, the hotel, a café, and an undertaker. Mary was tempted to stop and talk to the sheriff's deputy, but remembered Detective Sauer's admonition against such an action in the absence of evidence. At the north end of Main Street was a livery stable, as well as a small lumberyard.

Along the way, Mary passed a little house with a sign in the yard that announced "Seamstress." She peeked in the front window and saw a dressmaker's form with a plain gray skirt and matching jacket hanging on it. The lady's suit looked a little old-styled. But they always did say that the further one was from the centers of fashion, the further one was from what was *à la mode*. Dillmont was thus well behind Duluth, as Duluth was well behind New York, let alone Paris.

She was just about to turn the corner by Dr. Applegate's office and head two streets over to the guesthouse, when the sharp report of a motorcar backfiring caused her to spin around. There, backing out of Dr. Applegate's driveway, was a runabout that looked very much like the Oldsmobile Mary's neighbors had back in Duluth. It was being driven by the good doctor himself. He eased the vehicle onto the road, put it into forward gear, and proceeded off in the direction of the train station.

Either his patient hadn't shown up or the doctor had performed a very quick exam.

Peculiar, Mary thought. *Very peculiar.*

Chapter X

Mary had not wanted Christena to come with her to the interview with Dr. Applegate. But afterwards, she wondered if it might have gone better with her aunt present.

Christena had a way of putting people at ease, so that they often revealed very personal aspects of themselves without even noticing. Mary envied that ability. She was herself perhaps a bit too intense, too pushy when trying to draw information from a reluctant subject. Next time, she vowed, she would model her behavior after Christena's, and take the slow, disarming approach.

But there was one thing her aunt had done that Mary still didn't approve of.

"Tena?" Mary said, as the two of them walked toward the Dillmont cemetery.

"Yes?" her aunt replied, holding her parasol high. Why she had bothered to bring it, Mary didn't know, as Christena already had her broad straw hat planted firmly on her head, and the sky was cloudy.

"Do you think Edmond and Paul will really come to Mackinac?"

Christena stopped in her tracks and turned to Mary.

"Why in the world do you ask? Do you think they *won't*?"

"I almost wish that they wouldn't," Mary said, a bit churlishly.

Christena looked puzzled. "But I thought we'd all agreed it would be great fun."

The two were standing right in the middle of the road and had to move aside for a two-horse van that came rattling slowly through. The white-haired driver nodded to them and they waved back, as they once again continued on their way.

"Yes, we did agree," Mary said. "But you know, I've never really been with Edmond in a social setting. Well, I mean…"

Christena gave her a sideways glance. "You mean you're concerned that Edmond won't fit in on Mackinac? Because he's not of the right class?"

Mary fidgeted with the bouquet she was carrying, feeling flustered. How could she explain what seemed to be a snobbish attitude on her part?

"I really don't give a fig about social classes. Or the fact that Edmond has Indian blood. One of the reasons I like him is because he's exactly who he seems to be. No pretense, no arrogance." She paused. "But the upper crust can be cruel to outsiders."

"Miserably cruel," Christena agreed. "But I think you might be too concerned about how Edmond would handle a slight. I suspect both he and Paul would merely shrug it off. They are both rich in talent, after all. No snotty aristocrat could ever snatch that away from them."

Mary smiled at her aunt. "You're really quite taken with Paul, aren't you?"

A slight blush came across Christena's cheeks. "I suppose I am. I find him such a delightful conversationalist. He's very interested in Egyptology, you know. Said he would love to visit the pyramids and the Valley of the Kings some day. And so would I."

By now they had reached the intersection where another, narrower lane led up to their destination. An ornate wrought-iron front gate informed them that they had arrived at the Shady Rest Cemetery. The graveyard occupied a rustic patch of three or four acres dotted with old oaks. Mary and Christena began to amble up and down the ranks of headstones, looking for a relatively fresh grave.

As Christena stopped to admire a particularly florid piece of funerary art—a flight of cherubim carved into a large marble tombstone—Mary continued her search for Mrs. Olcott's grave.

Mary had never much enjoyed funerals and cemeteries. It depressed her to think that every vibrant life ended up here, huddled under the earth. The awful memory of her own mother's funeral still haunted her. Mary had been only eight years old, but she could still remember the morbid details. Vividly. Especially, how that person in the coffin had not looked anything like Alice MacDougall. More like some awful waxworks effigy.

Nearing the cemetery fence, she spied a mound of dirt a couple of rows away. "There's something over there, Tena," she yelled.

The new grave had a wooden cross standing over it, just as Merton Olcott had described. A little brass plate affixed to it was engraved with the initials "A. O." Sparse grass and weeds were starting to grow on the raw patch of soil. It certainly didn't show much care or concern.

First, Mary took out her Kodak Brownie box camera and snapped a picture. Then she placed her bouquet—lilacs from Mrs. Wingate's backyard—on the grave and took another snap.

"Poor woman," she said to Christena, who had joined her. "Put in the ground so far from home. No one to visit or tend to her grave."

"Poor dear, indeed," came a voice from behind.

Both Mary and Christena twirled around to find a middle-aged woman standing there, wearing a solemn expression. She was quite short and had the sturdy build of a farmer's wife.

"But then they're all poor dears that die in that place," she continued, moving closer to Mary and Christena. "My cousin works there at Westerholm, you know. Sometimes in the asylum, sometimes in the infirmary."

"It's not just an infirmary?" Mary asked, surprised.

"Not at all," the woman answered. "Westerholm Institution for Women, it's called. Mostly an asylum, you know, for those females that are…" She tapped her temple with an index finger. "Mrs. Westerholm built it and her trust keeps it going. It was because of her daughter, who wasn't quite right in the head. The old lady saw a need for such a place in this part of the state. She had a generous heart, no doubt of that."

"Very generous," Christena echoed.

"Now the infirmary has twelve beds, more than enough for the inmates who get sick. So the superintendent opened it up to locals. That was a godsend, let me tell you. Otherwise people in Dillmont had to go all the way up to Sault Ste. Marie when they needed a hospital." The chatty woman finally paused and looked Mary and Christena up and down. "Did you know the deceased?"

"No, not personally," Mary replied.

"A terrible way to die," the woman said.

"So I hear." Mary gave an involuntary shiver. Dr. Burns's description of the disease was still lodged in her mind.

"My cousin said she died in the morning, after quite a struggle. But now she is finally at peace."

"Did you hear anything about her symptoms?" Mary asked eagerly. "The details of her case?"

The woman looked a little uncomfortable. "Well, no. Why would I want to know such things? Makes me feel sick just to think of it."

Christena broke the ungainly silence that followed. "My name is Christena MacDougall and this is my niece Mary. We are here on our way to Mackinac. And you are?"

"Mrs. Tilda Gray." The woman smiled broadly, revealing a gap between her teeth. "Well, I suppose I'd best get over there to my husband's plot. I try to visit him every few weeks, rest his soul. He left us four years ago, but my sons handle all the work at the sawmill just fine. You ladies have yourselves a wonderful time on the island." And with that, she briskly strode off.

Mary and Christena went in the opposite direction, heading for the cemetery gate. As they approached it, a black buggy came rattling in, so sharp and clean that it almost glinted. On the side of the buggy Mary spied a name in handsome silver Roman type: *Van Pelt & Sons, Undertakers.*

There was a thin young man in the driver's seat, in an old-fashioned black suit—no doubt one of the sons. He tipped his bowler hat to the two ladies and continued on into the graveyard.

Mary stopped in her tracks, staring at the receding buggy.

"What is it, Mary?" asked Christena.

"One final opportunity, perhaps," Mary answered and began trudging after the Van Pelt buggy. "Come on, Tena."

They caught up to the gentleman in front of a shed not far from Agnes Olcott's grave. He was standing there talking to some laborer holding a spade, a string bean of a fellow in dirty dungarees. Probably the gravedigger. They both regarded Mary and Christena a bit curiously and quickly concluded their conversation. The laborer went off and the suited man turned his attention to the Mac-Dougalls, doffing his bowler hat.

"Good afternoon, ladies. How may I help you?"

"Are you one of the Van Pelts?" Mary asked.

"That I am," he nodded. "Abraham Van Pelt. I operate

Van Pelt & Sons with my older brother and my father. Do you have some need of our services, miss? Or is it missus?"

He had a pale, clean-shaven face shaped like a V, severe and clearly not given to any frivolity.

"Thankfully, not just yet," Mary replied. "And it's Miss MacDougall. But my aunt and I have stopped off in Dillmont as a favor for a friend of ours, whose mother died here some weeks ago. The grave is just over there, the new one with the wooden cross."

Mr. Van Pelt peered in the direction that Mary pointed. "Ah yes, the poor woman from Westerholm."

"We were hoping you could give us some details of her burial, to convey to our friend." Mary clasped her hands, as if about to pray.

Mr. Van Pelt maintained his sober demeanor. "Yes, of course. I remember that day well, Miss MacDougall. Dr. Applegate handled the details. He came to my house early that morning and said that he needed a coffin immediately for someone at Westerholm."

"So the body was put into the coffin soon after she passed away?" Mary asked.

"I don't know the exact hour of death," he said. "I just know that my brother and I and one of our employees brought in the coffin, a modest pine model that we make here in our shop. Embalming was not asked for."

At that point his features turned mournful.

"The dearly departed was wrapped in a shroud. Only her face and a few tendrils of red hair were visible."

Looking down, he paused and shook his head, as if at the wonder of it. "I have seen death in many forms. But, apart from the passing of children, few things have ever touched me so deeply as seeing the doctor and his attendant place the deceased—very gently and respectfully, I might add—into that plain wooden coffin."

Mary couldn't tell if he really meant it, or if he was merely exercising the morose drama inherent in his somber trade.

"And then you conveyed her here?"

"Yes, we buried her that very afternoon. Reverend Pascal said a few words, as he always does for the folks from Westerholm. Dr. Applegate, bless his heart, came as well."

"And her husband was there, of course," Mary said.

The undertaker shook his head, looking puzzled. "No. No one else attended."

Mary frowned. Even if Merton Olcott wasn't a killer, it was inexcusable that he had not attended the graveside service.

"It is a rather primitive marker," observed Christena. "Is it not?"

"Yes, you're right," he said. "But that was what was asked for."

"Have there been any other burials from Westerholm in recent months?" Mary was curious to know if Mrs. Olcott's cholera was an isolated incident.

The young undertaker pondered for a moment, then shook his head. "I don't believe so. Typically, they are interred at the little graveyard at Westerholm. But I gather her family asked that she be buried here."

"Well, thank you so much, Mr. Van Pelt. I'm sure your account will give great comfort to my friend."

They once again headed toward the cemetery gate.

"Do you believe it?" Christena grumbled. "The man didn't even attend his wife's interment. The gall of him. Incredible!"

"Yes," Mary agreed angrily, "it does beggar belief. Why wouldn't he have been there? I'll bet he was too anxious to get home and start plundering the company accounts. What a dreadful man. I felt it about him from the first moment we saw him in his office."

They walked a few minutes more in silence. "Well," Christena observed, "short of digging up Mrs. Olcott and reanimating her, I think you've done all you can on Clara McColley's behalf, wouldn't you say?"

Mary wrinkled her forehead. "I guess I have. But it doesn't feel like I've learned much. I hate to charge Mrs. McColley even five dollars for such threadbare results." She thought a moment. "I wonder if I should go to the infirmary and talk to someone there."

"If Dr. Applegate wouldn't tell you anything, why do you think someone at Westerholm will? Besides, Mrs. Wingate said it's quite a hike to get there, and it's almost dinnertime. And to be perfectly honest, my feet are getting sore."

Mary supposed her aunt made a good point. As inadequate as it seemed, she had done what she could to find out about Agnes Olcott's death. The only thing left was to write up her report once they got to Mackinac Island, and send it back to her client in Duluth.

There was, however, one small question that lingered in her mind.

Chapter XI

Mary and Christena made their way down the ferry's gangplank Friday morning, jostled along by dozens of other vacationers. In front of them, Mackinac Island's commercial district—actually the backside of the district—spread out along the shore. Above and behind it was a broad hill, with an old army fort off to the right. They followed the crowd between two fish sheds and out onto the island's main thoroughfare.

Colorful little shops lined the sandy street, selling all manner of curios and candy to the thronging tourists. Carriages and wagons slowly made their way through the promenaders and the flocks of bicyclists that flew this way and that.

The two women spotted the Grand Hotel's omnibus and climbed aboard. After a hearty welcome to Mackinac from the young, heavily-freckled driver, the conveyance clattered into motion. As it swept up the hill, Mary caught her first sight of the magnificent hotel. A smile blossomed across her face. The sprawling, five-story structure of white, perched at the top of the hill, seemed to go on forever. She prodded Christena in the ribs.

"Oh, Tena, it *is* grand, isn't it?"

Christena shook her head in wonderment. "The pictures in the brochures don't really do it justice, do they? If ever there was a place made for summer magic, this is it."

"Will you look at that front porch?" Mary asked in amazement, as the vehicle drew near to the central staircase into the hotel. "It must be a city block in length!"

The omnibus lurched to a halt, and the passengers stepped down. A bellman greeted Mary and Christena and directed them to the red-carpeted steps. When they finally reached the porch above, they had to quickly step aside, to avoid the traffic in and out of the hotel's doors. Guests up and down the porch's length were seated on benches and rockers on either side, while revelers flowed between. Children capered around in front of mothers and grandmothers who were enjoying cups of tea.

Mary took Christena by the arm and attempted to forge through the crowd, managing immediately to walk right into a young man striding by with a tennis racquet. He dropped it as Mary dropped her purse.

"Oh, I do beg your pardon," she apologized. "Wasn't looking where I was going."

"No apologies needed," he laughed, stooping over to retrieve both the racquet and the purse. "My fault *entirely*. I was daydreaming about the match I just fumbled."

He wore white trousers and a short-sleeved white shirt that revealed muscular arms, and he did look a bit flushed and a little sweaty. Mary guessed his age at about that of her brother Jim—in his early twenties. Probably just out of college for the summer.

"I'm Thad Watkins, by the way."

He extended his hand and Mary shook it.

"Pleased to meet you. I'm Miss Mary MacDougall and this is my aunt, Miss Christena MacDougall."

"Good heavens! I thought you two were sisters."

Christena gave him a polite smile, but Mary could see she wasn't buying the young man's line of guff. If this fellow thought he could charm Mary's aunt with transparent flattery, he was greatly mistaken.

"How long have you two been on the island?" he asked, pushing a thick mop of flaxen hair back on his head.

"Just arrived," Mary replied. "From Duluth. We've been looking forward to it for months."

"I'm from Chicago myself. My grandmother brought me and my chum up here. Kind of her reward for doing so well in college."

"How lovely," Mary said.

"Yup. Just finished my first year at Wharton School of Finance and Commerce in Philadelphia."

"A distinguished institution," Christena observed.

"That it is," the tennis player agreed. "Well, best get inside and tidy up. It occurs to me, if you like to dance, there's always a band playing in the ballroom. Maybe I'll see you two there." He gave them a brisk salute with his racquet and marched into the hotel.

Christena arched her eyebrows. "I must say, the guests here seem a tad bit shy and reserved, don't you think?"

Mary chuckled. "Thank goodness the hotel is packed.

Hopefully we won't run into him again."

She locked her arm into Christena's and the two made their way through the doors and into the spectacular lobby—walls painted green, with opulent furniture and art and flowers all about. After checking in, they took the stairs up to the third floor, to their adjoining rooms, where both had excellent views of the Straits of Mackinac.

Mary quickly changed out of her traveling clothes and went down to the lobby, where she dispatched a telegram to Duluth. A short time later, she and Christena were sitting in rocking chairs out on the Grand Hotel's great piazza.

"That telegram you just sent in the lobby," said Christena, gazing out onto the water. "What was that about?"

"Something's been nagging at me ever since we spoke to the undertaker," replied Mary. "Chances are there's nothing amiss, but I just need to confirm a certain fact with Mrs. McColley. Once I've received her reply, I'll sit down, compose my official report, and post it off to her."

Christena rocked slowly forward and backward. "You know, Mary, I'm all for women getting out of their ruts and pursuing serious interests, even careers. But I must say, the life of a detective seems a bit, well, improbable. Even for a strong-willed person such as yourself. If you're dead set on a career, why not medicine? Like your friend Lillian. I'm sure you've learned a lot already at Dr. Burns's practice. Wouldn't helping patients get well be a lot more rewarding than helping someone find a stolen piece of jewelry?"

Mary wrinkled her nose. "To tell you the truth, I don't find sick people all that interesting. But the psychology of criminals? The unraveling of their tricks and their subterfuges? Now that's fascinating. And to be able to reveal malefactors, and see them brought to book..." She puffed herself up a little, thinking of her twin triumphs of 1901. "To have done some good for the victims and for society. That's the best part—justice."

Christena narrowed her eyes and peered evenly at Mary. "Very fancy words, my dear. But, I think, disingenuous."

"What do you mean?" Mary huffed.

"I don't think you want to pursue detection for society or for the victims or for justice. I think you're doing it because it's exciting. You have remarkable self-confidence and intelligence and you want to do something extraordinary. It gives you a thrill that being an unremarkable rich girl cannot."

Mary scowled at her aunt, but couldn't think of a retort. Because everything her aunt had just said was true.

"Tell me quite honestly, Mary. Are you not even a little tempted to live the life you're entitled to? To party and dance and travel pretty much constantly, until some handsome young man with good prospects marries you? Didn't you ever think that might be..."

"Fun?" said Mary. "No. From the time I was little and Emma Beach talked about it, I thought it sounded dreadful. I want to work, Christena. I want to be in charge of my life. I want to be in control." She frowned at her aunt.

Christena smiled at her. "I understand, Mary dear. But if I'm going to defend you to your father, I need to be very sure that you know what you're doing."

After a generous breakfast Saturday morning in the hotel's big dining room, Mary and Christena, both in white summer frocks, set out to explore their new environs. They strolled down the long porch at the front of the hotel, nodding and saying hello to other guests.

Below the hotel, a lovely beach stretched along the shore. As the two women made their way down it, the wind attempted to snatch their broad straw hats from their heads. Christena tied hers down tighter, while Mary took hers off and carried it. Though the sun wasn't that high, Christena still opened up her parasol.

As luck would have it, they ran into young Mr. Watkins and his friend. Both men were dressed rough and carried fishing rods and kits.

"We chartered a small boat," Thad Watkins explained, "and aim to see what we can pull out of the straits for dinner tonight. The kitchen manager said they'd be happy to fix up whatever we catch. Perhaps you ladies would care to join us for dinner? My grandmother will be there, too."

Mary was about to say no, but Christena surprised her by piping up first.

"We'd be delighted, Mr. Watkins. Just leave word for us at the desk. The name, as you may recall, is Miss Christena MacDougall."

"Right," said Thad Watkins. "The Misses MacDougall. Easy to remember."

As the two anglers tramped away, Mary shot her aunt an annoyed glance. "Why in the world did you accept his invitation?"

In return, Christena looked annoyed at Mary's annoyance. "Mr. Watkins comes across as a bit swell-headed, I will grant you. But he was being polite. He may be able to introduce you to some of the other young people at the hotel. There's nothing wrong with meeting new people."

The comment irritated Mary.

"I know you enjoy Edmond's company," her aunt continued. "But he won't be here for a while. It wouldn't kill you to have some fun in the meantime with some other folks your age."

Mary did not want to continue in this vein of conversation. She was nervous about Edmond's visit. What would it be like to spend so much time with him—some of it out of Christina's sight? Thinking about him made her feel a little crazy. She knew she wanted him in her life. But as what? And of course Edmond must have his own expectations of Mary. How did he see *her* in *his* future?

It was all so confusing. Maybe time alone with him would clarify things. But she didn't need her aunt to complicate the situation by trying to thrust her into the social whirl at the Grand Hotel.

They walked off the beach and back up the hill in silence. After lunch, Christena positioned herself in a rocker on the verandah, starting a new book, while Mary took a long bike ride through the bucolic, woodsy interior of the island. When she got back, she stopped by Christena's room. Her aunt informed her that Mr. Watkins and his chum had hooked several fat lake trout, more than enough for a generous dinner for five. The two MacDougalls would be expected in the dining room at seven.

Mary groaned inside but accepted her fate. "Well, I suppose it would be rude not to show up."

"*Quite* rude," Christena agreed.

A crisp rapping of sharp knuckles came through Christena's open door from the hallway outside. Mary opened the door, looked out, and spied a bellhop waiting with a silver tray in hand, in front of her own door.

"Yes, may I help you?" she asked.

The young man, almost painfully thin, turned to her. "Miss Mary MacDougall? Telegram for you."

She took it from him, thanked him, and gave him a quarter for his tip. He looked quite pleased to receive such a generous gratuity.

It must be the reply from Clara McColley, she thought, as she tore the yellow envelope open. But it wasn't.

She looked at Christena. "It's from Edmond. He and Paul are coming."

Christena beamed. "Excellent. When will they arrive?"

"On Monday. *In just two days!*"

Chapter XII

Almost as soon as Mary and Christena sat down at the table in the Grand Hotel's bustling restaurant, Thad's "Grandmama" Richardson attempted to find out who Mary was—to ascertain her bloodline.

"What is it that your father does?" the old lady asked.

"Oh," Mary said, "he dabbles in stocks and buys the odd property here and there." She didn't mention that the "odd property" included iron mines and vast tracts of timberland. "We have a nice little house on Superior Street in Duluth."

"And you came out a year or two ago?" Grandmama asked. Her beady little gray eyes looked as if they never missed a thing.

In fact, Mary might have debuted a year ago, if she had been willing. But she had refused the honor. What a silly thing, being a debutante. Had she not existed before that?

"No, Mrs. Richardson," she answered, "never did anything like that. I just said, 'Hello, world, here I am.'" She gave a silly little laugh, hoping to end this particular line of questioning.

It seemed to do the trick. Grandmama leaned back in

her chair, glancing around the dining room, no doubt looking for a young lady more suitable to her grandson's attentions.

All around them were scores of vacationers gotten up in their summer best, creating such a din with their conversations that Mary very nearly couldn't hear Mrs. Richardson. Waiters scurried about. A string ensemble sat off in a far corner of the big dining room, knocking out popular songs and favorite dance tunes by Strauss, Brahms, and Dvořák.

Although the lake trout almondine was mouthwatering, Mary's thoughts were focused less on the dinner than on the telegram she had just received. Her dining companions nattered on about the new president. Thad, his grandmother, and chum Ronald McNulty were of the opinion that Mr. Roosevelt, though of the right class, might not be loyal to that class. Mary, barely paying attention to them, mulled over the many ways in which Edmond's impending visit might go awry.

What if the couple quickly ran out of things to say? What if they really had nothing in common, apart from a love of art? What if Edmond made some dreadful social misstep? What if someone belittled the impecunious artist, shaming him in Mary's presence? What if Christena and Paul Forbes went off together, leaving Mary and Edmond to their own devices? What if Mary and Edmond somehow ended up alone in her room? Would he be able to restrain himself? Would she?

"Miss MacDougall? Mary?"

Mary started and blinked across the table at Grandmama, who, along with Thad and Ron, was staring at her. The stocky, white-haired old lady looked mildly concerned.

"Are you all right, my dear?" she asked. "You look quite distracted and a little flushed."

"Yes, Mary, are you feeling ill?" asked Christena, leaning toward her niece.

Mary felt a bit embarrassed. "Fine. I'm fine," she reassured them. "Just daydreaming, you know. What you say about President Roosevelt is very interesting. About how he's a bit of a loose cannon and perhaps not perfectly trustworthy with regard to business concerns. It got me thinking."

Thad looked pleased with himself. "Then you're suspicious of him, too. I mean, a cowboy! In the highest office in the land? There's no telling what outrageous thing he might do. Not a few of my professors at Wharton have their eye on him."

Mary very nearly observed that the most powerful man in America, who had suffered terribly in his personal life yet accomplished so much, would hardly lose any sleep over the opinions of a bunch of fusty old professors of finance and bookkeeping. But she held her tongue. She and Christena had agreed to be agreeable with anything their dinner companions said tonight, however small-minded.

Since Thad and Ron and Grandmama had done little but pontificate amongst themselves—with occasional nods to Mary and Christena—Mary decided to do some pontificating of her own.

"Well," she said, "I don't know about Mr. Roosevelt's business acumen, being neither a student of politics nor finance. But I do know that I very much admired President McKinley."

Thad attempted to leap in and take back the conversation, but Mary ploughed ahead.

"Several years ago, when I was still in school, the president came to visit Duluth and I was privileged to attend a speech of his before a large crowd. I stood not twenty feet from him, and I can tell you that he was quite a handsome man. A wonderful orator. And he seemed so kind and concerned about us young people and how education would help us make our ways in the world and..."

Mary kept on this track for a good five minutes, before she finally ran out of steam. In the midst of her monolog, she caught a glimpse of Christena suppressing a smile.

"A very interesting account," observed Grandmama Richardson dryly.

"Why, thank you so much," Mary said, now smiling herself. "I should add that I haven't decided yet if I myself will go off and earn a college degree. It's an open question."

The old lady curtly shook her head. "My dear, that is a *terrible* idea. A waste of time and money. Your duty is to find a gentleman you would want to marry, and then to start a family."

"My father," replied Mary sweetly, "has said something along the same lines."

"Then your father is a wise man," the old lady pronounced.

There was a slightly awkward silence, until Thad took the floor again and shared everything he had learned about Mackinac, in the way of entertaining activities.

"Say, I have swell idea," he said. "Do you ladies play tennis?"

"I do," Mary said, "but rather badly."

"Same here," tossed in Christena.

"Well then, what do you say to a mixed doubles match in the morning, after church? Ron and I have a court reserved. We can decide who plays who tomorrow."

"What do you think, Mary?" asked Christena.

Mary shrugged. "Fine with me. Sounds like fun."

Only a tennis match, Mary thought. How bad could it be?

"And I hope we'll see you ladies at the big dance." Thad was grinning at Mary, his perfect white teeth glinting. "Tomorrow night. They're bringing an orchestra down from Sault Ste. Marie especially for it. I'm very much looking forward to twirling you two ladies around the floor."

"Oh, we'll be there," gushed Christena. "I do love to dance."

"And so do I," Mary said. But she wondered if she looked as insincere as she felt. Thad's arms were not the arms she dreamed about having around her.

A single-set mixed doubles match was played late Sunday morning on the courts below the hotel. Mary and Thad defeated Christena and Ron 6-3 without too much trouble. Mary actually enjoyed herself. Thad showed that he had a fine sense of humor, cracking jokes and falling to the court in mock agony when one of Christena's wild volleys barely missed his head.

Saying goodbye to the gentlemen, Mary and Christena dragged themselves up the hill and the several flights of stairs, back to their rooms.

"I don't think I'll be able to move the rest of the day," groaned Christena, as she unlocked the door to her room. "What was I thinking? A woman my age playing tennis with three young people?"

Mary was still grinning as she opened her own door and went in. When she noticed a yellow envelope on the carpet, a telegram, her pulse quickened. This had to be the reply from Mrs. McColley to the telegram Mary had sent on Friday.

Snatching it up, she ripped it open. Her heart racing, she read the contents, then rushed out down the hallway and into Christena's room, without even knocking.

Her aunt, who was sitting with her feet up on a hassock, looked surprised.

"Mary, what's wrong? And what's that in your hand?"

"I have to go back to Dillmont, Tena," Mary said breathlessly, waving the telegram in the air. "As soon as possible."

"But whatever for?"

108

"As you recall, I wired Clara McColley. I asked her one question—what color was her mother's hair? She tells me it was black, with flecks of gray." Mary paced back and forth as she spoke. "Whoever the undertaker saw in that shroud at the infirmary... Whoever he buried... That woman with the wisps of red hair... She was not Agnes Olcott."

Mary stopped pacing and looked her aunt in the eye.

"Oh, Tena, I'm beginning to think something truly is rotten in Dillmont!"

Chapter XIII

Christena and Mary stared at each other for a long moment, as the revelation sank in.

Clara McColley's deep suspicion about her stepfather might well be justified. Agnes Olcott had certainly not been put in that grave in the Dillmont cemetery. Where she had been put, Mary realized, was now the mystery.

"I have to go back to Dillmont," she repeated. "First thing tomorrow morning."

Christena glared at her niece. "You most certainly are *not* going to Dillmont tomorrow. Have you already forgotten that Edmond and Paul are coming? As our guests! You will not be heading north on the train as they are heading south. It would be incredibly rude of you to vanish just as they arrive."

Mary blinked at her aunt, a bit astonished. Sometimes she forgot that Christena was more than twice her own age, old enough to be her mother. And that Christena might feel it necessary to impose limits on her niece when she felt Mary needed the voice of a responsible, mature adult.

Of course Mary hadn't forgotten about Edmond and Paul's imminent arrival. Perhaps, on some level, she was exaggerating the urgency of a return to Dillmont because she just wasn't ready for Edmond.

She slumped into a chair. "You're quite right, Tena. I was being a bit too impulsive. But getting that news—I guess it overexcited me."

"I think so," said Christena. "In fact, the tone of your voice leads me to believe that you're actually hoping for some dark doings. But clearly waiting a few days shouldn't make any real difference in your investigation. Whoever is in that grave won't be going anywhere anytime soon."

"I certainly hope not," Mary answered. "Though it would be quite the lark to track down a perambulating corpse." She gave her aunt an impish grin.

Christena's expression softened a bit and a tiny smile appeared on her lips. "Yes, that would be quite a caper. Now how about we have some lunch brought up to the room. Then we can go try to find a place for Paul and Edmond to stay."

"I'll run downstairs and order something," Mary volunteered. "What do you have a fancy for?"

The concierge in the lobby pulled out a room-service menu and Mary made her selections. Then she asked the man if he could recommend a nice, inexpensive guesthouse on the island for friends who were arriving Monday.

He thought a moment. "I'd try the little inn by the old Presbyterian church, right in the shadow of the spire. Used to be the rectory. It's plain, but comfortable." And he told her how to get to it.

After they finished eating, Mary and Christena set out

and found their way to the little hotel by the church. They were impressed with how tidy and quiet it was.

They booked two rooms and trudged back under the hot sun to the Grand Hotel. Off in the distance they could see the cheerful red roofs of summer cottages peeking through the trees, probably owned by wealthy families from Chicago and Detroit. Mary wondered what it must be like, staying in one of those instead of a hotel. For a summer-long sojourn, it would make more sense—and would offer the peace and quiet that was lacking in the bustling Grand Hotel.

As they walked, the niece and the aunt discussed the mystery of the strange woman in Mrs. Olcott's grave. Who could she be? Where was Agnes Olcott? Had Merton Olcott been referring to the cemetery at Westerholm, not the town cemetery of Dillmont? Had there been some mix-up on Mary's part? And what was Dr. Applegate's involvement in all this?

Christena asked Mary what she intended to do once she got back to Dillmont. She had agreed to allow Mary to return to the little town on Wednesday, as long as she promised to be back on Mackinac Island the next morning.

"I'm going to find Mrs. Gray, the woman we met at the cemetery," Mary explained as they neared the Grand Hotel. "And I hope she will take me to her cousin, who works at Westerholm. She may be more amenable to answering my questions than the doctor was."

Mary had packed three evening dresses for her stay on Mackinac—all made by Madame Zoya. For this evening's appearance on the dance floor, she selected a dress in pale green silk with a raised waistline. It was simple, but lovely. For her part, Christina wore a dark blue dress with light blue piping, which beautifully complemented her pale complexion and deep red hair.

As soon as they entered the ballroom, Thad and Ron rushed over to greet them and claimed their first dances. Grandmama Richardson was there, as well, ensconced in one of the chairs at the side of the hall, whence she could admire the dancers and chat with other old ladies.

As Mary waltzed around the floor with Thad, she caught Mrs. Richardson's ravenous gaze following her. The old woman, while reasonably cordial, had hardly seemed taken with Mary over dinner the night before. But now she appeared quite intrigued with her. Or was she merely watching her grandson, to gauge his reaction to each of the young women he danced with?

To her surprise, Mary found Thad a reasonably interesting conversationalist, more open-minded than he had first seemed. It turned out that he was a musician, and played cornet and wrote tunes for a student band at Wharton. He wondered if she played golf, as the island's little Wawashkamo course was rather nice. She replied that, alas, she did not. He talked about his studies and teachers, too, especially a professor who was a reluctant advocate of labor unions.

"He believes the future of American prosperity

depends on workers being able to afford the goods that they make. He thinks unions could make that happen," Thad said as they took a break from the dance floor. "I don't know if I'm entirely persuaded."

"I know my father isn't," said Mary. She recalled her uncomfortable encounter with Edmond's friend Simon Skelton on that very topic.

The next tune was a waltz, and the two of them took again to the floor. As they twirled about, Thad mentioned that on Tuesday he intended to rent a little sailboat and, if the wind and waves cooperated, go out onto the straits.

"Have you ever been out in a sailboat?" he asked.

"Not a small one like that. It sounds like barrels of fun."

"Indeed it is. And I'd be delighted if you and your aunt came along."

Mary very nearly said that it sounded wonderful, but remembered in the nick of time that she and Christena would be spending the day with Edmond and Paul. "Oh, I wish we could go. But we're expecting some guests tomorrow afternoon, and we want to take them around on Tuesday."

"Oh, I see. Who's arriving, then?"

"Just a couple of friends from Ishpeming. We persuaded them to join us for a few days."

"Well, if they need anyone to show them the ropes, I'd be happy to help. I know the island backwards and forwards."

Mary danced for another hour, mostly with Thad but

occasionally with one of the other young men. She finally made her excuses, saying she was quite done in, and went to find her aunt.

As she threaded her way around the perimeter of the dance floor, she passed by Grandmama Richardson. Mary nodded at her and had almost escaped, when she heard the old lady's husky voice.

"Miss MacDougall?"

She turned around, hoping that Thad's grandmother didn't have too much to say. Mary really was exhausted.

"Yes, Mrs. Richardson, how are you this evening?"

"I am well, my dear." The old lady patted the empty chair next to her and Mary could hardly refuse to sit down.

"My memory isn't what it used to be," Grandmama began. "But sometimes I am able to dredge up what I'm looking for. And it occurred to me that last night you mentioned your father was in investments and property."

"Yes," Mary agreed, "I did say that."

"Well, this evening, watching you dance with Thad and Ron and the other young gentlemen, I recalled that John MacDougall—*the* John MacDougall—lives in Duluth. I read the business news every day, you know."

Caught out, Mary thought. *Blast it!*

"Is *he* your father?"

Mary knew she couldn't lie. "Well, yes."

The look of satisfaction on the old lady's face almost made Mary laugh. Grandmama reached over and patted her hand.

"I understand why you might want to go incognito.

Don't worry, I won't tell a soul."

Mary finally spied her aunt on the dance floor and, excusing herself, headed in that direction. Christena, in spite of her morning tennis and hike to the rectory hotel, seemed to have replenished her store of energy. She was waltzing enthusiastically around the floor with a tall, bearded gentleman of about fifty. Mary stood off to the side and waited for the music to stop. When it did, she joined Christena and her partner.

"Oh, hello Mary," her aunt panted. "What a wonderful evening it's been, hasn't it?"

"Yes, wonderful," Mary said, though she felt the adjective a bit hyperbolic.

"Let me introduce you to my partner these last few dances. This is Judge Anson Tolliver from Sault Ste. Marie. He's here vacationing with his wife. Judge, this is my niece, Miss Mary MacDougall."

"So pleased to meet you, Miss MacDougall." He offered his large hand and Mary shook it. He had craggy, Lincolnesque features and he stood nearly a head taller than Christena.

"Pleased to meet you, Judge Tolliver. And where is Mrs. Tolliver?"

"Normally, she loves to dance. But, sadly, she twisted her ankle this morning. Swollen and painful, she tells me. She's in our room, reading some novel or other. But she said, 'Anson, you go down there and find a pretty lady to dance with.' So, by heavens, I did. And a redhead, to boot."

"I've told the judge that we'd very much enjoy having dinner with him and his wife," said Christena. "He has some wonderful stories about life in the Upper Peninsula."

"So, you're a judge in Chippewa County?" Mary asked.

"That I am, for eight years now. Elected three times. I plan to keep running until they carry me off the bench feet first. Best job in the world."

"Dillmont's in Chippewa County, isn't it?" Mary asked.

"It is," the judge nodded. "On the Duluth South Shore line between Soo Junction and Trout Lake. I would imagine if you came from Duluth, you passed through there. Fine little town. Lot of timber operations around there."

Mary was curious to find out if the judge knew anything about Westerholm, where Agnes Olcott had supposedly died. "We heard there's an asylum and infirmary there," she said off-handedly.

"That's right," the judge said. "You're not feeling ill, are you?"

"No, no, no," Mary assured. "I just happen to know someone whose mother lately has been suffering from severe moroseness. Does the place have a good reputation?"

"Well, it has a first-rate infirmary. But most of the patients are in the asylum. Westerholm Institution for Women is, in these parts, the best place for unfortunates with mental trouble. Females exclusively. It takes on indigents at no charge. But it's especially known for handling wives and daughters of affluence. That's what pays the bills."

"So that's where well-to-do gentlemen park their balky wives?" Christena joshed.

A dark shadow came over the judge's face. "Well, all joking aside, Westerholm has acquired that reputation. Very often the wife does need help. But I've heard of other times where she's merely argumentative or hectoring. For better or worse, husbands can commit their wives, in my opinion, rather arbitrarily."

Mary looked at Christena as they both took in the judge's comments. Westerholm, it seems, was a convenient dumping ground for inconvenient wives.

But before either woman could say anything, music again began to fill the hall.

The judge's expression brightened. He turned to Christena and offered his arm. "Ready for another spin around the floor, Miss MacDougall?"

Christena took his arm and said good night to Mary. The judge wished her a pleasant slumber, as well.

But as Mary left the ballroom, sleep was no longer on her mind. All along, she had been trying to ascertain whether Merton Olcott had killed his wife. Now she wondered if he had instead imprisoned her in an asylum.

Chapter XIV

The events and revelations of the evening did not make for a restful night's sleep. Mary kept thinking again and again about the very real possibility that what had been an inquiry into the cause of death had now become a rescue. Though Mary could not know for sure, Agnes Olcott at this very moment might be slumbering away in Westerholm, as she herself tossed and turned in the Grand Hotel.

When she finally rose from bed at seven, having long since given up the pretense of sleeping, she quickly washed and dressed and went down the hallway to Christena's door. She knocked, but no answer came. She knocked again. Not even a peep emerged from inside.

When she returned from breakfast, she knocked again. This time, a frazzled Christena opened the door a crack and told her she would meet her on the porch at about ten.

Frustrated by her aunt's sluggishness, Mary headed out on a very vigorous walk, mulling over her next steps in the Agnes Olcott case. This investigation was turning into something much bigger than anticipated. But she needed to proceed cautiously. She didn't want to bungle things through precipitous action before she actually found out the true fate of Mrs. Olcott.

And what if the woman was alive? What if Mary's investigation resulted in the reunion of mother and daughter? Mary couldn't imagine a more gratifying outcome.

She was waiting impatiently in her wicker seat at about ten, when she finally saw Christena emerge into daylight. Her aunt was wearing a hat with the brim adjusted to block out as much sun as possible. She shuffled along, looking pale and tired, and sat down next to Mary. As soon as a waiter appeared, she ordered "a nice cup of your strongest tea."

Clearly, she was in no mood to talk, answering Mary's queries with curt responses. "Slept poorly," she muttered, by way of explanation.

Mary knew her aunt to be an adventurous and intellectually curious person. But she was surprised by how vivacious Christena had seemed on this trip. Particularly when handsome men of all ages were paying her so much attention. First Paul Forbes, then Thad and Ron, and last night Judge Tolliver. Evidently, Christena, was not immune to the charms of the opposite sex.

But why, at this particular critical juncture, had she decided to go boy-crazy? Mary needed her aunt's sharp reasoning to figure out how to proceed with the Olcott case. And all her aunt was capable of at the moment was sipping her tea and complaining about the bright sun.

There was nothing for it but to wait until Christena rejoined the living.

So Mary got back to reading *My Brilliant Career*. She

was determined to finish the novel as soon as she could. Given that the next week would be tied up entertaining Edmond and Paul, and re-visiting Dillmont, she'd best plow through as many pages as possible this morning. It was hard to concentrate, though, with thoughts of Mrs. Olcott bouncing around in her head.

Bit by bit, Christena seemed to wake up. The strong black tea apparently was having the desired effect.

"Don't look now," she croaked, peaking out from beneath the brim of her hat, "but Mr. Watkins is rapidly steaming in our direction, from starboard."

Mary glanced up from her book and caught sight of Thad approaching with three other people, all in white tennis clothes and carrying rackets. One was Ron, and the other two were a pair of pretty sisters from Cleveland, whom Mary had met at the dance the night before. The four were engaged in an animated discussion. As they passed Mary and Christena, Thad doffed his cap with a smile, but kept on walking. Mary watched the group continue on, then saw him quickly glance over his shoulder in her direction, perhaps to gauge her reaction.

It was one of relief. Now maybe both he and his grandmother would focus their attentions on other matrimonial prospects at the hotel, and leave Mary in peace.

Christena finally pushed back the brim of her hat a bit and looked at Mary. "I gather the judge's comments about Westerholm last night didn't escape your attention."

Mary laid her book down and sat up straight. At last, she could discuss the case with Christena.

"Indeed they did not, particularly the one about wealthy men who commit their perfectly sane if contentious wives there. One can only wonder if a certain middle-aged wife from Duluth has been so deposited. Out of sight, and out of mind."

She didn't know what made her angrier. The fact that a husband would do this to his wife. Or that a wife would let herself be abused in this manner. If ever there was a single reason for remaining an unmarried woman, this was it.

"But how could Olcott have pulled it off?" Christena wondered. "Surely his wife would have protested being committed."

"Yes, she might have protested. But as the judge inferred, the husband has the final say."

"And what about the death certificate? It was signed by Dr. Applegate, after all."

Mary furrowed her brow. "I'm beginning to wonder if the good doctor might have some involvement in Agnes Olcott's disappearance. All I know is that my work is cut out for me when I go back to Dillmont on Wednesday."

"So the first order of business will be to see if Mrs. Olcott is at Westerholm?"

"Of course not. They're not going to let a perfect stranger waltz in and start questioning the staff about the patients. For all they know, I could be a reporter from some yellow-press newspaper, trying to dig up dirt about the crazy wife of some millionaire or senator. No, I'll start with Mrs. Gray's cousin, the one who works at the asylum. If I go about it the right way, she might just tell me if

Agnes Olcott is one of her patients there."

Just then, another acquaintance walked by—Judge Tolliver, with his wife. Introductions were made, and the couple invited Mary and Christena to join them for dinner some evening that week.

The judge and his wife strolled away—she limping noticeably. As Mary watched them go down the red carpet that bisected the porch, she saw something that made her catch her breath. There, about a hundred feet away, carpet-bags and equipment cases in hand, came Edmond and Paul. When Edmond caught sight of her, a smile lit up his face.

At that moment, all other thoughts flew right out of Mary's head. She stood and turned to Christena. "They're here," she said, trying to keep her voice calm as they approached.

"A hearty welcome to Mackinac," she pronounced as the men joined them.

"We are your official if not very energetic welcoming committee," Christena added, not bothering to get up. "We had quite an exhausting day yesterday, and slept poorly, so you'll have to excuse us if we're not prepared to show you around the island this afternoon."

"I'd enjoy just sitting here on the porch all day," Paul enthused, gazing around the vista. "What a glorious spot. I can't wait to start shooting. I hope you have some thoughts about good locations."

"As a matter of fact, we do," Christena said. "But first things first. We've booked you into a little inn near an old Presbyterian church. The old rectory, in fact." At that, she rose slowly from her chair. "Why don't we go inside," she said to Paul, "and see if we can arrange a cab for you to the inn. You can rest and freshen up, and then you can come back here for dinner tonight."

"And make plans for the rest of the week," Paul said, following her. The two of them disappeared through the hotel's front doors.

Mary, smiling shyly, reclaimed her chair while Edmond took Christena's. She had been nervous about his visit, about spending so much time with him, with no prying eyes. Christena, of course, was supposed to play the role of chaperone. But considering her recent effervescence, she might need a chaperone herself.

Mary looked down at Edmond's case and little fold-up easel. "I hope you've brought enough paint. There are so many breathtaking spots on the island that you'll be in danger of running out."

"I have plenty. In fact, I thought I could start you off on watercolors. After all, I owe you some lessons. The ones that I so rudely ran out on."

She gave him a mock scowl. "Yes, well, you've got your work cut out for you. I haven't held a brush since last fall. I barely remember which end to paint with."

He sat back in his chair and grinned at her. "It's good to see you again, Miss Mary MacDougall."

Mary cocked her head. "It's good to see you too, Mr. Edmond Roy."

Chapter XV

They requested a quiet table for four well away from the entrance to the restaurant that evening. After catching Mary and Christena up on the latest news from Ishpeming, Paul and Edmond put forth their ideas for the next week's activities. They both wanted to end their stay with work they could take back to Ishpeming and embellish upon. Paul would make prints from his negatives and Edmond would use his sketches and watercolors to start a new series of oil landscapes. With any luck, this trip would turn into a profitable one for the two of them.

"Tomorrow we'll hire a carriage in the morning and show you some of the island's natural beauty," Christena said. "There are spectacular coves and caves hidden all over the place. You'd think they'd be overrun with tourists, but it seems most visitors here prefer to spend their time eating and socializing."

"All the better for us," Edmond said. "We can paint and photograph to our hearts' content, without being interrupted by curious onlookers." He turned to Mary. "And let's start your lessons on Wednesday."

Mary's smile faded as she realized what she had to tell

him. "I won't be able to see you on Wednesday."

Edmond looked baffled. "Why in the world not?"

"I'm going back to Dillmont for the day. I won't return until the next morning."

Edmond did not look pleased with this news. "You're going back? I didn't know you'd been there in the first place."

"What's so fascinating about Dillmont?" Paul asked. "From what I've heard, it's just a sleepy town along the rail line."

Mary had planned to tell Edmond about her investigation *after* it had been wrapped up. Should she give both men all the details right now? Or just say she was doing a favor for a friend whose mother died there? Before she could decide, a look of comprehension came over Edmond's face.

"Good Lord," he said incredulously. "You're working on another case, aren't you?"

She gave a sheepish nod.

"In Dillmont. But why? There's nothing there."

So Mary decided to tell them. Everything. About the whole affair of Agnes Olcott's alleged death by cholera and the behavior of her husband. The daughter's suspicions. The slow strangulation of the family firm. The peculiar puzzle of the red-headed corpse.

"I came this close to saying 'Done.'" She held up her index finger and thumb, a fraction of an inch apart. "Then that dratted undertaker mentioned the red hair. And I knew the body couldn't be Agnes Olcott's. So my plan is to interview an attendant who works at Westerholm, to see if she can tell me who the red-headed woman was. And maybe she can even tell me about Mrs. Olcott."

"Christena is going with you, I should hope." Edmond shot Mary a sort of disapproving look that was more endearing than chastening.

"As a matter of fact, Edmond, no," Christena said. "As long as there's no danger involved, I've agreed to let her go sleuthing alone in Dillmont."

Edmond, now clearly frustrated, looked back at Mary. "Then at least let me come with you. I'd feel a lot better if there was someone around to help if you get in a fix."

Mary took his hand and squeezed it. "You're very sweet to be concerned. But, for heaven sakes, I'll be in Michigan, not Manchuria. I think I'll be perfectly safe. I'm just going to ask a few people a few questions and I'll be back before you know it."

Edmond gave her that look again. "What in the world can one do with such a willful woman?" he grumbled.

Willful? Mary thought the comment a bit unfair. She considered herself perfectly reasonable. She only was doing what she had to do, given the situation.

Christena chuckled. "I learned a long time ago that Mary, like my brother Johnny, has a stubborn streak a mile wide." She took a sip of her wine.

Mary peered at her aunt and thought that this was a classic case of the pot calling the kettle black.

"Now," Christena continued, "I want to be sure that we're all in agreement about going to the show Thursday evening. *Florodora.* I saw it in New York and it's quite delightful. And I'm told the theater company here is rather good."

The next morning, the foursome rented a two-seat wagon and headed north into the bucolic districts of Mackinac Island. They went up and around on narrow, woodsy lanes, stopping along the way to take little walks and view water vistas on the lakeshore byway. The island wasn't that big—a bit under three miles long and half that wide—but they managed to find more than enough to explore.

Paul had brought along his camera equipment and film. To begin, he insisted on making a dual portrait of Mary and Christena on the bank of Carver Pond. It fascinated Mary to watch the fastidiousness with which he worked—setting his focus and aperture precisely, moving his camera and tripod around for the best angle, posing her and Christena just so.

She supposed that, despite its eroticism, the gauzy, come-hither image of the unclothed Mrs. Lehmann was the result of hard work rather than passionate improvisation. It was difficult enough sitting there with Christena on the grassy bank for well over half an hour, fully clothed, as Paul fussed with his camera. What must it have been like standing naked for that long, especially if there had been a cool breeze blowing? One would have been goose bumps all over.

The morning went quickly. As Paul was making his pictures, a tourist couple stopped by and wondered if they might hire him to make a souvenir portrait of them out in an island setting. He took their names and set a date for the following week.

Lunch was a picnic on a grassy knoll, with sandwiches and beer that the hotel had provided. They sat on blankets on the ground in a semi-circle, facing Lake Huron. By now they were all rumpled and sweaty and not a little bushed. The morning had been wonderful. Mary would see more of Edmond later that day, but she planned an early evening. She needed a good night's sleep before her journey the next morning.

As the wagon rattled back to the hotel midafternoon, Mary and Edmond, jammed delightfully close together in the back seat, talked about his mural. A visiting banker had seen it in its almost completed state, and asked the painter if he might be available to do another. The new bank was in Eau Caire, Wisconsin, and the fellow wanted something similar, mixing history and commerce.

"Another five-thousand dollar commission," Edmond bragged. "With the money I make, I'll be able to afford to finally put together my gallery show. Of course, if I get the job, I wouldn't start until I'm done with Mrs. Ensign's portraits."

"You'd better not," Mary scolded playfully. "I plan to spend a lot of time watching you work at Mrs. Ensign's house. It's just a few blocks up from our place, as you recall."

Edmond smiled. "I would warn you that the only thing more boring than watching paint dry is seeing me put it down on a canvas. A sure cure for insomnia."

129

"Well, I'm willing to take that chance. And I'll bring a pillow, just in case."

The wagon trundled along a split-log fence built around a rustic cottage, and all four companions fell silent. If the rest of the week went as well as the first day, this would be the best vacation Mary ever had.

Mary caught the ferry to St. Ingace the next morning, and boarded the train heading north and west for Duluth. She got off in Dillmont at about ten o'clock. Carrying her leather valise, she walked over to Mrs. Wingate's guest-house and found that her old room was available.

The hike to Tilda Gray's house was a hot and sweaty one. Along the way Mary munched on the ham sandwich Mrs. Wingate had made for her. The sun beat down merci-lessly and Mary was grateful for her broad-brimmed hat. Soon her dogged trudging brought her to the two-story house that Mrs. Wingate had described. A few ginger-colored hens were pecking through the yard in a rather desultory manner. From not too far away, she could hear the fierce metallic whine of a powered saw ripping through wood.

She strode up to the front door and rapped on it. No one answered. A few more knocks were administered to the door, with no results.

"Not home," she muttered under her breath. "I proba-bly should have sent a wire yesterday."

Hands on hips, she surveyed the yard, thinking she might have wasted her trip here. There was a small barn to one side of the house and a chicken coop with more pecking chickens about. Walking around the house, Mary spotted a long, low structure banked up to its roof in grass-covered soil. The earth-sheltered building had its own separate driveway that wended through the woods out of sight. Mrs. Wingate had told her that Mrs. Gray and her sons operated an icehouse, in addition to the sawmill.

She still didn't see anyone about, though, and was almost ready to admit defeat when Mrs. Gray stepped out of the chicken coop, carrying a wicker basket full of eggs. She wore a simple blue dress and apron, and a sunbonnet on her head. She stopped in her tracks when she saw Mary. Then a smile spread across her face.

"Hello, miss," she said. "Welcome, and how may I...?" She looked at Mary for a few seconds. "You're the young lady from the cemetery, aren't you?"

Mary walked toward her. "I am, Mrs. Gray. Miss Mary MacDougall."

The two women shook hands. The older one regarded the younger rather curiously.

"Why in the world are you here? You aren't needing any eggs, are you?"

"No," Mary laughed. "I've no need of eggs, but I do need some information you might be able to provide."

"And what would that be?"

"When we met at the cemetery," explained Mary, "you said you had a cousin who is employed at Westerholm."

"Yes, she works in both the asylum and the infirmary, as she's needed. Mostly the asylum, though."

"May I ask her name?"

"It's Olive Handy. She's a strapping woman six feet tall, but gentle as a kitten. When the poor dears get, well, rambunctious… She's able to gather them up without hurt and restrain them from injuring their own selves or others. But what could you possibly want with Olive?"

"As you remember, we encountered each other at the grave of a woman who died recently at Westerholm."

"Indeed, we did."

"And I was under the impression that the woman in that grave died of cholera last April when on a trip with…"

"Heavens to Betsy!" Mrs. Gray exclaimed. "She died of cholera? I never heard that. I thought it was cancer. Cholera's terrible catching, isn't it?"

"Correct. But you see, this woman's daughter sent me to…"

"You said her *daughter* sent you?" Mrs. Gray looked baffled.

"I did. I'm not surprised you're confused…"

"I had no idea she had a daughter."

"Mrs. Gray, please," Mary said, seeking to gain control of the conversation. "Perhaps you could tell me who you believe is buried in the grave with 'A.O.' on the marker?"

"I don't believe it—I know it. It's Annie O'Toole, of course. Poor mad Annie."

"Did Annie have red hair?" Mary asked eagerly.

Mrs. Gray nodded. "Oh, yes. Long, beautiful red locks.

The attendants at the asylum loved to help her brush it and braid it. How did you know?"

Finally, some progress, some clarity! The initials on the wooden cross at the cemetery didn't stand for Agnes Olcott, but for Annie O'Toole.

This was by far the most important clue Mary had uncovered. While it provided no definitive proof that Agnes Olcott was yet among the living, it gave Mary the encouragement to dig even deeper. She had solved one important piece of the puzzle. Now, onto the next.

"Mrs. Gray," she said. "For a small remuneration, would you be willing to take me to your cousin's house and provide an introduction for me? I have some questions I'd like to ask her."

Chapter XVI

Olive Handy lived alone in a log cabin even further out in the woods than her cousin. She looked to be in her forties, tall, almost manly of figure. She was wearing a blue gingham wrapper with an apron tied over it and was pulling radishes up from a well-tended garden next to her rustic little house. Mary couldn't imagine any of the ladies of the asylum being her match in a contest of strength.

Olive seemed quite surprised to see the wagon coming up her driveway, but her welcome was warm and sincere. She quickly shooed her two guests into the house and sat them at her kitchen table, where she put a bottle of root beer in front of each of them. Mary found the sweet, fizzy drink just the thing after a hot carriage ride.

As her hostess put a few cookies on a plate, Mary surveyed the large, open room. Though timber-walled and rough, the place was clean and neat as a pin. A narrow brass bed sat in a corner and a bent-hickory rocking chair rested before the fireplace. Atop an ancient sideboard was a framed photograph of an old couple, no doubt Olive's parents.

"Now you mentioned, Miss MacDougall…" Olive

said, taking one of the chairs and placing the ginger cookies on the table.

Mary interrupted. "Please call me Mary."

The woman smiled at her. "Then you must call me Olive. You said that you have a friend whose mother died of cholera at Westerholm. Yet the only patient I know of that died there in many a long month was poor Annie O'Toole. And she certainly did not die of cholera and did not have a daughter."

"Yes, well, obviously my friend was given faulty information," Mary responded. "But, tell me, why was Annie O'Toole buried in the Dillmont cemetery. I was told there was a graveyard at Westerholm, just for its inmates." She had considered the possibility that there had been some mix-up—Annie in Agnes's grave and Agnes in Annie's.

"That there is. But Annie's cousin, her closest relative, said it was bad enough Annie had to spend so many years at Westerholm, she shouldn't have to spend eternity there. So she paid for Annie's plot in Dillmont."

"And you can't think of any other burials in the Westerholm cemetery in the past several months?"

"None that I recall."

Mary still intended to visit the asylum cemetery herself. If Agnes Olcott was there, she would find a fresh grave. No fresh grave, no Agnes Olcott.

"Do you remember any woman of about fifty being admitted to the asylum in the last few months?" Mary asked. "A woman with black hair beginning to show signs of gray?"

The tall woman frowned and shook her head. "Doesn't ring any particular bells."

"Have you ever heard of anyone named Agnes Olcott? Mrs. Merton Olcott?"

Olive Handy pondered the question briefly. "No, never heard of the lady. Though there's much that goes on at Westerholm that we ordinary attendants never hear of. We have well over two hundred unfortunates who are being cared for. And some sixty of us who work there."

"May I ask what your duties include?"

"I'm mostly with the ones who are more troublesome or need lifting or moving. Those that are curled up in bed, yet must be washed and put upon the commode. Or those who, really meaning no harm, might have fits and strike out. I gather them up and hold onto to them, or wrap them tight in a warm, wet blanket. The really violent ones we don't take. They have to go up to the state hospital in Newberry."

It was probably too much to have hoped that Olive would have known of Agnes Olcott. But this friendly woman could still provide some vital information.

"Tell me about Westerholm," Mary said. "How is it laid out? Who belongs where? That sort of thing."

Olive explained that Westerholm had two five-story wings joined in the middle by a three-story administration building. The west wing housed a large communal dining room, kitchen, and commons area on the first floor, with four floors of dormitories above it. The first floor of the east wing was devoted to the infirmary, along with examining rooms, and an operating room, as well as a second, smaller kitchen.

"The infirmary's where patients and local folk go if they're sick," Olive said. "If this Agnes Olcott woman did really have cholera, and came to Westerholm, the doctor would have put her in the infirmary's quarantine room."

Silent up to now, Mrs. Gray gave an audible shudder. "Cholera. Horrible. That's the last thing this town needs. But I'd think that if there had been a case at the infirmary, we would have heard about it."

The second floor of the east wing, Olive went on to say, was where well-to-do patients were housed. These ladies had their own dining room, parlor, library, and sunroom, separate from the general population. Even their own nurses and attendants.

"I've never worked on the second floor," Olive said. "But I know it's quite plush, with all the comforts of home, you might say. I think most anyone would enjoy staying there. Of course, their families pay a lot extra to keep them there, compared to the women in the dormitories."

"And what about the floors above that one?"

"Directly above is another general dormitory. Then on the fourth floor, the little apartments for the nurses and attendants that live on the grounds. And on the fifth floor they have more storage and a locked ward for extremely troubled patients. Most of the time there's no one in there. Our ladies are all pretty well behaved."

"Is that the only ward under lock and key?" Mary

asked.

"That's correct. Everyone else is allowed to roam, so long as they don't make trouble or wander too far. Many of the women are fit enough to help out in the fields, in the laundry and kitchen, and around the place. Healthy work can do a lot to help mend a troubled mind, after all. Even the wealthy ladies are encouraged to take on some of the chores, if they wish to."

"What other buildings are on the grounds?"

"There are barns for the animals, a chicken coop, the maintenance shed, a greenhouse, and the chapel. Mrs. Westerholm insisted on a separate chapel, and quite a lovely thing it is."

"And you said about sixty are employed at Westerholm?"

"About that many, I should think. The two doctors, their secretary, the folks in the business office, the farm manager, housekeepers, the engineer. And of course a lot of nurses and attendants."

Mary thought about the delicate situations the nurses and attendants might have to deal with, given that all the inmates were women. Surely men would not be allowed to handle some of the more intimate tasks. "Are all the nurses and attendants women?" she asked.

"Pretty much. But we have a few male attendants. Once in a while an inmate gets a bit too rambunctious for even me to handle. That's when Willis comes to help." A little smile flitted across her lips.

From the look on Olive's face, Mary figured that

Willis, whoever he was, had a real admirer.

"And we've a couple of other male attendants, as well. They're all big, strong men."

"Who are the doctors?" she asked.

"Well, Dr. Stanley is our superintendent," Olive replied. "A surgeon with training as an alienist. Our assistant superintendent is the town physician, Dr. Applegate."

Mary sat back in her chair. So Dr. Applegate didn't just treat patients at the infirmary. He was also the second-in-command at Westerholm. Suddenly things began to fall into place in her mind. The doctor would have been in a perfect position to take Agnes Olcott off her husband's hands and write up a false death certificate in her name. While she might not have been murdered, she could have, in effect, been removed from existence, clearing the way for Olcott to claim her estate. And what was in it for the doctor? Money, no doubt. Mary presumed he could make quite a nice income, helping rich men rid themselves of bothersome wives.

Given what she had just heard, Mary was fairly certain she knew what Merton Olcott had done. But now she needed to find out if he had accomplices. She understood her next question might not be well received.

Taking a deep breath, she looked Olive Handy square in the eye. "Would there be any chance that Dr. Applegate forged a death certificate for Agnes Olcott? In your opinion, would the doctor engage in such activities?"

The transformation of Olive's face could not have been more remarkable—from a friendly curiosity to a cold hostility in a wink. Even Tilda Gray looked angered by Mary's insinuation.

"You could not possibly be more mistaken about our Dr. Applegate," said Mrs. Gray with a chilly tone. "He's saved dozens of lives in these parts, delivered many and many a child. Dillmont would be in a bad state without him."

"To suggest that he's corrupt..." Olive Handy shook her head and glared at Mary. "He's a good man, a good doctor. Saw me through the pneumonia two years ago. He does naught but help people. And he has his own personal burdens to bear." She snorted, like a fuming bear. "I won't tolerate anyone speaking ill of him in my house. Now, Miss MacDougall, if you don't mind, I must get back to my gardening."

Mary had known there was a chance the women would not take kindly to her question. Still, their vehement reaction surprised her. Yet it taught a good lesson: As a detective, one ought to save one's most provocative queries for the end of the interview. She tried to find out more about Annie O'Toole, but the big woman and her cousin were having none of it. Mary apparently had over-stayed her welcome.

A moment later, she was in the wagon with Tilda Gray, who had become quite taciturn. She dropped Mary at the guesthouse and rattled off without even saying goodbye. After having a buttered biscuit and tea with Mrs. Wingate, Mary headed out, making for Main Street. She had one more thing to do before she could return to Mackinac.

At the livery stable she found a man who agreed to take her around the town and countryside in a buggy. "Just drive me to the scenic spots," Mary said. "And I'd like to see where Westerholm is."

The man, middle-aged and walrus-mustachioed, was a talker. And with a wink he wondered if Mary was feeling "a tad squirrelly in the brain box."

She laughed along with him. "That might be closer to the truth than you would ever know."

"I had a good interview with Mrs. Gray and her cousin, Olive Handy, the attendant at Westerholm," Mary recounted. "Though they turned a bit cool when I questioned the character of Dr. Applegate, the fellow who signed Agnes Olcott's death certificate. Apparently he is well liked by the townspeople."

Mary had arrived back at the Grand Hotel just before noon, the day after her visit to Dillmont. She was sitting in her aunt's room with Edmond and Christena, Paul Forbes being occupied elsewhere with something or other photographic.

"Olive claimed she had never heard of Mrs. Olcott, though I have no way of knowing if she was telling the truth. Apparently, the lady with the red hair—the dead woman in the shroud—was someone called Annie O'Toole, who just happened to have the same initials as Agnes Olcott. I can only presume that when Merton Olcott saw Annie O'Toole's wooden cross with 'A.O.' on it, he decided to seize the opportunity and use it to help weave his little story of death in Dillmont.''

Edmond was sitting in a side chair, leaning intently toward her, his elbows on his knees, his chin in his hands. Christena, looking very serious, shared the sofa with Mary.

"Then I went to have a look at Westerholm itself," Mary continued. "An impressive edifice, two wings joined in the center. Inmates out working in gardens and tending the flock of chickens. Not an unpleasant place to be confined, I should think. And the little cemetery was quite pretty, beneath a number of spreading oaks and maples. Perhaps forty or fifty graves with simple stone markers. Names engraved on every one. No recent burials, though. No sign of Agnes Olcott there."

"So really," said Christena, "you've come to a dead end."

Mary was about to disagree, when Edmond piped up.

"Don't you think it time, Mary, to send your report to Mrs. McColley and call it a day? You've discovered certain suspicious facts that your client can present to the sheriff. A fine job of sleuthing, I should say. You've done more than enough."

No, it is not nearly enough, thought Mary. It irked her that Edmond and Christena didn't understand how vital it was to soldier on.

Because if Agnes Olcott was alive, it wasn't unreasonable to think that she might be in Westerholm under Dr. Applegate's orders. If the doctor found out that Mary was snooping around the place, he might move Mrs. Olcott to another location. Time was of the essence.

Mary had a good idea now of what needed be done. On her trip back from Dillmont that morning she had thought of little else. But she knew she couldn't finish her investigation without the help of Christena or Edmond, or both. And they seemed intent on persuading her to call it quits. She had to make them see things from her point of view.

"Christena, Edmond," she began, "you have been very tolerant of my... What shall I call them?" She paused and deliberated over her choice of word. "Adventures, let us say. I'm sure that neither of you feels happy that my current case has become *more* adventuresome. Heaven knows I don't. I wish I had an easier answer to this puzzle."

She stopped again, hoping to gauge their reactions, but both remained inscrutable. Christena was peering at her though narrowed eyes and Edmond was fiddling with the edge of a doily on the table next to him.

Mary attempted to lend a certain gravitas to her voice, as if she were a lawyer summing up her case to the jury. "I could, as you suggest, send a report back to Clara McColley, telling her I believe her mother might yet be alive and encouraging her to follow up with the police. But, of course, I have no actual proof to present to her. What I do know for certain is that Mrs. McColley has no one else on her side. She has been told by her husband to accept reality and move on with her life. Even Detective Sauer thinks she's merely overwrought."

Mary looked first at Christena, then at Edmond. "I truly

believe that I am Clara McColley's last hope. And I think a great injustice would be done if we don't go the extra mile and make one last push to discover the true fate of her mother."

"But how in the world do you propose to do that, Mary?" sighed Edmond wearily. "Even if you could?"

Mary almost felt sorry for the man. He no doubt had thought he would be spending his time on Mackinac Island painting watercolor scenes and squiring her around. What she had in mind for him was certainly no picnic.

"We know that Agnes Olcott is not buried in the Dillmont cemetery under a wooden cross bearing the initials A. and O.," she said. "That dubious honor belongs to poor Annie O'Toole, of the lovely red hair." Mary stood up and started to pace. "And there are no fresh graves in the asylum cemetery."

"Yes, so you noted," said Christena. "But that still doesn't explain what you have in mind."

Mary stopped pacing and crossed her arms. "If the woman is not in Westerholm, then it would likely be impossible for us to ever know what Merton Olcott has done with her—even to know whether or not she is alive. Agnes Olcott, or her remains, could be hidden away anywhere. She might never resurface. Or she might be found wandering a street somewhere, disheveled and penniless, after her husband has vanished with the funds he looted from the family firm."

She paused one final time for dramatic effect.

"The only thing that I can do now for Clara McColley

is to answer this one, final question: Is her mother, Agnes Olcott, an inmate at Westerholm asylum?"

Christena and Edmond both regarded Mary with expressions of dread, as if anticipating an appalling end to her soliloquy.

"To do that, I'll need you two to take me there. And have me committed."

Chapter XVII

Mary wished she had her Kodak Brownie handy to take snapshots of Edmond and Christena's faces, after she had proposed her own committal. Clearly her two companions were appalled by her audacious plan.

"Good grief, Christena," Edmond finally said, "did I just hear what I thought I heard?"

For her part, Christena said nothing. She didn't need to. She only needed to stare at Mary through those narrowed eyes to sum up her simple response: *No! A thousand times no!*

"Please, just think about it awhile before you decide," Mary begged. "A woman's fortune—perhaps her life—is at stake. Time may be running out for Agnes Olcott, if indeed she's alive. We've been given the opportunity to save her from a terrible fate. Don't you think we should give it our utmost effort?"

Edmond evidently did not, standing to leave. "This morning, Paul asked me if I would help him lug his camera equipment up to the Arch Rock so he could spend the afternoon taking pictures. I told him he was crazy to go clambering about on such dangerous ground with camera and tripod and whatnot. But in comparison to what I've just heard suggested, his plan sounds quite sane. So I think I'll take my leave of you two ladies and go climb a cliff." He nodded curtly and left.

Mary was taken aback. Edmond had never been so abrupt with her before. She looked at her aunt. "You're mad at me, too, I suppose," she said with a tiny pout.

"I'd say that 'vexed' more describes my state of mind," answered Christena. "I figured that your little detecting escapade would only involve asking a doctor a couple of questions and visiting a cemetery. I hadn't considered that it might include incarceration in an insane asylum."

"But it wouldn't be for long. If Mrs. Olcott truly is in Westerholm, I should be able to locate her in a few winks. I'll be in and out in no time." Mary gave her aunt a pleading look. "How else can we find out if she's in there?"

Christena let out with an exaggerated sigh. "Have you ever considered just knocking on the front door and asking if Mrs. Olcott is a patient there?"

"Of course I have. But if I did, it might set off alarms. Dr. Applegate would be told, and perhaps even Merton Olcott, that someone had inquired after Mrs. Olcott. I'm afraid it would make finding her even more difficult."

Her aunt just shook her head, as if trying to dislodge the whole, preposterous idea from her brain. "By the way," she finally said, with a baiting smile, "did you know that when a woman goes into a place like Westerholm, her hair is cut *very* short and she is paraded naked to a dirty old bathtub, where she is scrubbed with lye soap to within an inch of her life?"

The look on Mary's face must have given her away.

"Ah," smirked Christena, "you *didn't* know that, did you? Doesn't sound like much fun, does it?"

"That may be the case for a state hospital, but I'm sure a private organization like Westerholm handles things much differently." Mary tried to sound certain, but the image of all her nice chestnut hair lying in clumps on the floor suddenly brought the risks of her scheme into sharp focus.

Mary spent the rest of the afternoon on a rented bicycle, pedaling around and about the island. She needed time to consider her options and she wanted to be alone. With Christena and Edmond opposing her scheme, the whole investigation was teetering on the brink of collapse.

It annoyed her that they didn't appreciate the cleverness of her plan. There were risks, to be sure. But Mary would only be inside Westerholm for a few days. Any qualms she had were outweighed by the satisfaction she imagined would come from reuniting Clara McColley with her mother.

As she swerved around a group of chattering tourists clogging one picturesque wooded lane, Mary lamented the fact that she was handicapped by a lack of support when she needed it most. Of course, she couldn't assume that family and friends would gladly lend a hand when she snapped her fingers—serving as lookouts or canvassing witnesses. She certainly couldn't expect them to put themselves in danger for her.

But if she was ever going to start a full-time detecting business, she had to have a collaborator—a Watson to her Holmes. Someone who was surefooted and quick thinking and handy in a tight spot. Her lack of such a companion right now was putting her at a great disadvantage—and possibly destroying all hope of exposing Merton Olcott for the scoundrel he no doubt was.

Flying downhill rather too fast, she promised herself that when she got back to Duluth, she was going to find an office downtown and set up shop. Then she'd place an advertisement for an assistant and see who showed up. She thought it best if her theoretical employee was a man, who could do things that she could not and go places that might be off limits for a woman.

Right now, though, she needed to get back to her room and freshen up. Christena had purchased four tickets for the musical comedy show that evening at the hotel's theater. Paul and Edmond would be joining them to see *Florodora*, with its reputedly hummable tunes and antic romance. Mary promised herself to behave and not spoil things by again arguing on behalf of her plan. There was no reason to involve Edmond and Christena in it, especially since they were so set against it. She would figure out another way to unlock the secrets of Westerholm, even if she had to break into the place in the middle of the night.

Four hours later, she was sitting between Christena and Edmond as the curtain came down on the final act of the musical. It had been a hilarious show with wonderful music. Paul, sitting on the other side of Christena, jumped to his feet during the curtain call and yelled "Bravo" several times.

The evening had been most pleasant. Paul, unaware of the Westerholm discussion, chattered happily away about the several landscape photos he had made with Edmond's help that afternoon. Earlier that day, he had dragooned a towheaded local boy and his gruff-looking father—fishermen both—into posing with their rods and reels for a picture upon the shore that he believed would be a sure money spinner.

Mary and Edmond had reached a détente of sorts. During intermission she had apologized to him for dropping such an improbable request in his lap.

"I had no right to expect you and Christena to join me in my little escapade. It was thoughtless of me to put you on the spot like that."

"You just caught me by surprise, Mary," he said with a shrug. "I'd been thinking all week about how nice it would be to spend more time with you. But I was imagining walks along the beach and picnics on the lawn. Just you and me. Alone."

The look in his deep dark eyes and the way he had whispered those last words made Mary catch her breath.

For a few seconds she didn't respond. "There *is* a way for you to have me all to yourself for an evening," she finally said. "Take me to a dance. They have one almost every night on the island. At the hotel or down on Main Street."

He beamed at her. "Splendid idea. I'm actually not too bad at a waltz or a polka, if I do say so myself. There's a fine little dance hall in Ishpeming and Rosie has been teaching me some of the latest steps."

At his mention of that name, Mary had felt another jolt of jealousy. She didn't want to dwell on the image of Edmond's arms wrapped around that very attractive woman, but there it was again. Certainly he had every right to enjoy the company of Mrs. Lehmann. And Mary needed to learn how to control her reaction. Still, it was a relief when the curtain went up on the second half of the show and she could focus once again upon the musical hijinks.

As they exited the theater, the foursome ran into Judge Tolliver and his wife. Introductions were made. The couple was quite interested to know that Paul took photos and asked if he might do an outdoor portrait of them. The photographer said he would be delighted to. Paul, it seemed, was turning his stay on Mackinac into a profitable venture. The Tollivers, in fact, were the fifth set of new clients that he had gained.

While Paul and Christena talked with the Tollivers, Mary and Edmond decided to take a stroll around the hotel grounds. At one point, Mary nearly twisted her ankle on an unseen stone and Edmond reached his arm around her, ostensibly to steady her. The arm stayed well after the danger of a sprained ankle was over. Thoughts of Rosie Lehmann vanished from Mary's head as she savored the half embrace of this man for whom she cared so much. But the magic of the moment was ended abruptly by a voice behind them.

"Oh, hello, Mary. What did you think of the show?" It was Thad Watkins, strolling arm in arm with one of the young women from the dance. As Edmond removed his arm from around her, Mary groaned inside but put on a pleasant smile.

"It was quite entertaining," she replied. "As good as anything I've seen in Duluth."

"Say, Mary, you remember Miss Peggy Booth from the dance last Friday, don't you?"

"Yes, of course." Mary nodded at the woman, who nodded back. There was no way around it. Mary had to introduce Edmond.

"And this is my friend Edmond Roy, temporarily of Ishpeming. Edmond, this is Thad Watkins of the Wharton School in Philadelphia."

Edmond shook hands with Thad, both saying how pleased he was to make the other's acquaintance. But Mary thought the look on Thad's face had all the friendly sincerity of a confidence trickster.

"And what is it you do in Ishpeming?" asked Thad.

"I'm a painter," Edmond said.

"Ahh," Thad responded. "Houses then? Commercial structures?"

Mary's jaw dropped. She knew Thad couldn't be so boneheaded. He was being rude, plain and simple.

"Edmond is an artist," she snapped. "And quite an accomplished one, at that."

"It's all right, Mary," said Edmond. "An honest assumption."

Thad seemed quite pleased with his little slight. And that smug look on his face incensed Mary even more.

"He is currently finishing up a new mural at the Pioneer Bank," she informed him. "And it's a masterpiece, if you ask me. When he's done with that, not one, but *two* portrait commissions await him. Have you ever heard of the Ensigns of Duluth?"

Thad confessed that he had not.

"Well, Mrs. Ensign is the wealthiest woman in the city and perhaps in the whole state of Minnesota. And she has commissioned Edmond to come later this summer and do portraits of herself and her granddaughter."

Miss Booth looked wide-eyed at the ferocity of Mary's lecture, but Thad seemed almost amused at her overblown response. "I *am* sorry. I just assumed your friend painted houses. My mistake. No offense taken, I hope."

"No, none at all," Edmond interjected.

"But I am curious about one thing, Mr. Roy."

"Yes, Mr. Watkins?" Edmond said in a quiet tone.

"Is it true that artists like yourself don't make much money? Go starving in garrets and such? Huddle around single lumps of coal in the winter? Plod around in shoes with holes in 'em?" He smiled, no doubt thinking himself very clever. Miss Booth managed a nervous giggle.

It thrilled Mary to see Edmond's dark eyes flare. The

questions had stung him, as Thad intended them to. "Well, it so happens, Mr. Watkins, that I'm making a decent income at the moment," he replied evenly.

"Glad to hear it," Thad said. "But it's not steady, is it? It's not reliable, like a paycheck. When your mural is done, and your portraits of Mrs… What's-her-name?"

"Mrs. Ensign," pronounced Mary through gritted teeth.

"Right, Mrs. Ensign. Why, you could go another year or two without making a nickel from your daubs. Don't understand why a fellow would want to be in that line. Makes no sense at all. Bet if you asked someone at that bank, they'd hire you on for a teller. Now there's a real career."

Mary had had enough. She glared at Thad. "You may know a lot about finance but you know nothing about art. To stick a talented painter like Edmond in a teller's cage would be a crime. When every bank teller is long gone and the Wharton School is dust, art historians will still be talking about Edmond Roy and his work. I wouldn't be surprised if someday his canvases sell for thousands of dollars each."

Mary glanced at Edmond and was surprised at the mortified look on his face. She realized she had overstepped herself.

Almost simultaneously, Thad Watkins seemed to have come to the same conclusion as Mary—that he had perhaps gone too far.

"Miss MacDougall," he said, looking sheepish, "I didn't mean to start an argument. I hope you're not offended. Nor you, Mr. Roy. Now, Peggy, let's go see if we can find a couple of chairs on the porch."

With another giggle from Peggy, the two departed.

Edmond's face finally relaxed. He turned to Mary, grabbing both of her hands in his. "Mary, you must realize that men like Thad Watkins don't bother me a bit. I have nothing to say to them. Their conversation usually bores me to tears. I intend to live the life I want to live and be with the kind of people I value."

He squeezed her hands and gazed earnestly at her. "I know you mean well, but you don't need to defend me from the Thad Watkinses of the world. Edmond Roy is quite capable of taking care of himself."

Mary lowered her gaze, feeling quite chastened. "I don't know what possessed me to go on like that. But his patronizing remarks about you just made me furious. I am sorry."

And she really, truly was.

Leaping to his defense as she had done had been more a reflex than anything else. Mary felt an overpowering urge to protect Edmond. He was so passionate, so idealistic. She had never heard him utter an unkind word. That's why Thad's mocking remarks seemed all the more offensive. But her reaction had embarrassed Edmond and that was the last thing in the world she wanted.

Mary took his arm and the two headed slowly back to the hotel. As they went, she again pondered her relationship with him. The number of days they had actually spent together did not add up to more than a dozen. They had exchanged letters, of course, but no deep emotions were discussed, no expectations were put forward. How well did they really even know each other?

She glanced up at him, and he smiled back down at her. *What is it you want from me, Edmond Roy?* she thought. *And what in the world do I want from you?*

At the moment, the answers seemed quite out of reach.

Chapter XVIII

Mary woke at six Friday morning and immediately began to plot her next steps in the Agnes Olcott matter. If she was going to find the woman, she would have to do it by herself. Perhaps she would just show up at Westerholm and proclaim herself suicidal or otherwise demented. If she had the money, they surely would take her in. She could give them a false name—she rather fancied the moniker Martha Patrick.

By seven, she was washed and dressed and ready for a hearty breakfast. Going down the hallway, she knocked on her aunt's door, to see if Christena wanted to join her for a bite.

"Come in, dear," came a muffled voice from inside the room.

To Mary's surprise, Christena was already up and dressed, and had a pot of tea and some buttered toast sitting on the table. Mary poured herself a cup and sat.

"About our little disagreement yesterday," Mary began, "I just wanted to say that…"

Christena put up her hand. "Mary, I have been thinking. While I don't believe that Edmond and I reacted unreasonably to your scheme, I perhaps was a little quick to dismiss Mrs. Olcott and her fate. The clues you have uncovered—rather cleverly, I must say—leave big questions unanswered."

Holding her tongue, Mary wondered where Christena was going with this line of reasoning. Perhaps she would agree to commit Mary to the asylum after all.

"So," said Christena, "let me offer you a slightly altered plan."

Mary nodded.

"I don't think you should be the madwoman in need of confinement."

"Oh?" Mary said, puzzled.

"I should."

Stunned at the suggestion, Mary shook her head emphatically. "Absolutely not! This is *my* investigation, not yours." There was no way she would put her aunt into that situation. The very idea! "Besides," she continued, "do you know how to pick a lock? I do. I spent hours training with a locksmith back home. Do you know the Fujian White Crane fighting technique? I do. At least I've started learning it. I'm much better prepared than you are for the risks involved."

"I would think I could learn fairly quickly how to pick a lock," Christena retorted. "Furthermore, I am a healthy, fit woman, and I'm quite confident that I could handle myself in a tight spot."

Mary gave her aunt a dubious look and Christena huffed in response.

"And if Westerholm is known as a dumping ground for unwanted wives, who better to portray a dreary old wife than me?" Christena ran some fingers through a few of the red locks at the side of her head. "Besides, I've been feeling quite youthful and spontaneous lately."

"And to what do you attribute that?" Mary asked suspiciously. She figured the answer involved the initials P and F. Christena and Paul Forbes had become quite fond of each other, and Mary didn't know what to make of this development. Was it romance a-budding? Or simply a holiday friendship?

"Well," Christena said, "what with hiking and dancing and playing tennis with people half my age, I feel quite rejuvenated. And I've been having such wonderful talks with Paul. We have so many interests in common. Art photography, for one. In fact, I've agreed to pose for him at a pretty spot up at the north end of the island next week."

Mary's eyebrows shot up, as she thought of Paul's photograph of an unclothed Rosie Lehmann. "What will you be wearing?" she blurted. "For Paul's photos?"

Christena blinked in surprise at her niece's question. "I hadn't given it much thought. One of my nice dresses, I should think."

Mary supposed that Christena was free to do what she wanted—and wear what she wanted—with Paul Forbes. But when it came to Agnes Olcott and Westerholm, Mary was in charge. She tried one more tactic to dissuade her aunt from taking on the role of lunatic wife.

"I'm sure Paul's pictures will be quite lovely," she said. "And they will help you to recall what your beautiful red hair used to look like, before they cut it off in the asylum."

Christena smiled at Mary's obvious attempt to discourage her. "For the sake of Mrs. Olcott it would be well worth it to sacrifice my tresses. They'll grow back eventually." She took a long, slow sip of her tea. "Well, what do you say?"

Mary pondered this new proposal. She realized that Christena's plan—to play the older wife to Edmond's younger husband—had a certain peculiar symmetry. It was perfectly in keeping with what Mary had suspected Merton Olcott had done to his older wife. But still she found it difficult to agree with.

"No. No, it has to be me." She crossed her arms as if to indicate her mind was absolutely made up.

Christena put down her teacup and fixed Mary with that penetrating stare. It was uncanny how much her aunt's fierce eyes looked so like John MacDougall's did, when Mary's father was in a stubborn mood.

"I think you don't quite understand, Mary. I go into Westerholm or no one does. I would regret that the fate of Mrs. Olcott is never resolved, certainly. But I will not put my brother's daughter into that predicament. And that is my final word."

Mary didn't like it. She didn't like it one little bit. But she so wanted to bring Clara McColley clarity about her mother's fate. If they could get Christena into the place for just a couple of days, the truth might finally be revealed. But there was another possible point of difficulty.

"I seem to have no choice but to agree," sighed Mary. "Now what we have to do is to convince Edmond to play your husband."

"Yes, just so," Christena replied. "And you'll have to do the convincing. I expect he will be quite horrified at the prospect."

"I should commit the *both* of you to Westerholm, is what I should do!" Edmond fumed.

The three of them were seated on the vast front porch of the Grand Hotel later that morning. The sky had gone slightly overcast and spat out a misty rain that didn't quite make it under the roof. Many of the guests had found shelter there, waiting until the precipitation ended.

"This is my very last effort to determine the fate of Agnes Olcott," Mary said. "And I can't do it without your help, Edmond."

"But what if Mrs. Olcott isn't even there?" he protested. "What if this is all just a wild goose chase?"

"Then I shall write my report for Clara McColley and that will be the end of it." Mary leaned toward her friend. "Please, Edmond. All that you will have to do is deliver Christena to the asylum and pay for a few weeks of its hospitality. We'll return two days later to claim your so-called wife, saying you've had second thoughts about admitting her."

"But Mary," he groaned, "I'm an artist, not an actor. The nurse or the doctor or whoever it is that takes admissions will see right through me."

"I'd wager they won't," said Christina, "not when you show them the cash that I'll provide you. And not when you make it clear that you're quite sick of your old wife, but you rather fancy your pretty, young secretary. I'm sure they'll buy it without giving it a second thought."

"We'll spend the next few days rehearsing what you need to say and how you need to act." Mary looked at him encouragingly. "You'll do just fine."

"Haven't you ever wanted to be in a real-life adventure, Edmond?" asked Christena playfully.

"No, not really," he answered plaintively. "All I've ever wanted was a roof over my head and plenty of paints and canvas. I'm as boring as they come." He frowned. "What will we tell Paul?"

Mary thought a moment. "We'll tell him it's a quick visit to wrap up my investigation, and you're just coming along to keep us company." Then her forehead furrowed. "But what if Paul wants to come, too?"

"From what he's told me," Christena said, "he's rounded up so many customers for portraits, that I doubt he'll have the time."

Edmond still didn't look convinced. "It's really not fair," he muttered, "the two of you ganging up on me."

"If you do this one little thing for me, I promise to be at your beck and call during the rest of your stay on the island," Mary said, relieved that he seemed to be wavering.

Edmond shook his head. "There's so much that could go wrong. So much has to go exactly to plan. And why should it?"

"Because we have justice on our side, Edmond," Mary pronounced. "Because a wrong has been done that must be righted."

"That's the best reassurance you can give me?" he grimaced. "Why am I starting to feel like Don Quixote before the windmill?" He sighed and looked at her. "You know, there's no one else in the world who could convince me to undertake such a lunatic caper. So, go ahead, lead me to my doom."

"Thank you so much!" Mary said gratefully.

But the relief she felt was tempered by the guilt that came with persuading him to do something he clearly did not want to. She hoped Edmond would not think that her affection for him depended in any part on his doing her bidding.

When this was all over, she would find some way to make things up to him. And she promised herself never to involve him in another one of her cases again.

As predicted, Paul Forbes didn't seem the least bit concerned that Edmond, Mary, and Christena would be abandoning him for a few days. He had several portrait engagements to handle and he had picked up another—that of

Thad Watkins and Grandmama Richardson. He had quoted them a steep price, but Grandmama had seemed quite amenable to it.

For their parts, Mary and Christena and Edmond spent several hours in Christena's room, plotting what they needed to do at Westerholm. Christena assumed the role of the severely depressive wife, all despair and slouching posture. She was even able to gin up a few tears on demand. Edmond had a harder time playing the haughty spouse eager to be rid of the old ball and chain. But his very real nerves made his portrayal ring true.

Mary, as the husband's secretary, figured she wouldn't speak at all, but would spend much her of time casting adoring glances at Edmond. Her posture and attitude toward him, she hoped, would alert the asylum staff that she and Edmond had something a little more than a professional relationship. And she would wear a hat with a veil she could lower, in case they encountered Dr. Applegate—who had met Mary and might recognize her.

It was decided that Edmond did not need to sail under false colors, so to speak. No alias was required. For no one that he was likely to meet at Westerholm had ever seen him or heard of him. Christena, though, entering fully into the spirit of things, rechristened herself as Mrs. Mabel Roy. And Mary would be Miss Martha Patrick.

Down on Main Street, a Bible with a clasp was obtained, along with a dapper white summer suit for Edmond, and a pair of cheap silver wedding rings. As they paid for the rings, Edmond wondered out loud if Mary could possibly turn a profit on this investigation, considering how much she was spending. She looked at him and laughed, the idea of a profit having never even entered her mind. The Bible was to be carved out to hold a few lock picks—from the set that they acquired at a locksmith's shop.

Mary made a quick visit to the backstage of the theater, as well, and was able to procure the use of a rather flirty-looking outfit that had been worn in a show the summer before. That, with a little rouge on the cheeks and lipstick on the lips, should provide her with the proper appearance of the calculating mistress.

The hardest part of their preparations came in teaching Christena not only how to pick a lock—in case the locked ward needed to be breached—but how to disable a person with a flurry of blows in the style of Fujian White Crane. Mary herself was only a beginner. But the strikes she was able to show her aunt, if delivered by surprise, should fend off even a fairly sizable man. Quite accidentally, Christena administered one blow to Edmond's stomach with full force, and doubled him over.

Mary rushed to him and started fussing, but he insisted he was fine. "My brother," he said, rubbing his stomach, "used to hit me a lot harder than that."

By Sunday night, Mary and her co-conspirators believed they were ready for their debut performance in Dillmont. Yet Mary couldn't help but feel nervous. Edmond, she had to admit, had been quite right.

There were so many, many things that could go

horribly, horribly wrong.

But if everything went well, Mary might just raise Agnes Olcott from the dead. And for that reason alone, she must proceed.

Chapter XIX

They stood before the central entrance of the Westerholm Institution for Women late Monday morning.

Christena had taken her plainest brown skirt and cotton shirtwaist, wrinkled them up ferociously, smudged them with dirt, and dropped several random items of food on them, for the stains they would leave. Her normally lovely red hair looked like a shattered haystack. There was a cheap, scuffed silver ring on her left hand. In her right hand she gripped a Bible. Inside it were secreted the lock picks. She slumped and peered down at the dusty driveway.

Mary wore her theater costume, along with the fancy, broad-brimmed hat she had purchased, with its drawstring veil that would partly obscure her features. It rather lent her an air of mystery, she thought with a certain wry amusement. She also carried a leather suitcase, which contained the things "Mrs. Roy" might need during her brief stay at Westerholm.

Edmond, for his part, looked dapper in a new white suit and straw boater hat. He clearly had a bad case of nerves, but he assured his co-conspirators that he was up to the task at hand.

Two sad-looking women came tramping down the steps of the big brick building, gotten up in gray work shifts, battered sun hats, and worn boots. They both muttered helloes and headed off toward one of the barns.

"Well, ladies," gulped Edmond, "the point of no return."

"Indeed." Christena sighed. "I do hope our little theatrical proves to be worth it."

Mary's feeling of guilt at putting her aunt through this ordeal—rather than herself—had not abated. But she knew the deed had to be done. At the very worst, they would fetch Christena on Wednesday, two days from now, and she would tell them, "Alas, no Mrs. Olcott in there."

The trio climbed the granite steps and went through the double doors into a spacious lobby area with benches to the side and a low, dark oak desk in the center. Behind the desk sat a stout woman in a brown-and-white striped uniform. A white nurse's cap perched atop her head and she was scribbling intently on a sheet of paper. She looked up at the new arrivals through pince-nez glasses.

"Good morning ladies, sir. How may I help you?"

Edmond drew in a deep breath and launched into his dramatic reading.

"We are here, miss, because..."

"It's 'ma'am,'" the nurse countered with a sour expression.

"Sorry, ma'am. We are here because my poor wife, Mrs. Roy..." He made a sideways nod in Christena's direction. "...has been suffering from the worst bout of melancholia that a person could imagine. She has spent the last weeks in bed, sobbing uncontrollably at times."

"I am sorry to hear it," the nurse said, first surveying Christena with a cold professional eye, then Edmond. Mary imagined she was trying to estimate the age difference between the spouses.

Edmond forged ahead. "My secretary here, Miss Patrick, heard that Westerholm does wonders for ladies with melancholia."

He gestured toward Mary, who flipped up her veil, and nodded at the nurse. Then she gave Edmond an adoring look, as they had planned.

It worked. A look of tired recognition showed in the nurse's features—she had seen it before.

"And we came over from Ishpeming to find out if you could do something to fix up the missus," Edmond continued. "Our own doctor's no good with mental troubles."

"So you would like to commit your wife permanently?" the nurse asked.

"Well, I don't know about permanently," Edmond said. "But for a little while anyway. See if you folks could bring her around. Miss Patrick and I are going down to Mackinac Island for a few days, on business."

The nurse's expression indicated that she doubted any business was going to be conducted, except in a bedroom.

"And we will check back in on our way home to Ishpeming, to see how Mabel here is doing."

Mary was rather proud of her two thespians. Edmond, a

little shaky with those first few words, now actually seemed the young, vital husband who had tired of his decrepit old wife. Christena had remained looking suitably down in the dumps.

"As you can well imagine," the nurse said, "before we take anyone in, our superintendent or our assistant superintendent needs to see them and make an evaluation. Our superintendent, Dr. Stanley, is not here today, but Dr. Applegate is. If you'll take a seat, I will go get him. Your full name and wife's name, Mr. Roy?"

He told her and the three of them went to sit on one of the long oak benches.

"So far, so good," Mary whispered to her compatriots after the nurse trotted out of the lobby. "I shall have to keep my mouth shut tight. The doctor might recognize my voice. And I'm glad I wore this veil."

"Is it too late for a change of plan?" Edmond asked.

A panic seized Mary. What was he talking about?

"We could still commit Mary. What do you say, Christena?"

Mary's aunt gave a grim chuckle. "Frankly, Edmond, I think all three of us ought to be tossed into the madhouse."

Steps came echoing from the corridor where the nurse had disappeared and Mary abruptly pulled down her veil.

"Now it's in the laps of the gods," whispered Christena.

Not two seconds later, Dr. Joseph Applegate strode energetically into the lobby, with the nurse clattering along behind him on the terrazzo floor. He stopped and regarded the threesome with a concerned look.

"Mr. and Mrs. Roy, welcome to Westerholm," he said warmly. "Nurse Gillis tells me that you may have need of our help with regard to a nasty bout of melancholia."

The man seemed quite sincere and charming, and Mary suddenly felt a tinge of doubt about her suspicions. Could he really be in league with such a shifty character as Merton Olcott?

"That is why we have come," said Edmond, standing and shaking hands with the doctor. "It is my earnest hope that Mrs. Roy here may be cured of this condition, however long it may take, and whatever the cost."

Mary could have sworn Dr. Applegate's eyes twinkled behind the lenses of his spectacles when he heard those last three words.

"Westerholm was founded to comfort the afflicted and, God willing, bring them back to normalcy," he pronounced. "Now why don't you follow me to my office." He started to turn, but stopped. "And the other lady would be?"

"My secretary," Edmond replied. "Miss Martha Patrick. She has been such a help during this trying time. I'd like her to come with us, if you don't mind."

All during this brief conversation, Mary observed that Dr. Applegate didn't direct a single word to the "afflicted" woman. Clearly in the doctor's mind, any decisions to be made would be made by the poor, encumbered husband, not the burdensome wife.

"Certainly," the doctor said. "Your secretary may join

us. Now come with me and let's find out what's been going on."

Her eyes downcast, Christena shuffled after the doctor, followed by her handsome young "husband." Mary brought up the rear, pulling a notepad out of her purse to take notes, as any proper secretary would. Christena and Edmond sat in straight chairs before the doctor's desk, with Mary seated off to their left, notepad in hand.

She had to give her aunt full credit for a fine performance. Her sniffling and mumbling were quite convincing.

At the doctor's behest, Edmond was recounting his wife's history—as it had been feverishly concocted in the hotel room on Mackinac Island. "People warned me against taking up with a spinster so much my senior," he said with a gloomy countenance. "But I came to like the old girl, and she me."

"What were your ages when you met?" the doctor asked, jotting his notes on a tablet of paper.

"I was twenty-four and Mabel was thirty-six. I was able to take her inheritance and parlay it into considerably more by careful investments in the stock market. And so we can now live quite comfortably in a big house with a maid and a secretary. And things were fine for a time, until the last year."

"Is that when Mrs. Roy began to suffer from her melancholia?" Dr. Applegate asked.

"I would say so," Edmond answered, as Christena brushed away a tear and nodded in agreement.

"And can you identify any precipitating event or series

of events?"

Edmond squared his shoulders and sniffed. "I think when it become clear after a few years that we were not to have children."

Christena, her chin quivering, reached for Edmond's hand, but he shook her off.

"I wanted children, too," she blubbered. "You know I did."

Edmond didn't even look at his "wife."

Dr. Applegate glanced from Edmond to Christena and back again, then shot a knowing glance in Mary's direction. "Surely you could have adopted a motherless baby, then. There are always foundlings and orphans that need homes."

"I have no interest in raising another man's child," Edmond said coldly. "I made myself quite clear on that point, didn't I, Mabel?"

Christena nodded once with a downcast look.

Mary nearly burst into applause. These two were both such good actors that she almost felt sorry for poor, barren Mabel, and angry at hard-hearted Edmond.

"Has Mrs. Roy shown any suicidal tendencies?" asked the doctor.

Edmond pondered this and shook his head. "Well, we have a gun in the house, but she's never shown any inclination to blow her brains out."

Dr. Applegate seemed a bit surprised at the crude response. "What I would propose, then, is to keep Mrs. Roy under observation here at Westerholm for a few weeks.

And with any luck, we will find some way to bring her back to her senses. We'll get her busy working and stop her feeling so sorry for herself. How does that sound, Mr. Roy?"

"Makes sense, I suppose," said Edmond, stroking his beard. "She can keep her Bible, can't she? It seems to be one of the few things anymore that gives her comfort."

"Yes, please, Dr. Applegate," murmured Christena.

"And we brought some of her things in that suitcase," Edmond continued. "I'd like her to have those, too."

"Of course," the doctor said.

Edmond gave Christena a pitying glance, then looked back at the doctor. "Just one more thing, Dr. Applegate. I do want your assurance that if I change my mind, I can come back and get the old girl. That you will release her immediately upon my request."

"That should be no problem," Dr. Applegate confirmed. "Now with regard to Mrs. Roy's time with us, I would recommend placement in our special ward on the second floor, where we treat ladies of means. Meals are of a better quality, patients have their own rooms, and they can continue to wear their own clothing. The cost runs to one hundred dollars per month."

"Sounds fine," Edmond agreed. "For however long it takes."

Dr. Applegate got to his feet. "Very good, Mr. Roy. You may leave your first payment with Nurse Gillis at the front desk and she will provide you with a statement. Now I'm going to find an attendant to take Mrs. Roy and prepare her for her stay with us. Be back in a few minutes."

All of a sudden, Mary felt almost queasy. Her scheme was about to enter its most dangerous phase and her aunt had to bear the brunt of it. She darted over behind Christena and whispered in her ear.

"We can still hotfoot it out of here, if you want to change your mind. It's not too late."

Christena shook her head. "No. We've come this far. In for a penny, in for a pound."

"All right then," Mary said. "But Edmond and I will come back in two days, on Wednesday. And no matter what you've found out—or not found out—we are taking you with us. Westerholm shouldn't mind, since we'll insist they keep the unused balance of what we're paying. A nice little profit for them."

Mary could hear Dr. Applegate approaching in the hallway, talking to someone. He strode into the room and right after him came none other than Olive Handy, all six feet of her. Fortunately, Mary still had her veil down, or certainly the big woman would have recognized her.

"Olive here will take Mrs. Roy and deposit her with one of our matrons, who'll settle her in," explained the doctor. "I'll let you say your goodbyes."

It was all Mary could do to restrain herself from hugging Christena. But that would have been a bit peculiar for the husband's secretary. So Edmond did just what they had rehearsed back on Mackinac.

He offered his hand and his "wife" shook it.

"I wish you well, Mabel," he said. "Hope we can get

your head back on straight."

"Thank you, husband," Christena muttered, looking down—now, finally, seeming genuinely fearful.

Olive took Christena by the arm and gently led her away.

Edmond and Mary left the book-lined office, made the payment, and headed out.

"Act one went very well," Mary said, as Edmond grabbed the brass handle of one of the asylum's front doors and held it open for her. Going out, she nearly bumped into a tall man in an attendant's uniform who was coming in through the door. He had a bony face with a long, sharp jaw and a muscular build.

"Careful, Willis," came a voice behind him. "You don't want to knock the lady over."

Mary recognized the name Willis from her visit with Olive Handy. He was the strong attendant who dealt with the hard-to-manage patients. Unfortunately, she also recognized his companion, coming up right behind him. And her heart stopped ever so briefly.

It was Merton Olcott, mounting the bottom steps.

He looked at her veil-covered face as Mary lowered her glance.

"Good morning, miss," he said, tipping his hat.

"Good morning, sir," Mary replied, as she quickly went past him.

Chapter XX

The rail station in St. Ignace was down on the main street, not far from the Mackinac ferry company. Mary and Edmond walked the dusty road to the dock with nary a word said between them. The train ride from Dillmont had been similarly silent.

Mary hoped that Edmond's reticence was due to his concerns about leaving Christena to the tender mercies of the Westerholm Institution for Women. It was far likelier, she hated to admit, that he was simply disgusted with Mary MacDougall and her whole idiotic scheme.

But at least he shouldn't be troubled about Merton Olcott's appearance. Edmond didn't know the man from the haberdasher down the street.

Mary, however, did. And seeing him come into Westerholm presented her with both good news and bad news.

The good news was that, if he was making a visit to Westerholm, he must certainly be visiting his wife. Ergo, Agnes Olcott was alive, and Christena should be able to find her and tell her what had transpired in Duluth during her absence.

The bad news was that, though Olcott wouldn't have

recognized Mary behind her veil, he might see Christena and remember her. And then he might feel compelled to do something desperate to protect the secrecy of his plot.

As they trudged toward the dock, Mary very nearly told Edmond about the danger that had just arisen. The words were right on the tip of her tongue, but at the last second she held them back.

Really, what *were* the odds, she asked herself, that Olcott would happen to see Christena in such a big place, teeming with over two hundred women? And even if he did, he probably wouldn't recognize her—now frumpy and slouching and haggard. Nothing like the handsome, well-dressed woman he had encountered in his office those weeks before.

She convinced herself in a matter of minutes that Christena would be safe. She would tell Edmond about Olcott. But she would wait until the ferry to Mackinac was well away from the dock. That way, it would be too late to return to Dillmont, should Edmond take alarm and insist on rescuing Christena posthaste.

When the boat was about one hundred yards from shore, churning into a healthy chop and brisk headwind, Mary turned to Edmond. "There's something I have to tell you about. Something that happened just as we were leaving Westerholm."

"Oh?" he asked with a tone of foreboding. "What's that?"

And she told him about Merton Olcott.

She had hoped that he would be more understanding.

But the first sound to come out of his mouth was a groan.

"Maybe you're right, and Christena will go unnoticed," he said, his worry and frustration clear. "But no investigation is worth endangering a loved one or even a friend. I truly think you've let your blasted detective books go to your head, Mary MacDougall. You have some cockeyed notion that nothing's more important than solving the case. But that's just wrong."

Mary tried to reassure him. "Westerholm is full of nurses and attendants. Olcott might want to do something, but how could he pull it off?"

Edmond just shook his head. "I have a bad feeling about all this. It looked difficult enough before. But now with Olcott on the loose..."

Mary felt perfectly awful, sitting there with Edmond brooding beside her. This whole mess would never have happened if only Christena hadn't invited the artist and his friend to vacation with them. Mary would have figured out another way to gain entry to Westerholm. And Edmond would be happily finishing up his bank mural back in Ishpeming.

But the plan now was too far in motion to stop. And Edmond was fully entangled in it. Mary needed him to stick it out until they could gain Christena's release on Wednesday.

As Edmond stared out at the water, Mary studied his face, which was wracked with worry. From her position of exceptional privilege, she needed to remember that Edmond hadn't lived anything like the life she had. If he found himself in trouble, he couldn't depend on a family retainer to come to the rescue, or to hand over a fat check to fix some problem. He had already spent time in jail, and now she had gotten him involved in a scheme that most people would judge to be quite misbegotten, if not illegal.

Edmond was an artist. He had a sweet and sensitive nature. Nothing gave him more joy than simply standing in front of a canvas, applying daubs here and there. Mary had never heard him express a desire to do anything else.

She, on the other hand, wanted nothing more than to solve crimes, to catch the villain and bring him to justice. She felt an incredible rush whenever she was on the hunt for clues. Her single-mindedness perhaps made her a little insensitive to what other people were feeling. Clearly, it had when it came to Edmond.

It occurred to her that if she pushed him too hard, he might decide that he had had quite enough of Mary MacDougall. At the very notion, her breath caught. She couldn't stand the thought of not having him in her life. After this whole affair was concluded, she would make amends. She would find him more commissions among her father's wealthy friends. If the painter had enough work, she might even persuade him to rent a studio and make Duluth his permanent home.

"Edmond," she said, grabbing his hand, "let's spend all day tomorrow painting. We'll hire a cab and go up to the old fort. Away from the crowds. You can start me on watercolors, show me how to paint with them. Perhaps a Lake Huron vista."

A reluctant smile appeared on his face. "Well, as a matter of fact, I had a little bit of a surprise planned for you," he said, straightening up from his gloomy slouch.

"Oh really?" said Mary brightly. "What kind of surprise?"

"I asked Paul to make a portrait of you and me in one of those pretty spots up north on the island."

For the first time since Mary caught sight of Merton Olcott, she saw a ray of sunshine. "That would be lovely, Edmond. Just lovely. What a wonderful idea. I'll order a picnic lunch at the hotel and we can make a day of it."

As he drove the hired carriage into Mackinac's rustic precincts the next morning, Paul Forbes wondered aloud why Christena hadn't joined them. Had the excursion to Dillmont worn her out?

Edmond, who was sitting next to Paul up front, turned around and glanced at Mary. "Why don't you explain the situation," he said, giving her a chiding look.

Mary and Edmond had agreed yesterday that the time had come to reveal everything to Paul. She took a deep breath. "Actually, Paul, Christena didn't come back with us. She's still in Dillmont, tying up some loose ends in the case."

This time it was Paul's turn to twist around and look at Mary. "Your case? The one with the lady whose husband claimed she died of cholera?"

"The very same," confirmed Mary from the back seat. To her eyes, it seemed that Edmond was squirming slightly.

"What's she doing?" Paul asked suspiciously.

Mary deliberated a few seconds over her answer. "You see, some new clues have come to light that indicate Mrs. Olcott might be sequestered in the women's asylum in Dillmont."

"Well, that's good news, isn't it? You can tell your client and be done with it."

"But we need to prove it, Paul. We need factual evidence that the woman is there."

"And Christena's helping with that?"

"Oh, very much so."

"So exactly what is she doing?"

Mary steeled herself for the answer. "Well, Paul, yesterday the three of us went to the women's asylum."

"Yes, go on."

"And Edmond and I had Tena committed."

Paul suddenly stopped the carriage in the middle of the road and turned around to stare at her. Or perhaps "glare" was the better verb.

"You put Christena into an insane asylum?" he sputtered in horror. "Oh, please tell me you didn't."

"It was the only way to find out if Mrs. Olcott is in there," Mary quickly explained. "I wanted to be the one committed, but Christena forbade me and insisted on doing it herself. There was no other way."

"Of course there was another way," Paul snapped.

"You could have told your client that your investigation had gone as far as practicable. You could have told her what you've uncovered, and she could have notified the police herself. Surely the woman doesn't expect you to take such extreme measures."

Paul had a point, of course. A perfectly sensible point that Mary had heard before. But she was absolutely convinced that she would be delivering Agnes Olcott back to her daughter within a matter of days—and stopping Merton Olcott's massive fraud in its tracks. The outcome was well worth the risk. And it frustrated her no end that her friends could not understand.

She glanced at Edmond, who looked embarrassed to have been a part of her little conspiracy. "Paul, I promise you that Christena is perfectly safe in Westerholm and we'll have no trouble extricating her tomorrow."

The normally jocular photographer did not look satisfied. "I say we all go back up to Dillmont *today* and free her, Agnes Olcott be damned. For heaven's sake, Mary, haven't you read Nellie Bly's *Ten Days in a Mad-House?*"

Actually, Mary had read Miss Bly's harrowing account of a public asylum in New York City, with its brutal conditions and harsh treatment of female inmates. But she had tried to put it out of her mind. It certainly did not provide much comfort.

"I understand why you're angry at us," Edmond finally said to his friend. "And I agree—it's a absurd plan that never should have been hatched." He shot Mary an accusing glance. "But another day in Westerholm can't make that much difference."

"She's perfectly safe," repeated Mary, earnestly endeavoring to believe it herself. She quite purposely did not mention seeing Olcott and, fortunately, neither did Edmond. That might have been the last straw for Paul. "And if something goes wrong," she continued, "I take all responsibility. Let the results of any misadventure be upon my head."

"But it's Christena's head that would bear the brunt of things, isn't it?" Paul snorted. "You're damnably irresponsible, if you ask me. The both of you. If anything should happen to her, I hope you two never catch a wink of sleep the rest of your lives. You should be ashamed of yourselves for what you've done. I mean, *really!*"

The temperature being close to ninety, the rest of the ride up to Point St. Clair was hot and sweaty, and was made even more uncomfortable by the tense silence. They arrived at the spot Mary remembered from an earlier jaunt—up on a grassy little hill dotted with maples, overlooking the shore and lake. It didn't take Paul very long to set up his camera and tripod under one of the trees.

From beneath the black cloth that let him see his ground glass in bright daylight, Paul posed them this way and that. Edmond standing behind Mary, his hands on her shoulders. The two of them sitting on the ground, before the trunk of an old, large maple. The pair gazing out on the lake. Paul exposed ten plates altogether.

And as the photographer became more and more absorbed in his work, his old, genial personality reasserted itself. He even teased Edmond that one pose looked particularly beautiful, except for the painter being in it. Mary felt herself relaxing, and sensed the same in Edmond. By the time Paul snapped the last picture, the gloom that gripped the trio had lifted like a cold fog.

"Now, shall we have our lunch?" Mary asked. "Ham sandwiches, cabbage salad, cookies, lemonade, and beer. Quite a nice rustic feast."

They ate on the blanket spread beneath the same maple where Mary and Edmond had posed. As they nibbled, Paul told them that the day before he had made the portrait of Thad Watkins and his grandmother. They had found a nice spot in the park down beneath the old fort.

"They were both rather interested in you, Edmond," he said between bites.

Edmond's eyes narrowed. "Were they now? Why?"

"I couldn't say," Paul replied. "Thad wanted to know how much money you really made, and I said his guess was as good as mine. Grandmama wanted to know where you grew up and who your people were. So I told her."

"And what did you say?" Edmond asked warily.

Paul kept a perfectly straight face. "I told the old lady that *that* was the problem. You never did quite grow up. Legend has it that your mother was a disgraced Indian princess who left you in the forest to be raised by wolves."

Mary bit her tongue to stop an incipient laugh, as she regarded Edmond's expression, wavering between amusement and horror.

"Some good folks took you in, I said, and civilized

you, to a degree," Paul went on. "Teaching you how to speak English and eat proper and paint a decent still life and such. But you continue to have a proclivity to go out at night and howl at the moon."

Edmond's mouth was hanging open. "You didn't really say that, did you?"

"Well, yes, as a matter of fact. She's such a sour old thing. I was trying to get her into a better humor."

"The problem," Mary said with a smile, "is that Mrs. Richardson actually doesn't have a humorous bone in her body, apart from her humerus. She'll be starting all sorts of rumors about our wild man of Ishpeming."

Mary could well understand why both Edmond and Christena had become so fond of Paul. He loved to talk and joke, and, if anything, enjoyed laughing even more. He was someone who, as he gazed at you with that rugged face and those kindly hazel eyes, made you feel as if you were the very center of the universe. That he was a talented photographer, a real artist, was merely a bonus. But he may have gone a bit too far this time.

"Well," Edmond sighed, "the horse is out of the barn. Let the old lady think what she wants. Maybe it will embellish my reputation as an artist, being raised by wolves and all."

Paul dropped Edmond and Mary off at the hotel a couple of hours later, and drove away to take the horse and carriage back to the livery. He made both of them swear that they would be on the first ferry the next morning, heading back to free Christena from her captivity.

After returning the wicker picnic basket to the hotel kitchen, Mary and Edmond went to browse through the little store off the rotunda. It sold books, magazines, fudge, cigars and pipe tobacco, and the knickknacks that guests bought for souvenirs and gifts.

Mary wanted to get something for both Emma Beach and Lillian Burns, and thought that the beautifully beaded coin purses or pincushions would be just the thing. She was closely examining a purse when Edmond sidled up to her.

"Pretty little thing, isn't it?" he said. "You have no idea the amount of work Indian women put into those, in return for chicken feed. It's really very demanding, finicky labor. The tourists just love them, though."

As Mary turned around to answer him, she saw, standing nearby, Grandmama Richardson, holding a recently popular book in her hands. She nodded to Mary in a chilly manner. Edmond noticed the old lady, too. He rather ostentatiously took the purse Mary had been examining and peered down his nose at it.

"Hmmm," he said over-loudly, "I wouldn't be a bit surprised if one of my cousins made this. I'm thinking maybe Simone Whitewolf. It looks like her style. She stills lives in a wigwam, you know."

Mrs. Richardson's eyes popped open. She made a sharp intake of breath, and turned back to the shelf of books, muttering to herself.

Mary tried to stifle a laugh. "Edmond," she whispered, "you really are a naughty boy."

He gave her a conspiratorial wink and it made Mary feel wonderful. It seemed that things were getting back to normal between the two of them. This was the Edmond Mary had grown so fond of—happy and relaxed and ready with a witticism.

She walked him to the front doors of the hotel and they said their goodbyes, arranging to meet early the next morning to catch the first ferry to the mainland. Mary walked back into the rotunda, heading for her room.

As she mounted the stairs up to the third floor, she glanced over at the concierge's desk. He was talking to a tall, trim man in a dark suit. A tourist, no doubt, looking for directions or advice. Mary continued her ascent, but something made her stop after three or four more steps. She looked back again at the concierge's desk. At that same instant, the tall man turned to face her.

It was Merton Olcott!

His pale gray eyes fixed on her and a shark's grin snapped into place. He strode toward her, weaving between clumps of other guests.

Mary's first reflex was to bolt—run up the stairs and hide in her room. But she couldn't allow herself to appear afraid. She had engaged this man in a contest, and retreating was not an option. She stepped back down to face him.

"Miss MacDougall," he boomed in his honeyed baritone, as he came up to her. "How delightful to see you again."

Mary was unable to reply. In spite of the hot, humid day, a cold chill ran down her spine.

"I thought it was you I saw when I was at Westerholm yesterday," he said, standing a bit too close for comfort. "I have a friend who works there, you know. Big, strong fellow named Willis. Handles the difficult women. But he seems to think your name is Miss Patrick."

Mary could feel herself trembling. This was a kind of fear she had never felt before.

"And he said you came with a red-haired lady and her husband," Olcott continued. "Odd that. I thought your aunt, whom I recall so fondly from our little visit in my office, was single."

"I'm sure, Mr. Olcott, that I don't know what you mean," Mary managed to say, trying to control her quavering voice.

"Now really, Miss MacDougall. A veil? That's the best you could do?" He gave a derisive little laugh. "After Dr. Applegate wired me about how you popped in at his office, I wondered if you'd turn up again. And sure enough Olive Handy gets a visit from you. She told Willis all about it—she's got a bit of a crush on him, you know."

As it happened, Mary did know. Not that it did her any good.

Olcott leaned even closer, and Mary could smell the rank odor of too much whiskey on his breath. "I pray that the good doctor doesn't need to use any of those powerful drugs on your aunt," he whispered, like a snake hissing. "I understand that some people are never the same after taking them. Good day, Miss MacDougall."

And with that he walked away toward the dining room, leaving Mary in a flat-out, heart-racing panic.

Chapter XXI

Mary felt utterly exhausted on the train ride up to Dillmont the next morning. The night hadn't given her a single wink of sleep, for all her agonized worrying. She kept imagining Christena being dosed with some dreadful medication.

After her encounter with Merton Olcott the afternoon before, she hadn't wasted a moment. She had rushed to the concierge's desk, demanding to know if there was any way humanly possible to get to Dillmont that evening. The man behind the desk was sympathetic, but said that the last ferry had gone. And, in any event, there wouldn't be a train from St. Ignace to Dillmont until morning.

It was only with a great deal of persuasion, over an early breakfast Wednesday, that she and Edmond had managed to keep Paul from joining them. He wanted to come along, he said, to prevent them from making an even bigger mess of things than they already had. But Mary pointed out that it would be hard to explain his presence at Westerholm. Who was he supposed to be?

No, she had insisted, it was best for him to stay on Mackinac and await their return Thursday morning. Besides, he was scheduled to shoot the woodland portrait of Judge Tolliver and his wife, who were leaving that afternoon to head back to Sault Ste. Marie.

Paul might not have agreed to stay, had Mary told him about her most recent encounter with Merton Olcott. But she had kept that unsettling story from both him and Edmond. What good would it do to tell them? The plan was already in motion to retrieve Christena, and that's what they all needed to focus on right now.

As the train rattled along the rails through the woods, Mary and Edmond discussed how they would handle things once they arrived at Westerholm. Their plan was to walk in and simply ask for the release of Mabel Roy, to explain that Mr. Roy had undergone a change of heart about her detention in the asylum. Edmond would express regret at having taken up the time of the doctor and nurses for no good reason, and would tell them to keep the balance of the one hundred dollar payment, for their trouble.

Once they had reclaimed Christena, Mary would find out if she had located Agnes Olcott. If so, Mary would immediately telegraph Clara McColley, and let her take up the matter with the police. That would truly be the end of Mary's case.

As she and Edmond trudged out of the Dillmont station onto the town's dusty main street, Mary glanced around nervously. She had not seen Merton Olcott on the ferry or the train, but she figured he would be heading back to Dillmont, too.

Their first stop was Mrs. Wingate's guesthouse, where

they booked three rooms for that evening. The landlady agreed to drive them to Westerholm, though she boldly wondered why. But Mary and Edmond politely revealed nothing. In fact, they said very little on the ride out to the asylum. The situation was so grave that normal banter seemed not only pointless, but depressing. Nothing would be right until Christena was safely in hand.

Mrs. Wingate dropped them off just outside the arched gate with the big sign that said WESTERHOLM in flowing script. Mary lowered her veil, and she and Edmond walked onto the asylum grounds. After climbing the entrance stairs, they once again found Nurse Gillis seated behind the desk in the main lobby. She was helping an older lady, and didn't seem to notice Mary and Edmond as they came inside.

"Now, Mrs. Nowak," said the nurse, "you're saying that your granddaughter, Miss Yates, will be coming to visit Mrs. Voelker tomorrow afternoon. Is that correct?"

"Yes, that's right," replied the visitor. "Mrs. Voelker is an old friend of the family and took care of Sally when she was little. Sally is in teacher's college, you know, but home for the summer. My granddaughter always makes a point to visit with dear Mrs. Voelker, even if the poor woman is not quite herself these days."

Nurse Gillis nodded. "I'll leave a note to let the attendants know that Miss Yates will be coming."

As the old woman departed, Mary and Edmond stepped up to the desk. If the nurse was at all surprised to see them again so soon, her tone and manner didn't betray it.

"Good morning," she said, "and welcome back to Westerholm. How may we help you?"

Edmond took off his hat and held it in his hands. "Well, as you know, I left my wife with you two days ago, and I wish to talk to Dr. Applegate about her."

The nurse looked from Edmond to Mary, then sniffed very subtly, as if still disapproving of the veiled hussy. "Dr. Applegate is not on duty today. I'll go see if Superintendent Stanley has time to see you." She left and returned a moment later, directing them to the superintendent's office.

Dr. Stanley, a somber, professorial-looking man, greeted Edmond and Mary from behind his desk, and invited them to sit down. He apologized that Dr. Applegate was not there to discuss Mrs. Roy's case. "But I have her records here and perhaps I could deal with any concerns you may have."

"Well," Edmond replied, "I've been thinking it over quite a lot and I realized that whatever Mabel's problems, it might be best to take her back home to Ishpeming and try to deal with them there. Fact is, I just feel a bit guilty about dumping her into this place. Not that there's anything wrong with Westerholm. But I miss the old girl. And I'd like to have her back. Of course, you folks can keep the unused part of the payment I made."

The doctor's expression grew grave. Mary suddenly felt uneasy.

"Unfortunately, Mr. Roy," he said, "it's not that simple."

Mary's stomach turned in knots. This was not what she expected.

"What do you mean?" Edmond snapped. "I understood it was my decision as Mabel's husband to place her in here. And now, as her husband, I require that she be released to me."

Dr. Stanley gave him a practiced look of concern, mixed with a bit of studied regret. "Normally we would abide by the husband's wishes. But when a patient exhibits violent behavior, we prefer to keep her under watch for a time. Mrs. Roy, I'm afraid, may be a danger to others, as well as to herself."

"I don't understand," Edmond continued, his voice quivering with a real anger that mirrored what Mary was feeling.

The doctor took a deep breath, as if preparing for an unpleasant task.

"Yesterday, on her first full day at Westerholm, Mrs. Roy was seen by one of the attendants stealing a piece of jewelry, a little emerald bracelet, that belonged to another patient."

Mary couldn't believe her ears. Never, ever would Christena do such a thing. Why would she, when she had money enough to buy all the emerald bracelets she wanted?

"Ridiculous," Edmond spat. "Chris... I mean Mabel would never steal anything!"

With the cool detachment of a skilled alienist, Dr. Stanley made his voice go even calmer in the face of Edmond's anger. "She was confronted by Willis Flugum, the attendant who witnessed the theft, and asked to produce whatever might be in her pocket. She refused. He attempted to remove the item, to display the evidence of her transgression, and she assaulted him. He ended up with several scratches on his face."

Mary felt a fury rise inside her. This little gambit had clearly been concocted by Olcott in cahoots with his friend Flugum. They had a good notion of what Mary and her companions were up to, and they needed to put Christena out of action—before she could expose Olcott's deceit.

If there were any scratches on Flugum's face, they were probably self-inflicted. Or Christena might have been defending herself. But it would have been difficult for her to convince anyone of her innocence. Mary didn't want to imagine what her aunt must be feeling right now. Would she ever be able to forgive Mary for making such a muddle of things?

Edmond finally seemed to have found his voice again. "Now, see here," he protested. "I'm not leaving without my wife."

"Don't worry about Mrs. Roy," the doctor said with maddening equanimity. "We find that solitary confinement is a very effective therapy. It allows the patient to consider her behavior in an environment with no external stimuli. So we have placed her in a locked room. I shouldn't think it would take more than a week for your wife to come around, Mr. Roy. And you'll thank us in the end."

Edmond gave Mary a desperate look, as if asking for

guidance, but she merely stood and nodded toward the door. Much as she wanted to reveal Olcott and Flugum's treachery to the doctor, she couldn't very well make that accusation without confessing to her own and Edmond's duplicity in the affair.

For the time being, Merton Olcott, it seemed, had the upper hand. But Mary MacDougall had no intention of leaving Dillmont again without Christena at her side. And she had a fair notion of what she needed to do to make that happen.

"Thank heavens Paul didn't come," Edmond muttered as they left the building. "He would have socked that sawbones silly, and tore down every wall in the place to find Christena."

"Don't think I didn't consider it myself," Mary huffed, as she marched double-quick back toward town.

"Well, we can agree that it's finally time to call the police." By now, Edmond was almost trotting to keep up with her, even with his longer legs. "It might take a day or two, but they'll get this disaster cleared up and fetch her out of there."

Mary stopped dead in her tracks and pivoted to face him. She had put the man through so much. But she needed to ask him for one more very big favor.

"I understand how you feel, Edmond," she said. "But they have Tena in a locked room. By tomorrow she could be drugged out of her mind." She gave him a pleading look. "I am begging you to indulge me one last time."

Edmond gave a desolate laugh, as if he expected as much. "What are we going to do then? What's the plan?"

"As you may recall," Mary said, "a certain Miss Sally Yates is scheduled to visit her grandmother's friend, Mrs. Voelker, tomorrow."

"Yes, I remember the old lady in the lobby telling that to the nurse. But I don't see how Sally Yates is going to be much help to us."

"Ah, but she is. Because Miss Yates is going to arrive early. Tonight, in fact. Just after supper. And she will look very much like Miss Mary MacDougall."

Chapter XXII

Mary looked in the mirror that hung on the bedroom door, turning from side to side in front of it. Yes, this would do. This would do nicely.

Her trip to the dressmaker's house on Main Street had netted her that plain gray suit she had spied two weeks before. The seamstress was hesitant to sell it, as it was intended for someone else. But she relented when Mary offered her double her price. The fit of the skirt didn't seem quite right—a bit too loose—but not so much that anyone would notice.

Mary had pulled her curly hair back into a severe, tight bun, and topped it with a cheap hat that she had borrowed from Mrs. Wingate. There was no need for Mary to wear her veil, since Dr. Applegate wasn't on duty.

Inside her purse were the lock picks left after she had given three to Christena. Nestled reassuringly at the bottom of the purse was her Smith & Wesson revolver, fully loaded.

Leaving her "Miss Patrick" costume strewn on the bed, Mary went out her door and knocked on the one across the hall. Edmond opened it.

"I had no idea you could look so ordinary," he said in mock admiration.

Mary made a little curtsey. "Thank you, Mr. Roy. So kind. And now Miss Yates is ready for her command performance."

They had already had a light supper in Mrs. Wingate's dining room, and arranged with the woman to borrow her horse and carriage. They warned that they might not return until quite late.

By seven o'clock Edmond was steering the horse toward Westerholm. When they arrived at the front gate and climbed down out of the carriage, he laid down the terms of agreement for his role in this assault.

"I will wait for you by the gate. If you don't reappear by ten o'clock with Christena, I'm going to go get the deputy."

"Agreed," Mary said. "It's good to know you'll be here, ready to bring in the cavalry if I need it."

Then she stood up on tiptoes and kissed him lightly on the lips. He wrapped his arms around her in a tight hug.

Snuggled up against his chest, Mary suddenly wanted nothing more than to stay right there. How frustrating that her moments alone with Edmond were always cut short. One day, she promised herself, things would be different. She would have time to get to know him, time to understand him. Time to be alone with him.

She finally pulled away from his embrace. "Duty calls, dear boy."

But before she could leave, he caught her arm.

"One more thing, Mary MacDougall," he said, brushing a strand of hair from her forehead. "When we get back to Mackinac, I want your undivided attention. No more adventures. No more escapades. Just you and me, and a little bit of Paul and Christena. And if we ever make it to the dance floor, you have to promise every dance to me."

Mary smiled at him. "Sounds heavenly." Then she turned and began her march up to the entrance of the imposing edifice.

Coming into the front doors, she was relieved to see that, as she had hoped, Nurse Gillis was no longer on duty. Her much younger replacement was positively gregarious, in comparison.

"Good evening, miss," the woman said brightly. "I'm Nurse Swenson. Isn't it hot in here? I hope we get some rain soon. Now, what can I do for you?"

"I'm Sally Yates," Mary lied, "and I've come for a visit with my grandmother's friend, Mrs. Voelker. I believe Grandmother informed you that I would be coming."

"Well," Nurse Swenson said, "let me look here." She riffled through some papers on the desk. "Ah, yes, here's the note, Miss Yates. But it says you're not expected until tomorrow afternoon."

Mary tried to look embarrassed. "You see, I arrived in town early and my cousins Grace and Annie want me to go with them to Mackinac for a few days. So I just thought I'd nip up here tonight to see Mrs. Voelker and then be free to have a little fun the rest of my stay. Is it a terrible imposition to visit her now?"

"Oh, no. She'll be through with supper. You just head over there into the east wing. Climb the main stairs up to the third floor and ask for Mrs. Voelker. One of the nurses will help you find her."

Perfect, thought Mary. She remembered that Olive Handy had said the locked rooms were on the fifth floor of the east wing. Just two flights up from Mrs. Voelker's floor. And the private rooms for the wealthy patients were on the second floor. If Agnes Olcott was at Westerholm, that's where they would probably keep her.

Mary thanked the nurse and started to turn away. But an idea popped into her head and she turned back.

"By any chance," she ventured, "do you have a patient named Mrs. Olcott?"

"Truth be told, I only started working here a couple weeks ago, so I haven't learned all the patients' names yet. Right off the bat, it doesn't sound familiar. But let me take a look."

She pulled a black ledger book out of a desk drawer, flipped through it, and scanned down a page. Her eyes stopped to read for a few long seconds. "No, Miss Yates," she said with a nervous grin, slamming the book shut. "We have no patients here by the name of Mrs. Agnes Olcott."

"I must have been mistaken then," Mary said sweetly. "Thank you anyway. Now I'll just go visit with Mrs. Voelker for a bit."

But as she walked away, Mary thought how interesting it was that Nurse Swenson knew Agnes Olcott's first name, even though Mary hadn't mentioned it. Whatever the young nurse had read in that book must have specified that Mrs. Olcott's presence at Westerholm was to be kept confidential.

Mary was sorely tempted to poke her nose behind the handsome glass door on the second floor that said "Special Ward" and go hunting for her client's mother. But she reminded herself that Mrs. Olcott was no longer her primary concern. At the moment nothing on earth was more important than liberating Christena MacDougall from her captivity.

As Mary made her way up the stairs, she bumped into two nurses coming down. They looked at her curiously, as if they wondered what she was doing there that time of the evening.

"I know I'm here late, but I'm trying to find my friend Mrs. Voelker," Mary said, anticipating their question. "Could you tell me if I'm heading in the right direction?"

They told her she was, then watched her head up to the landing on the third floor. Mary decided she had better actually go find Mrs. Voelker, to keep suspicion at bay. Then she'd figure out how to ascend those two additional flights to the locked ward.

At least a dozen women were sitting at chairs and tables in what felt like a reasonably homey common room. Some of them were playing cards, some were reading books, some holding dolls, and some were just staring into space. They all had on unadorned, homemade dresses.

As Mary walked in, several of them turned to scrutinize her. Their expressions were neither friendly nor unfriendly—merely impassive and expressionless.

However, one of the inmates, a moon-faced, fidgety blonde girl of eighteen or so, bounced to her feet from behind a table littered with dominoes and scampered over to Mary.

"Hello, hello, hello, hello, hello, hello," she chirped, leaning in uncomfortably close to the visitor. "They say my name is Ethel. But they're lying you know."

The words came out of her like a Gatling gun—*rat-tat-tat-tat*.

"I'm really Alice Roosevelt the daughter of the president and they put me in here because I know a state secret that would help our enemies and they think I can't keep my mouth shut but I can. I can. I most definitely can. I'm no traitor. They think I saw Father do something very, very, *very* bad. What's your name?"

She stared expectantly at Mary with saucer-wide, vivid blue eyes.

Mary was so shaken, she almost gave her real name to the girl. "I'm, I'm Miss Yates," she said, backing away a step. "I've come to visit Mrs. Voelker."

"You look like someone I can trust," the girl observed. "So I'll tell you what I saw Father do because I…"

"No you will *not*, Alice."

Out of nowhere, a nurse appeared and took the young woman firmly by the arm, leading her back to the table with the dominoes. Alice seemed not to take any offense. The nurse returned to Mary, shaking her head.

"I'm sorry that Alice… Her name really is Ethel, but it

upsets her when we call her that. I'm sorry she waylaid you. She likes to tell her little story to anyone who comes. And who can blame her? Her make-believe life is a lot more pleasant than her real life was."

"What do you mean?" Mary asked.

The nurse briefly shut her eyes and shook her head. "Poor Ethel saw her father stab her mother to death. He put that knife into her dozens of times. Then he sat down at the kitchen table, covered in blood, as if nothing had happened, and ordered the girl to fix him his dinner. He's up in the madhouse in Newberry. Mrs. Westerholm's trust pays for Ethel to stay here in a dormitory bed."

Mary was appalled. How could such things even be possible?

"Can I help you find someone?" asked the nurse.

Mary told her she was visiting Mrs. Voelker and the nurse pointed at an older patient, sitting in a rocking chair and paging through a magazine. Mary went over to her and knelt beside her.

"Hello, Mrs. Voelker," she said. "I'm a friend of Sally Yates. She said I should come visit you if I was in town."

Mrs. Voelker focused her rheumy eyes on Mary and smiled. "Oh, little Sally. She's such an adorable girl. How old is she now? Four? Five?"

The woman seemed delighted to have a visitor, so Mary pulled up a chair, seeing no harm in spending a few minutes chatting with her. It would, after all, lend credibility to her story if she were to be questioned later on during her search for Christena. She would just claim that she had gotten lost after visiting with Mrs. Voelker, and the nurse would confirm that Mary had been there.

Except for being a bit mixed up about her location in time and space, the woman was an amiable conversationalist. Listening to her prattle on, Mary glanced around the room at the other inmates.

Her eyes fell upon someone sitting by a window who looked almost like an angel. She was a beautiful, pale woman, staring out into the early evening. Although she had flowing white hair, her face looked oddly young. She held a picture frame in her hands. In this room full of people, she seemed to be in a place all by herself.

"Mrs. Voelker, do you know who that lady is by the window?" Mary asked when the old woman had paused for a second.

"Oh that poor dear. She's waiting for her children, you see. But they're never going to come, you know. They're dead. The doctor takes extra good care of her. Visits her often."

After a few more minutes, Mary finally stood, telling Mrs. Voelker that Sally Yates would be up to see her tomorrow, which was quite true. As she turned to go, Mary almost ran into another patient who had come up behind her.

"Thank you for visiting Mrs. Voelker," the woman said. "She gets quite lonely here."

Mary saw kindness in the warm brown eyes that regarded her. The woman had a solidness about her that seemed out of place here. If it weren't for the faded pink and blue dress she wore, Mary might have mistaken her for one of the nurses or attendants. She looked normal, and sounded quite normal, too.

"Please excuse my presumption," Mary said tentatively, "but might I ask why…"

"I'm here?" the woman said dejectedly. "Simple. My husband didn't want me anymore. Dr. Applegate diagnosed me with hysteria and malicious disposition. I didn't even have a say in the matter—they just hauled me off to the bathtub." She gave a frustrated laugh. "I wonder if Dr. Applegate ever met a wife he couldn't help a husband get shed of."

Another victim of Dr. Applegate, Mary thought angrily. When Christena was out of harm's way, Mary would make damned sure that Dr. Applegate was held accountable for his actions.

"This place isn't all that bad," the woman said. "Homer is paying for me to stay here. But once he divorces me…" Her voice quivered. "The money will stop and they'll likely send me to the state hospital up in Newberry." She pulled a hanky out of her pocket. "That place makes Westerholm look pretty plush."

Mary felt horrified at the woman's prospects. "Don't you have people who can take you in?"

"Homer has poisoned the children's minds against me. Beyond them and the in-laws… I'm not wanted by anyone. But I'm a fine cook and I took good care of the young ones." She bit her lower lip and shut her eyes, as if to hold back the tears. "I do my best," she finally said. "But some days, life just doesn't seem worth living anymore. I don't understand what's happened to me."

Throwing a seemingly levelheaded woman like this into a madhouse just because her husband found her wanting—now that was true insanity. "What's your name, ma'am?" Mary asked.

"Still Mrs. Alvina Tiegland. For a little while, anyway. I wonder if I must give up the name 'Tiegland,' when I'm no longer his wife."

"Mrs. Tiegland, I have to leave now. But please look for a letter from Miss Mary MacDougall in a few weeks. I know she will be able to help you with your predicament."

"Who is she?" Mrs. Tiegland asked. "This Miss MacDougall?"

"You'll find out."

Mary left her and made her way across the room. The nurses were moving some of the patients toward a dormitory filled with dozens of narrow beds in rows. Most of them were tidily made up, but some were already occupied by huddled and curled-up women.

As Mary came out onto the landing, she looked about. No one was in sight. This was it. Things had gone well so far. Now it was time to finish the job. Time for action.

She rummaged in her purse for her lock picks. She found the slender black case and jammed it into the right pocket of her gray jacket.

A couple of moments later she was up on the fifth floor, which to all appearances looked abandoned. Down the corridor to her right, she saw a solid-looking locked door. This is what Olive Handy had described to her. Mary only hoped that her huge gamble—that Christena was behind that door—was a winning one.

She closely examined the heavy commercial lockset on the door. It looked much more daunting than any she had worked on before. She selected the short-hook pick and the tension tool. One last time, she glanced over her shoulder and was relieved to see she was still quite alone. With a deep breath, she inserted the tension tool, then the pick, and began to work.

As she had when she practiced picking locks at home, Mary went into an almost meditative state. Her eyes shut, she focused all her senses into her hands and fingers, and the two tools in them. She applied rotational force to the lock's plug with the tension tool and moved the pick around inside the lock, trying to lift the pins one at a time. When she had lifted the final pin the proper distance, the lock would open with a sweep of the tension tool.

But this particular lock resisted her, and she went back to again attack the pins with her pick. It took a few seconds for the sound of the soft padding footsteps that came up behind her to penetrate through her single-minded concentration, just as the lock snicked open.

Mary spun around to see the raw-boned, equine face of Willis Flugum leering at her, as if out of a nightmare. She tried to dart sideways. But Flugum moved with supernatural agility.

With brutal swiftness, two powerful arms locked around her like a python's grip, and they squeezed until

Mary could barely breathe. A sweaty slab of a hand clamped over her mouth, smothering her screams of outrage.

She tried to struggle, but her captor was far too strong.

"Any more kicking or shouting," Flugum growled hoarsely, "and I'll break your pretty neck. Understand?"

Mary went limp as her heart pounded wildly.

"*Understand*?"

She nodded twice, fighting off a wave of nausea.

"A single squeak and you're dead. Right?"

Mary nodded again.

She was in no position to argue.

Chapter XXIII

Flugum gripped Mary with his left arm, opened the door that she herself had unlocked, and dragged her down the hallway of the isolated corridor. As they passed one of the rooms, she caught sight of a face watching them through the porthole in the door. Someone with eyes and mouth wide open in shock.

It was Christena.

She was all right!

Mary felt a momentary surge of relief. Her aunt gave a frantic wave, but Mary could only communicate back with a raise of the eyebrows.

Flugum quickly unlocked the door next to the room Christena was in and gave Mary a shove. She went sprawling onto her fanny, ripping her skirt in the process. The indignity of it enraged her, but at last she could see the fellow clearly as he glared down at her. He had red, scabby scratches across his left cheek—no doubt self-inflicted.

"I was warned about you, girl. And here you are, trying to break into a locked ward. With a lock pick, no less." Flugum crossed his arms. "We've got ways to deal with troublesome bitches like you."

Mary had never, ever been called that word, and had rarely heard it said. But if Flugum thought to shock her into submission, he had another think coming.

"You have no idea who you're dealing with," she snarled. "I demand that you let me go, or my father will have your head on a platter!"

"Ah, poor little millionaire's brat," he taunted. "Well, Papa's just going to have to wait a week or two to get his precious darling back. There's still money on the table. Can't have you go blabbing to the coppers until the big deal is closed." He got down on his haunches and stared her in the eye. "This ward is my domain, missy. They let me handle the unruly ones how I see fit. So don't expect anyone to come to your rescue." He reached out and stroked her face.

Mary tried to back away, but wasn't quick enough. He grabbed her arm again and touched her neck. His fingers felt like sandpaper.

"You are a pretty little thing, I'll grant you that. Now, be a good girl and I'll move you and your auntie to a nicer spot later tonight. I've got a cozy house out in the woods, where no one can hear you scream."

He stood and closed the door behind him. Mary heard the key click in the lock.

She wanted to yell. She wanted to curse. She wanted to cry. But she had no time for any such self-indulgence. No time to ponder how things had gone so spectacularly wrong.

Flugum had said he would be back later. She needed to

be ready the next time he swung that door open.

If she didn't show up at the front gate on schedule, Edmond would head into town and alert the police. But by then, Mary and Christena might not even be on the grounds anymore. No, the two women couldn't depend on the authorities arriving in time.

Mary hopped up, dusted herself off, and examined her surroundings. There wasn't much to work with. A stained mattress was thrown on the floor and an enameled metal chamber pot sat in the corner. A window with bars looked out on the top of some maple trees.

Mary tried the door. It was rock solid. Somehow, she had lost what remained of her lock pick set in the struggle with Flugum. And of course he had taken her purse, along with the revolver inside it.

She knocked three times on the wall between her room and Christena's. In a few seconds, she heard three knocks from the other side. It was a primitive form of communication, but at least she could assure Christena that she was all right.

Sitting down on the mattress, Mary thought long and hard about her lessons with Mrs. Chin, mistress of the Fujian White Crane fighting technique. Their most recent session had been just a few days before the *tableaux vivants,* which seemed like a million years ago. "You have one chance when man attack," Mrs. Chin had said. "You surprise him. Fast, sharp, quick. Adam apple. Groin. Knee. Face. Then you *run*." The old lady had scowled fiercely. "Do not stay fight him, Mary MacDougall. You *run*."

Well, the contingency Mrs. Chin described had arrived with a vengeance. It seemed, absent some *deus ex machina*, that Mary herself would have to take Flugum out of action.

She laughed a bleak laugh. She had never once struck anyone in anger in her entire life. Well, except for Jim. Her brother had been the recipient of not a few punches and kicks when they were growing up, but she never intended to disable him. With Flugum, though, she had no qualms about doing damage.

Grabbing the hem of her skirt in back, Mary pulled it between her legs in front and up. She jammed it behind her waistband and practiced a few kicks. The improvised bloomers worked well, nicely augmenting her freedom of motion.

She couldn't tell how long it had been by the time she finally heard the key click back in the lock. It had grown dark outside and there was no light in her prison cell. When the door swung open, she was on her feet, ready for Flugum.

"Evening, Miss MacDougall," he said, standing in the doorway with a lamp in his left hand. The quivering shadows made his face look like a skull.

Her pupils having been dilated so long, the light almost blinded Mary. It wouldn't work to attack immediately, she realized. She needed to wait until her eyes adjusted. She squinted and said nothing.

Flugum put the lamp down on the floor. "The way it's going to work is this. You and me are going to spend some time here." He glanced at the mattress on the floor. "Get to know each other, nice and personal. Then I'm going to give you a little something to put you to sleep. When you wake up, you'll be in my house." He grinned a toothy, ravenous grin.

Mary kept her silence, as her heart raced and her hands sweated. That rictus smile! She wished she had a shovel to smash his face with, to make that awful smile go away.

Flugum edged toward her. He grabbed her left wrist.

"Now how about you give good old Willis a nice kiss? Then we'll have some real fun."

Mary froze in place.

His other hand went around her back and he pulled her toward him. He leaned over and pressed his rough, chapped lips against hers. He stank of sweat. Mary almost gagged, he was so revolting. But she needed to keep calm, to focus on what she had to do.

Flugum backed off a foot or two, looking her up and down, like a wolf eyeing a piece of meat. He smiled that leering grin again. Mary regarded him coyly and forced a smile onto her face.

"I've never been with a man before," she said meekly. "You'll need to show me what to do."

Flugum seemed amused by her words. "Don't you worry, missy," he said, relaxing his grip on her wrist. "Old Willis here is a very good teach—"

With vicious suddenness, Mary shot her right arm forward and smashed the heel of her palm up into Flugum's nose. The nasal cartilage cracked like cheap tinder.

Then she instantly followed with a powerful hit to his Adam's apple with her left fist—putting her whole body into it.

Before he could even bellow his outrage, she repeated the two blows, and backed away.

He tottered in front of her, blood streaming from his nose and onto his shirt, a look of astonishment on his face.

"Why, I oughta—!"

But before he could finish the sentence, Mary spun sideways, kicked up with her right leg, and smashed her hard-heeled Oxford shoe into the man's groin.

He bent over double, gasping, groaning, looking down, staggering toward the open door. As he got closer to it, Mary darted in and kicked his left knee out from under him. He lost his balance and lurched onto the floor, ramming his head straight into the wall.

Mary stood there, panting, as astonished at her handiwork as Flugum undoubtedly had been. She couldn't wait to tell Mrs. Chin that surprise was indeed the key to disabling an attacker.

But then she noticed that Willis Flugum was lying terribly still. Not a movement, not a twitch.

Suddenly Mary had a dreadful thought.

What if she had broken his neck? What if she had killed him?

Chapter XXIV

Mary loathed Willis Flugum. How could she not?

But all she wanted to do was put him in jail. Not in his grave.

Her adrenaline pumping, she rushed over to him. He was lying face down on the floor, terribly still.

Leaning over him, Mary touched a finger to his neck. She could feel no pulse, and her own heart quickened. It didn't help that her hand was shaking.

"Don't be dead," she pleaded. "Please don't be dead."

Moving her finger to a second spot, she finally found a pulse, and let loose a sigh of relief.

She patted the unconscious man and found the ring of keys on his belt. Stuck in the top of his white pants in back was Mary's own Smith & Wesson. She reclaimed it. Then she felt through his coat pockets and discovered a brown bottle of ether and a rag.

Flugum was moaning now. Mary needed to act quickly. She dribbled some of the clear liquid onto the rag, taking care to keep it away from her own face. Then, hands still shaking, she pressed it over his nostrils and mouth for three or four seconds. She hoped that was enough and not too much. Having nearly killed him once, she didn't want to chance doing it for real the second time.

The moaning stopped and Flugum once again went still.

There were at least twenty keys on the ring, and it took Mary a moment to find the right one. She grabbed the lamp and locked the scoundrel into her former cell. Allowing herself one calming, deep breath, she then went to Christena's door and held the lamp up.

Christena's face was plastered to the glass in the porthole, wearing a look of utter incredulity. Her mouth was working away, but Mary had no idea what she was saying.

She put the lamp on the floor. It took another minute to find the right key for Christena's cell. And the instant the door swung open, Mary found herself in a rib-cracking, smothering embrace.

"Oh, Mary," her aunt blubbered. "You're all right. I was so afraid that awful man had hurt you."

Mary held Christena at arm's length and gave her a good examination. She seemed none the worse for wear, although the shabby gray dress she now wore did nothing to flatter her—even the stained brown skirt and shirtwaist that she had arrived in at Westerholm had looked more deluxe.

"I'm fine. And *I'm* the one who hurt *him*. But right now, we have to get out of here. And that means sneaking down four flights and out the front door as quickly as possible."

They descended the stairs in starts and fits, pausing in ink-black nooks when activity was heard. They had removed their shoes to avoid clicking and clacking, and Mary had transformed her makeshift bloomers back into a skirt, albeit a ripped one. When they finally got to the first floor by the infirmary, they put their shoes back on and went slowly across the windowed passageway between the east wing and the administration building. Christena peeked out into the lobby.

"There's someone sitting at that desk," she whispered. "And someone else is talking to her. An attendant, I think. They most certainly will try to stop us from leaving. Any ideas for persuading them that we're sane?"

With a wry grin, Mary hefted her Smith & Wesson.

The shock on Christena's face was priceless. "You're going to *shoot* them?"

"Of course not," Mary muttered. "But *they* don't know that."

"Ah, a grand bluff."

"That's the idea."

But just as they were about to move forward with their plan, a loud pounding resonated through the lobby. Mary stole a look. It was the gregarious Nurse Swenson who was at the desk, talking with a female attendant. They both turned in the direction of the main door.

"Who the devil could that be at this hour?" Nurse Swenson said.

She went to the big double door, followed by the attendant. The pounding continued and so did muffled shouting. Mary couldn't see who was outside.

"Westerholm is closed at this hour, sir," the nurse hollered through the glass and wood. "If you wish to visit a patient or see one of the doctors, you'll have to come back in the morning."

The angry shouting and pounding continued.

"I am not opening the door," Nurse Swenson insisted. "And if you keep pounding, I'll call the police."

Looking a bit concerned, she turned to the attendant. "Sadie, go find Oscar or Willis. Whoever it is out there sounds crazy."

Briefly savoring the irony of the woman's observation, Mary turned to Christena. "It could be Edmond with the deputy."

"Or it could be Olcott," Christena countered. "This may be a case where discretion is the better part of valor."

Mary thought a moment. "Right. We'll find a place to hide out of sight until the dust settles. Olive Handy told me the east wing had its own kitchen. No one should be in there this time of night."

The two women made their way back past the infirmary entrance to the kitchen, and slipped inside. A single gas sconce flickered weakly up on the wall, casting barely enough light to see. It showed stacks of plates and wood trays, pots and pans, sinks, tables, cupboards up and down one wall, and two stoves. The gaping opening of a dumbwaiter sat centered in one of the walls—doubtlessly to send meals up to the well-to-do ladies on the second floor.

Next to a large icebox was a single door. Mary swung

it open but could barely see anything from the sconce light. It seemed to be a stairway down into the basement. Without a lamp, though, it would be dangerous to try to descend into that utter blackness. A single little misstep could lead to disaster.

"Well, what do we do now?" Christena asked.

Mary groaned. They were in a terrible fix, almost certain to get caught, sooner or later. She dreaded to think what might happen if Flugum got hold of them again.

"I'm afraid there's no way out, Tena, but the way we came."

"*Oh, yes there is. Yes there is. Yes there is,*" sang a girlish voice out of the shadows.

Chapter XXV

Christena let out a yelp that was probably loud enough to be heard back in the infirmary. "Who…who is it?" she stuttered. "Who's there?"

Mary desperately scanned around the kitchen, seeing no one. Only when she caught some movement in the darkest corner, and a figure in a shabby white nightgown began to materialize, did she realize who their late night "ghost" was.

"Alice, is that you?"

"Alice Roosevelt" stepped into the puddle of light, her pale moon face grinning. "Bet you didn't think you'd see me again, did you, lady? Who's this other lady?"

Mary wasn't sure there was any point in actually introducing Christena, but she did so anyway—just to be polite.

"Now what are you doing out of your bed, Alice?" she asked a little sternly. "It's awfully late to be rambling around by yourself."

Alice leaned in toward her. "I like to wander the White House at night. Sometimes the president's guards catch me, sometimes they don't."

"White House?" squeaked Christena.

Mary knew she needed to play along with the unfortunate young madwoman. "Well, Tena, where else would the daughter of the president live?" She turned back to Alice. "But you really should be in bed."

"I know." Alice frowned. "But it's hard to sleep. I have bad dreams."

Mary could only imagine how bad, considering what this poor girl had gone through. "You've lived in the White House quite a while, haven't you?"

Alice nodded. "Yes, since Father became president."

"Is there any way out of the White House, other than the front doors?"

Alice smiled like a cat that just caught a canary. "There is. Would you like to know where?"

"I would," said Mary. "Very much."

Alice scampered over to a counter and lit a small lamp that Mary had failed to notice. "I'll take you on a tour," she said proudly. And she led them to the stairs that descended into the basement.

They followed her down into a vast, dank chamber that was full of boxed and crated supplies. Mary saw shelves crammed with items that inmates must have brought with them—suitcases, stacked articles of clothing, books, shoes, hats. It was a poignant sight, representing hundreds of sad stories. Off in a corner, next to a coal bunker, a huge dark steam boiler hunkered, its pipes going off in all directions. It was hibernating just now, unneeded in the summer heat. Alice made a beeline for the north wall. She stopped in front of a solid wood door, which she opened.

"A tunnel," murmured Christena. "Where does it go?"

"You'll find out," Alice teased in her sing-songy way, wiggling with delight. "You can keep the lamp."

Mary did not like having to take a tunnel to an unknown location on the word of a lunatic. But at the moment it seemed their only option. If need be, they would turn around and come back—hopefully no worse off than before.

After thanking Alice with a hug and walking her back to the stairs—Mary had to promise to come visit her again—Mary and Christena made their way slowly through the dark, mildewy passageway, where seepages of filthy water trickled across the floor.

They had gone only a few dozen feet when Mary stopped so quickly that Christena ran into her. They faced each other in the lamp's wan circle of orange light. Mary realized she had forgotten to ask a very important question.

"Did you find her, Tena? Did you find Mrs. Olcott?"

Christena's face lit up. "Yes, I did. Almost immediately after I arrived. In fact, I was talking with her—what a charming woman—when her husband came upon us. That proved to be my Waterloo."

"I bet it was right before you purloined that emerald bracelet," Mary said, continuing through the tunnel.

Her aunt snorted. "It looked like a cheap little trinket worth all of fifty cents. If I were going to steal anything, it would have to be from Tiffany. And I did not touch that man."

"Well," Mary grinned, "at least they didn't chop your hair off."

A moment later they came to a steep, narrow staircase going up to a closed door. Mary started climbing, hoping that one of Flugum's keys would unlock the door. But the door handle turned easily and she stepped out into a darkened room. She held up the lamp and turned around.

"Ah," she said, smiling, "it's the chapel, Tena. And a fine one it is."

Though not nearly as opulent as the great chapels she and her aunt had visited in France, it was a lovely Gothic church of brick and marble, complete with a vaulted ceiling. It had a sense of peace and serenity about it, as though many a troubled soul had found comfort there. Handsome mahogany pews lined either side of a central aisle, and an altar stood up front with a triptych of Jesus, Mary, and Joseph looming behind it. Benches for a little choir sat at the side, next to a handsome pump organ.

"Well," Christena said with admiration, "old Mrs. Westerholm certainly spared no expense, did she?"

Mary didn't answer. Going to the front door, she found it locked. And not a single one of Flugum's keys would open it.

"If we're going to get out of here, Tena, it'll have to be through a window."

The chapel had a dozen windows. Eight of them were inset with stained glass depictions of Biblical scenes. The other four were merely double hung and should have been capable of opening. But as hard as Mary and Christena tried each one—grunting and straining—they couldn't budge them. The windows were frozen shut, the sashes wouldn't move.

"I suppose there's a Sunday service," Mary said, plopping down into a pew. "What day is it? Wednesday? Almost Thursday? We'll be awfully hungry by then."

She looked down at her torn and dirtied suit, and then at Christena's rumpled, soiled dress, marveling at their ragged appearance. She would not have wanted to run into two such disreputable-looking characters in a darkened alley.

Christena came and sat next to her.

"Being an inmate," she observed, "has given me a lot to think about. I look at all those women in Westerholm who used to have lives. Through bad luck or God's will or what have you, they lost most of what they had or were. After Flugum locked me up, I wasn't sure if I was to live or die. I have never felt the preciousness of life more."

Mary didn't know what to say. She grabbed her aunt's hand and held it tight.

"I'm forty years old, Mary. If I'm lucky I'll have another forty. It hasn't been a bad life so far, but I don't want to waste what's left. I'm thinking I need to be a bit bolder."

"Good heavens, you're not planning on taking up snake charming?" Mary said with apparent seriousness. "Are you?"

Christena gave her a withering look. "Ha ha."

The mood having been lightened, Mary stood and went over to a folding chair that was leaning against the wall.

She approached one of the double-hung windows, chair in both hands. Eyes tightly shut, she swung the thing, smashing the glass. Then, using the barrel of her revolver, she knocked out what remained of the muntins and the glass shards that might have cut the fugitives as they climbed out.

"There, liberty is ours." With her left hand Mary made a flourishing, chivalrous gesture toward the now-open window. *"Aprés vous, madamoiselle."*

And, one after the other, the two women crawled into the warm, humid night.

They crept off the grounds of Westerholm, to the spot where Mary had left Edmond many hours earlier. She hadn't expected to find him there, and indeed there was no sign of him or Mrs. Wingate's carriage. By now the ruckus at the front door seemed to have stopped, although the lights on the first floor of the administration building all were blazing.

The pair headed down the road that would lead them back to Dillmont. The sky was blue-black and peppered with a thousand glinting stars. A half moon provided adequate illumination. Both went silently, alone with their thoughts. Mary, for her part, pondered how she was going to deliver Merton Olcott and Willis Flugum into the hands of the authorities. All she could do, she supposed, was report the facts as she knew them. The next order of business would be wiring her client, Clara McColley, with the good news that her mother was alive.

A few minutes later, they spied a dim light bouncing in

the distance.

"That looks like a carriage lamp," Mary said. "Maybe the driver will take us into town."

"A ride would be lovely," Christena agreed. "I'm quite exhausted."

"We *have* had an exciting evening, haven't we?" laughed Mary. And she hoped she would never have one as exciting ever again.

They stood by the side of the road. Mary, to avoid alarming any Good Samaritan who might be approaching, tucked her revolver into the back of her skirt. As the carriage got closer, they waved their arms.

The man in the driver's seat reached for the lamp that had been swaying on a hook by his side. He lifted it up in front of his face.

"Hullo," he said in an eerily familiar voice. "What have we here?"

"Oh hell!" Mary groaned. It was Merton Olcott.

Again!

Chapter XXVI

"Looks to me like two lunatics escaped from the asylum," the fraudster sneered from his carriage seat. "Would you ladies like a ride back to Westerholm?"

"No, thank you, Mr. Olcott," Mary snarled. "If that's even your real name." She couldn't believe how this horrible man kept turning up like the bad penny. "And I'm afraid that I shall not be giving your company that order for Sunday school furniture."

Olcott roared out a laugh. "I'm glad you have a bit of good humor about the situation. I mean, it is very amusing, isn't it? That an heiress like yourself should have gotten herself into such an awful pickle by poking her nose into something that didn't concern her."

"I think when a husband commits a perfectly sane woman to a madhouse, and tells her loved ones she's dead, it should be everyone's concern."

Olcott shrugged with irritating composure. "That was strictly a business decision. The daughter of the great John MacDougall should understand. Now, you may disapprove of the way I treated my wife. But I never intended her harm. I only meant to unburden her of her fortune. In fact, we went to a great deal of trouble to keep her alive." He scowled. "But after all this fuss, I almost regret my scruples."

"Quite the moralist you are," Christena observed.

Olcott ignored her sarcasm. "We could have arranged a very real death for Agnes here in Dillmont. A push off a cliff. An accident on the road. No one could have proven foul play. It would have been much easier for us. But Willis and I have never been murderers. We prefer not to have blood on our hands. Don't want to dance at the end of a rope, you know."

"You *will* be going to prison," Mary said. "That I can promise you."

Olcott gave her a pitying, condescending smile and shook his head. "Oh, I don't think so. As soon as we stash you two away, we plan to disappear for good. We aim to enjoy our profits in a warm, sunny place where no one knows us." He leaned over, as if to grab something from the floor of the carriage.

It's a gun! Mary thought in a panic.

She reached around her back and snatched the Smith & Wesson from her waistband, cocking the hammer as she swung the weapon forward.

Just as Olcott began to straighten up, she fired a shot well above his head.

The man sat bolt upright, empty-handed, looking flabbergasted. "You could've killed me, you little bitch!"

Mary almost laughed. That was the second time this

evening someone had called her that. She must be doing something right.

"Hands up, Mr. Olcott," she said as evenly as possible, though quivering inside. "We're taking you to the deputy sheriff and making our charges against you."

"Mary," whispered Christena.

"Yes? What?"

"There's another carriage coming, at rather a quick pace." She pointed in the direction from which Olcott had come.

Keeping her pistol on the man, Mary sidestepped a few feet and confirmed what Christena had seen. Perhaps it was Edmond with the police. She could only hope.

Half a moment later, the second carriage rolled up alongside of Olcott's and stopped. The light from Olcott's lamp barely showed the stranger who was driving, a fellow in a derby hat and a plain dark suit.

"Sir," Mary said as forcefully as she could, "this man is a criminal and confidence trickster who stole his wife's money and kidnapped my aunt. He has an accomplice who works in the asylum. We would be ever so grateful if you would go back into town and fetch the deputy sheriff."

"She's lying, sir," exclaimed Olcott in the tone of an aggrieved innocent. "Both these women are complete lunatics. They jumped out of the bushes and shot at me. They tried to make me get out of my carriage so they could steal it."

"That's a lie!" Christena retorted.

The stranger hopped down and walked slowly toward

Mary, who still was holding her gun on Olcott. He reached into his coat pocket and pulled something out, which he showed her. It was a large silver star attached to a leather wallet.

"Miss," he said in a raspy voice, "the deputy sheriff would be me. And I would be grateful, for my part, if you gave me the gun, nice and slow with the grip forward. And then we can try to sort this all out."

Finally, some good luck. What were the chances of having the lawman turn up at just the perfect moment? "Of course, deputy sheriff," she said with relief, handing him her gun.

"Did you hear me?" Olcott blustered from his perch. "This madwoman shot at me. I demand that you arrest her and her accomplice immediately for assault and attempted robbery. And she's accused me of the most awful things! Though I've never even met her before. Terrible slanders!"

"He's lying!" howled Mary. The pure gall of the man! "Let me tell you what happened."

"I'm lying?" snapped Olcott. "*I'm lying?* Look at these two. Ragged, dirty wretches. Shooting guns at innocent people. Outrageous!"

"If I've never met you before," countered Mary, "how is it I know your name? Merton Olcott, from Duluth."

"She knows my name, officer," Olcott retorted, "because she forced me to tell her at gunpoint. She was threatening my life. Of course I told her my name. And I'm not from Duluth. I'm from Detroit."

The deputy glowered at both of them. He turned to

Mary.

"What's *your* name?"

"Mary MacDougall of Duluth."

"Daughter of John MacDougall," Christena slipped in. "Who happens also to be my brother."

The deputy, a slender man of middle age with a large, bushy mustache, raised his eyebrows. "The mining millionaire? You're his daughter? And you're his sister?" He looked them up and down and snorted. "Seems a peculiar place and time to find wealthy ladies out on constitutionals. And looking as you both do. That old gray dress is just what the gals at Westerholm wear, as I recall."

"I told you, officer," Olcott chimed in. "Lunatics. Both of them."

The deputy glared at him. "You wait your turn while these two explain themselves."

Mary told the tale of Agnes Olcott with commendable brevity. She ended with an urgent plea that her client be informed of her mother's whereabouts as quickly as possible. She asked that he contact Detective Robert Sauer of the Duluth police.

"All right, miss," said the deputy when she finished. "You're alleging this gentleman married this widow and fooled the folks in Duluth about her supposed death so that he could take control of her company and bank accounts. And when you and your supposed aunt here came snooping around, fancying yourselves detectives, you were both captured and held captive by his supposed accomplice in Westerholm."

"Yes, that's it," Mary agreed. The officer's use of the terms "alleging" and "supposed," however, worried her.

"And you shot at him because he was about to pull a gun on you."

"Correct, deputy."

"Mr. Olcott." The deputy turned to the man in the carriage. "Were you reaching for a weapon?"

"It so happens I was," Olcott confirmed, "because this woman was aiming a gun at me."

"That's not true," protested Mary. "He made the first move and…"

"Shut up, miss," barked the deputy. "Now, sir, tell us your side."

Olcott insisted that he had never even been to Duluth, knew nothing of widows or asylum attendants, was merely in Dillmont to view the nearby scenic rapids and waterfall, and had been innocently driving along when these two crazy women waylaid him.

The deputy ruminated a moment, looking from Mary and Christena to Olcott, as if he wished a pox on all three of them.

"I was called about a disturbance at the asylum," he said, eyeing the women suspiciously. "Now, sir, where are you staying?"

"The hotel in Dillmont," Olcott answered.

"I'll ask you to remain in town for the next day or two," said the deputy. "You can come to the sheriff's office in the morning and swear out a formal complaint."

Olcott nodded briskly. "I shall do that, deputy. I shall

do that with pleasure."

Mary felt like she had been hit in the chest with a sledgehammer. It was just too appallingly incredible! Unfair!

The smug, amused look on Olcott's face would haunt her forever. He drove around them and up the road, still smirking.

"No!" she wailed. "You can't trust him! He's a professional liar! And he's got two accomplices! An attendant in the asylum. And Dr. Applegate."

"Mary," groaned Christena. "I meant to tell you about the doctor." But before she could finish her comment, the deputy interjected.

"You two, *shut up*," he growled. "I'll not have you slandering Dr. Applegate. He's very well regarded in these parts. As honest as the day is long. He delivered my second granddaughter not a month ago."

Mary understood all too well that she shouldn't try to argue with the lawman. "What happens now?" she asked in a tone of utter dispiritedness.

"Funny you should ask," the deputy responded. "Fact is, you're under arrest, the both of you. Hands out, please, so I can put on the manacles."

Chapter XXVII

Mary's back was sore and stiff from having spent two nights in a row in jail, upon lumpy straw-filled mats, with no pillows. But Christena, being twice her age, suffered even more, and appeared visibly crooked by the time the deputy brought the two of them up to the courtroom in Sault Ste. Marie on Friday after lunch.

There were only a few people in the gallery. One of them was Paul Forbes, who managed to reach out and touch Christena's hand as she was being led to the defendants' table. When Mary, Christena, and Edmond had failed to show up on Mackinac Thursday morning as promised, it seemed that Paul had sounded the alarm—immediately wiring Mary's father in Duluth.

Which was no doubt why John MacDougall's personal attorney, Archibald Cullen, was seated next to Paul. "Uncle Archie," Mary had always called him. He had been a family friend since she was little. He nodded to her, but the look on his face was not as good-humored as Mary was used to. She could only imagine what the conversation had been like between her father and Uncle Archie when they learned of her and her aunt's predicament.

The third man who was with them, Mary didn't know. But as soon as she and Christena were seated at the defendants' table, he walked up to join them.

"Phinneas Wilcox," he said, shaking hands with each of them. "I'll be representing you. Mr. Cullen said Mr. MacDougall wanted the best criminal-defense man in the Upper Peninsula to represent his daughter and sister. And that would be me."

Mary grimaced when she heard the word "criminal." She had never thought that she would ever be associated with that particular noun, except in the ferreting out of them.

"How in the world did Uncle Archie..." Mary wondered. "I mean, Mr. Cullen get here from Duluth so quickly?"

"Traveled all night, I understand," the attorney explained. "Hired a private car and engine out of Superior."

Mary, cringing, could only imagine what that must have cost her father.

Mr. Wilcox began to pepper the two of them with questions about what had happened two nights before. Christena, closer to him, answered most of them.

Mary knew she should be listening, but her mind wandered back to the misadventures of Wednesday evening.

She had been informed by the deputy sheriff in Dillmont that it indeed had been Edmond Roy who had made that terrible ruckus at Westerholm's front door. In his effort to get into the asylum, he engaged in fisticuffs with a male attendant who, unceremoniously, tossed him down the granite steps. He had been arrested, but spent the night in the infirmary at Westerholm, where Dr. Applegate treated him. Mary was worried sick about his injuries, but no one could give her any details.

And this all happened to him because of stupid, bone-headed Mary MacDougall!

Not only had she been wrong to involve Edmond and her aunt in this disaster. She had also apparently been terribly wrong about Dr. Applegate's character.

During her brief residency on Westerholm's deluxe second floor, Christena had learned from one of the nurses that the doctor's liberality in committing men's wives came from his personal experience. His own wife, at the loss of their two young children to diphtheria, fell into extreme melancholy; and, in fact, tried to kill herself. She had been the white-haired woman Mary saw, who clutched the photograph of her dead son and daughter as she stared out the window, awaiting their return.

A couple of the wealthy inmates at Westerholm had told Christena that they actually *preferred* to be there, rather than at home. Putting up with their husbands was a considerably more distressing situation than living comfortably and simply on the second floor of the east wing.

Mary's thoughts were interrupted as the door at the rear of the courtroom creaked opened. She turned to look. A tall man came limping in, being steered by a deputy.

It was Edmond. She had not seen him since they parted just outside Westerholm.

His summer suit was covered in dirt and dried spots of blood, and torn in at least two places. A bandage covered the left half of his handsome forehead. And a plaster cast encased his arm. His right arm. *His painting arm.*

She gasped and could feel tears forming in the corners of her eyes.

He waved at her with his good left hand and managed a despondent smile, as Mary waved back. The deputy nudged him into a seat at the rear of the courtroom.

Mary turned back, moaning, overcome with guilt. Edmond had reluctantly agreed to help her in this misbegotten scheme and this was his reward—a broken arm and another encounter with the law.

How would he ever finish his mural? Or manage the portraits of Mrs. Ensign and her granddaughter?

She slumped in her seat. The world would be a much safer place if the judge simply tossed Mary into jail and threw away the key.

Christena put her arm around Mary and tried to comfort her. As she did, the bailiff entered the room and called out, "Hear ye, hear ye. Please rise. The District Court of Chippewa County is now in session, Judge Anson Tolliver presiding."

"Good Lord, it's dear old Anson," Christina whispered to Mary as they rose.

Mary blinked at the lanky gentleman in the black suit who mounted the bench and sat in the tall chair behind it. It was none other than Christena's dancing partner, from the ballroom of the Grand Hotel on Mackinac Island.

The judge told everyone to be seated, then spent a few minutes reading through the documents on the desk before him.

"Well, well, well," he said, finally looking up. "It really is Miss MacDougall and Miss MacDougall here before me today. And I believe your friend Mr. Roy is also among us. You three are charged with offenses I would not have expected of you. Some of them *serious* offenses."

He fixed his penetrating and Lincolnesque gaze first on Mary and then on Christena.

"I assume that, as the sister of a millionaire, you have not taken up a career in crime as a matter of choice. Would I be correct?"

"You would, your honor," Christena concurred.

"And your response, Miss Mary MacDougall, would be the same?"

"It would, your honor," Mary meekly confirmed.

"And Mr. Wilcox is counsel for both of you?"

Mr. Wilcox nodded and said, "I am, your honor. And I will also represent Mr. Edmond Roy."

Mary's heart jumped. Knowing that Edmond would have a proper defense took at least a little of the sting out of her feeling of guilt.

"All right then," the judge said. He picked up a sheet of paper and summarized the contents. "The county attorney enumerates the following charges against Miss Mary MacDougall. We have criminal trespass at Westerholm Institution, malicious damage to property at Westerholm, first-degree battery against a Willis Flugum, and assault with a deadly weapon with regard to a Mr. Merton Olcott. Against Miss Christena MacDougall the charge is malicious damage to property." Judge Tolliver turned to look at the assistant county attorney, sitting alone at his table. "Is that everything, Mr. Phelps?"

"It is, your honor," replied the prosecuting attorney.

"Are your clients prepared to make pleas, Mr. Wilcox? If they are, I am inclined to be lenient, except with regard to the charges of assault and battery."

Mary leaned across Christena and whispered urgently to Mr. Wilcox about Olcott and Flugum. He nodded several times and stood.

"On behalf of Miss Mary MacDougall, I can say she's willing to take her medicine for the damage she did to the chapel at Westerholm, by way of paying restitution and more. And so is Miss Christena MacDougall. But the matter of the battery against Mr. Flugum and the assault against Mr. Olcott raises this question. Are the gentlemen prepared to make their complaints and provide testimony in person or by deposition?"

The judge peered down his nose at the assistant county attorney. "A fair question, don't you think, Mr. Phelps? Are Mr. Olcott and Mr. Flugum available to this court?"

The prosecutor rose, a bit of red showing in his cheeks. "Well, your honor, both gentlemen said they would swear out complaints at the time of the incidents. I have word from the deputy sheriff in Dillmont that he's looking for them. But they seem to have vanished. Mr. Flugum's house is empty and the hotel never heard of Mr. Olcott."

"I knew it!" Mary exclaimed, jumping to her feet. "The two of them have gone to ground."

"Miss MacDougall," the judge snapped, "you will please control yourself. If you don't, I will find you in contempt of court."

Mary apologized and sat down. This nightmare, she hoped, might finally be ending.

Chapter XXVIII

It had been two weeks since Mary had arrived back in Duluth, after legal arrangements were made for her departure from Chippewa County. She kept pondering everything that had happened—the good and the bad. There was plenty of both. It was quite incredible, all that she had gone through.

She was sitting in the library of the big house on East Superior Street, late on a warm Thursday afternoon in July, knitting. Emma Beach had placed the basket full of wool yarn and needles in front of her. "Best to occupy yourself with something worthwhile," she had said. And so Mary began on a pair of mittens that would join others destined for the orphanage this Christmas.

She couldn't quite say which disaster had made her father angrier. The matter of Agnes Olcott, and Mary's unintended crime spree at its conclusion? Or his sister Christena's decision to stay with Paul Forbes for a time, then have him come to Pittsburgh for a visit with her?

Was John MacDougall more aggravated by having his daughter brought before a judge in Sault Ste. Marie? Or by having his beloved little sister take up with a free-spirited photographer? Christena hadn't even bothered to come back to Duluth, only letting a surprised Mary know of her plan on the platform in Ishpeming. Mary wished she could have stayed there with her aunt, but she had no choice but to return home alone and face the music.

She had never seen her father's face quite so red or heard his intimidating voice sound quite so fierce. She winced again and again, and very nearly started to cry. But Mary had determined she would sit there and take it. She had earned her dressing-down the hard way, and wasn't going to sully it—or evade it—by some feminine trick. By sheer force of will, she kept the tears at bay.

"Not only did you go snooping about that asylum quite improperly, and shoot a gun at a man, and damage property, and get arrested, for God's sake," John MacDougall had fulminated, standing over her. "You exposed yourself to assault by a dangerous criminal. You put your own dear aunt into a madhouse on the off chance that she would discover a woman thought to be dead. You involved your friend Mr. Roy in the affair and got him arrested. And you got his arm broken, as well!"

"Father," Mary had replied tremulously, "I am more than willing to repay you for all your costs." Those, she knew, included the attorneys' fees, mending the chapel window, and the fines that Judge Tolliver exacted on her, Christena, and Edmond. Not to mention the cost of hiring an engine and carriage to bring Uncle Archie to Sault Ste. Marie. There was also the five thousand dollars that John MacDougall had donated to Westerholm's trustees by way of apology.

His eyes had widened. "*Young lady, that is not the bloody point!*" he roared. "You have made a fool of yourself in society. You have my colleagues laughing at me behind my back. You have caused our family name to appear in the newspapers, and not in a flattering way."

He paused and caught control of his temper. "I would be entirely justified in demanding that you cease this ridiculous detecting obsession of yours. But I have a feeling that, short of locking you up, I wouldn't be able to stop you. Understand, though, you could have gotten yourself killed." His voice quieted. "And I would take very cold comfort indeed if, at your funeral, some fellow came up to me and said, 'Ah, Mr. MacDougall, your daughter, she was a fine detective.'"

Mary had nodded abjectly. However, a little voice in her head riposted that it was a much better epitaph than "She died a boring young woman with piles of money, and not a thought in her head." Still, she understood her father's point and genuinely regretted causing him pain.

"I should hope that your recent debacle has convinced you to apply your intelligence and energy to more sensible pursuits." Her father had finally slumped into the chair opposite her. "Lord knows, I cannot keep an eye on you every moment of every day."

Thank goodness, thought Mary.

"But you'll be happy to hear that I've arranged for the next best thing."

Mary steeled herself for an undoubtedly unpleasant

surprise.

"You know that your mother's cousin Jeanette has been through some hard times down in St. Louis."

Mary did indeed. Emma Beach had already told her that Jeanette had been found and was in straitened circumstances. John MacDougall had only been able to track her down by hiring a detective—a "real detective," as the housekeeper had said pointedly. The news had come when Mary was off on Mackinac.

"I've asked Jeanette to come live with us for a while, and she has agreed. She's to be your personal secretary and *constant* companion."

Mary had been appalled. She liked Jeanette Harrison well enough. But the woman was a little too straight-laced and prudent. A kind of stick in the mud. Not nearly as fun as Christena. And Mary knew perfectly well that Jeanette would serve as a spy for John MacDougall.

"But I don't need a secretary, Father," she tried to persuade him. "I'm perfectly capable of taking care of my own affairs."

He didn't need to say a word. His expression said it all: *Recent events would indicate otherwise.*

"As to my sister," John MacDougall continued, his face darkening again, "the consequences of her little holiday with you are dismaying. And I have no idea how to stop her. You know that Tena hates being told what to do. I've never known anyone as stubborn as she is."

Mary almost said, *Well, look in the mirror then*, but thought better of it.

After the dust had settled, she had one final thing to be grateful for. Her father—having correctly suspected Detective Sauer's part in the matter—made no attempt to get him discharged. And when Mary had sought out the policeman at his favored luncheon spot, Salter's, he expressed his gratitude. But still he had unhappy news for her.

"My boss has told me that he does not want to hear of you visiting police headquarters," the detective said. "Off limits, I'm afraid. Or next time I really may get the sack. And to be frank, if I'd have known what you planned to get yourself up to out there in Chippewa County, I never would've given you the lead. Didn't I tell you to merely observe and interview and report?"

Mary nodded sheepishly. "That's what I intended to do. The assault on Westerholm was just sort of improvised."

He gave her a smile, a rare occurrence. "Yes, well, I have to hand it to you, though. You proved the fraud and unmasked the fraudsters. And at least they didn't get Mrs. Olcott's every dime. There's enough left that she and her company will survive."

"Have you heard anything more about Olcott and Flugum?"

"Still at large, I'm afraid. Not their real names, of course. They had worked a big flimflam down in Tennessee. Memphis. They used different aliases then. While Olcott cooked the books up in the office, Flugum stole the goods from the warehouse. They managed to disappear back then, too."

Mary had also sent a letter to Mrs. Tiegland at Wester-holm—the poor lady whose husband had abandoned her. Mary told her that the law office of Wilcox and Jameson in Sault Ste. Marie would be in touch with her, regarding representation for her divorce, and possible employment as a cook or housekeeper. This would be at no cost to her good self.

And then there was Edmond Roy.

The parting at the Ishpeming station had been nothing like that in Duluth last December.

They had stood regarding each other nervously, almost as if they had only just met. Mary was already upset because Christena had just walked off with Paul Forbes—having not bothered to tell her niece of her impromptu stay-over until moments before.

"So, I'll see you in Duluth in a few weeks," Mary had said.

Like a shy boy, Edmond had kicked at the bricks that paved the platform. "I hope so. I do hope the arm heals up in time."

"It will," Mary had said encouragingly, trying to wish that outcome into reality. "Of course it will."

Edmond's face showed skepticism.

"We did have some fun, though, on Mackinac, didn't we?" Mary gave him a bright smile.

"We did," he nodded with a smile not so enthusiastic. "You are a charming companion." He averted his eyes. "Most of the time."

That stung Mary a little. But he was right.

She almost said something about her feelings for him. About how very, *very* much he meant to her. And about how she couldn't imagine not having him in her life. But before she could say anything, he quickly leaned over and kissed her.

It was a light brush of lips on her cheek with no hug. Then he offered her a clumsy handshake with his good left hand, said goodbye, and walked away.

Mary couldn't blame him for having had enough of her.

A few days ago a typed letter from him had arrived that did nothing to cheer her up. In a worryingly formal tone, he explained that Miss Jursik of the Pioneer Bank had graciously agreed to help him with his correspondence while his arm was in the cast. Mary recalled how the young woman's almond-shaped blue eyes had gazed so admiringly at Edmond, when Mary had met her those many weeks before.

Unable to paint, Edmond had hired Rosie Lehmann to help him finish the bank mural. Rosie—the talented painter and beautiful nude model. They would be spending a lot of time together, Mary thought despondently.

Even worse, Edmond wrote that he had resigned Mrs. Ensign's commission, as she expected him to come in late July. His arm could not possibly mend by then, according to the doctor in Ishpeming.

For half a year, Mary had been planning for his return to Duluth. Now, because of her own stupidity, he would not be coming. It made her want to scream in frustration.

"Excuse me, dear."

Mary started and looked up from the knitting in her lap. Emma Beach, the housekeeper, was standing in the library doorway.

"Yes, Emma?"

"You have two visitors. Mrs. McColley and Mrs. Larson."

Mary's former client had come calling, along with the woman who had been the focus of so much worry and effort during those days in Dillmont. Mary put her knitting down and jumped to her feet.

In the vestibule she found Clara McColley standing next to a stout lady with black hair going gray.

"Mrs. McColley," she said, offering her hand, "how good to see you again."

Clara McColley took Mary's hand and shook it.

"And this must be Mrs. Olcott," Mary said. "Finally we meet."

The older woman scowled. "I'll never use that name again. I'm having my attorney get me an annulment. Please, call me Mrs. Larson. And I am honored to finally meet my rescuer." She offered her right hand and grasped Mary's firmly.

Agnes Larson had a square, well-lined face that still showed the effects of fatigue and worry. But for the most part, she seemed to have weathered her ordeal quite well.

"Your heroics came just in the nick of time, Miss MacDougall," said Clara McColley. "Some of the money from the company accounts is gone for good. But much remains untouched, and thank heavens the sale of the firm did not go through. We've put our old manager back in charge and we have great hopes."

Mary smiled. Despite all the disasters in Dillmont, she had, in the end, been able to reunite mother and daughter, and save a well-respected enterprise.

"Mrs. Ol... Pardon me. Mrs. Larson. May I ask you a few questions?"

"Certainly."

"How was Merton Olcott able to get you into Westerholm? Was it against your will?"

"Quite the contrary," Mrs. Larson replied. "I confess now that I was suffering from severe melancholia for some time, ever since my real husband's death. Merton suggested I needed professional help and I agreed to go to Westerholm, with the hope that their therapy would mend me. Merton insisted that we keep my committal secret, to prevent any rumors that might hurt Garlock & Larson. He said he would only tell my daughter and a few of the top men at the factory."

She shook her head angrily. "Instead, he told them that I was dead, and he went about appropriating the company and its bank accounts."

"Do you feel that Dr. Applegate acted properly, accepting your husband's opinion of your problem?" Mary asked.

Mrs. Larson's expression softened. "The doctor was horrified to learn that he had played a role, however innocent, in the fraud. But I do think he sincerely believed his diagnosis of my mental state was correct. He did *not* do what he did because my husband persuaded him to. He put me into Westerholm because he genuinely believed I would get better there. We had several long talks, and he helped me to realize that losing my husband could never be gotten over. Those wounds ache until your very last day."

Mary thought of Dr. Applegate's own losses. The two young children who died despite his best efforts to save them. The mute wife and mother who sits by the window day after day at Westerholm, waiting for her son and daughter to return. Mary regretted yet again how she had misjudged the doctor in her rush to make sense of things.

"We are made of our scars as much as we are made of our bones and muscles," Mrs. Larson reflected. "But one must keep on living and loving the people who are still with us." She looked at her daughter with transparent affection.

"And the death certificate?" Mary asked.

"Dr. Applegate never wrote or signed that death certificate," answered Mrs. Larson. "He assured me of that before I left Westerholm."

"The doctor didn't know you or have any reason to trust you, Miss MacDougall," explained Clara McColley. "He told Mother he wired Merton right after you brought up the death certificate. My stepfather promptly assured him that you were some unhinged flibbertigibbet who had become obsessed with Merton Olcott. He said you imagined the supposed death certificate."

That, realized Mary, was why Dr. Applegate had left his office so quickly after she had visited him. He was rushing to the train station to send a telegram. And that was what brought Merton Olcott to Dillmont double-quick, to reassure and placate the ruffled physician.

"Probably Willis Flugum stole a blank certificate from Dr. Applegate's office at Westerholm, and he or Merton forged it," Mrs. Larson theorized. "That and the coincidence of poor Annie O'Toole's death gave Merton exactly the conditions he needed to put the final touches on the fraud."

"But now Mother is home, safe and sound," Clara McColley said with a grateful smile. She reached into her purse and pulled out a small, folded piece of paper. "We've come to pay you for your services. Since we never received a bill, we could only guess at the figure. We decided on one thousand dollars, after all that you suffered for us. If it's not enough, please say so." And she held out the check.

Mary was frozen on the spot. She hadn't even expected to receive a payment, after the fiasco she had presided over. Let alone such a large payment.

"You're very kind," she said, pointedly not taking the check. "But it was hardly a well-handled case. I made so many mistakes. I really don't deserve any reward at all."

"Mary?"

The three women turned as John MacDougall strode toward them through the foyer. He held a lit cigar in his right hand and wore an amused expression on his weathered face. He stepped into the vestibule, with Emma right behind him.

"If you're to be a businesswoman, my girl, it doesn't do to turn down payment from satisfied customers. Even if the job was a little slapdash."

Mary beamed at him. Finally, a note of approval from her long-suffering father. "Thank you," she said, taking the check from Clara McColley.

"Now ladies," John MacDougall said, "if you're not in any rush, may I invite you out to the porch in back for a cup of tea or coffee. I understand we have some fresh-made shortcake with strawberries. Emma, would you lead the way?"

As Mary saw her two visitors out the front door an hour later, she noticed that the day's last post had arrived and was sitting on the side table in the vestibule. Riffling through the items, she found a thin brown parcel from Ish-peming. She ripped it open and extracted a piece of cardboard wrapped in tissue paper. She pulled off the tissue and smiled.

There, mounted to the cardboard, was one of the *al fresco* portraits that Paul had made of Edmond and Mary. Smiling, Edmond leaned against one side of that old maple, his arms crossed, his gaze focused on Mary. She stood on the other side, her hat in hand, regarding him with equal fondness—as if the two of them were sharing some sweet secret. The memory of that morning came flooding back to Mary, in a bittersweet rush.

The accompanying note was from Paul. He wrote that he had wanted to get the photo mailed to Mary before he left for Pittsburgh, where he would be visiting Christena for a while. *Well why not*, Mary thought. Christena and Paul had found each other. Apart from saving Agnes Olcott, it was the only good thing to have come from this horrible holiday.

But there was one other item in the large envelope. A small tablet with a simple white card attached to it. On the card, in block letters, were written the words:

I MAY NOT BE ABLE TO PAINT VERY WELL, BUT I CAN STILL DANCE.

WITH STEADFAST FONDNESS, EDMOND

What on earth did it mean? Mary examined the tablet and then understood.

On each page, Edmond had drawn—obviously with his left hand—a bearded stick figure with his right arm in a sling. As Mary flipped through the tablet sheets with her thumb, the stick man danced a jolly little jig.

Relief washed over her like a wave. Edmond seemed to be saying that he had forgiven her. She put everything into the brown envelope, tucked it under her left arm, and headed back to her mittens.

Mary MacDougall the detective vowed she would live to detect again. And Mary MacDougall, ardent admirer of Edmond Roy, hoped that one day soon she would feel his strong arms twirling her around the dance floor.

—The End—

Coda

The Unfortunate and Mysterious Disappearance of Jeanette Harrison

From the Papers of Jeanette Harrison Sauer

January 1902

If I had in my possession a time machine of the sort Mr. H. G. Wells writes about, I would climb into it, pull the lever backward until I reached the summer of 1900, climb out, track myself down, look me in the eye, and say, "You, Jeanette Harrison, are a total and complete dunce!"

My younger, less-enlightened self would surely take offense, but I would give her no time to reply.

"You are a partner in a somewhat profitable secretarial bureau. You own a modest but beautiful house in Benton Park, bought and paid for by the hard labor of your dearly departed Daniel. You have a small nest egg in a savings account at the bank, thanks to the generosity of your cousin

Alice MacDougall, who so kindly remembered you in her will. For a 30-year-old widow, you are in a very good situation financially. And yet you plan to gamble all your reserves on some insane scheme suggested by a total stranger."

"But I'm almost guaranteed to increase my money four-fold," this naïve me would protest. "And I'd like to think I'm a good enough judge of human nature to know who I can and can't trust."

It almost makes me smile now, to think how self-confident I was back then. And to look at me now. Well, as the Good Book says, pride goeth before a fall, and fall I did. Right into the wretched hole from which I fear I may never climb out.

If only I could sleep. But the infernal noise won't let me. I refer not only to the several working men next door snoring away like approaching thunder, but also the scrawny old woman in the swaybacked, spring-screeching bed next to mine. Where the men rumble, Gertie makes a din not unlike a dull saw hacking at tin. Poor thing—she has had a hard life. I shouldn't begrudge her the little respite she has from it.

But because of her nocturnal racket, slumber and pleasant dreams escape me. When I drag myself out of my own sagging, decrepit bed at four in the morning, to bake the breakfast biscuits, I usually climb down the stairs bleary-eyed, foul-tempered, and a bit lame in the left leg.

And so I lie in bed all night, staring at the ceiling and going over and over again and again the chain of events that led me here, knowing that I have no one to blame but Jeanette Harrison for the state in which I find myself.

It was a lovely July morning in 1900, a Tuesday as I recall. I was busily typing out my shorthand notes from a board meeting of a charitable organization that helps indigent folks around St. Louis. Our office was in a shabby old building on the fringes of downtown, up on the fourth floor, the top floor—where it got blastedly hot in the summer. But it was still not unpleasant by about ten. My partner had gone to visit another regular client, and the two girls who typed for us part-time weren't expected in until after lunch.

I was banging away on my new Underwood, when I heard a rapping on the doorframe behind me.

"Hullo," said a woman's voice, a voice rich and melodious. "Excuse me."

Rolling my secretary's chair around 180 degrees, I caught sight of a middle-aged lady in a fancy gray dress, its collar and cuffs outlined in a lovely pink-colored piping. She had on a broad summer hat decorated with red feathers, and was a good deal shorter than me, and somewhat plump. A bit of perspiration glistened on her forehead, no doubt from climbing the stairs.

I hopped up from my chair. "Yes, ma'am. How may I help you?"

Removing her gloves, she stepped into the office and

smiled at me—a lovely smile, as it happened. "I was told that I could find the Summit Typing Bureau at this location. But the sign says…" She turned and peered at the door, which was open and extending into the office. "…Antonio Di Cicco, Attorney at Law."

"You'll have to forgive us," I said. "We just moved in a month ago and haven't gotten around to getting Mr. Di Cicco's name removed and our own painted on. At any rate, you've come to the right place. I'm Mrs. Harrison, one of the proprietors of the Summit Typing Bureau."

I offered my hand to her. She shook it once or twice, with a light grip that Daniel would have called "tepid." I noticed that she wore a rather gaudy diamond wedding ring.

"I am Mrs. Von Wassenburg and I am in need of someone who can type a dozen documents without so much as a single error."

She looked at me, not in an unfriendly way, mind you, but somewhat imperiously. She seemed a woman who was used to getting her way. The name was German or Austrian, and she had a trace of an accent. But her English was quite good.

"No erasures, Mrs. Harrison. No corrections with pencil. They must be absolutely perfect. Is this something that you would care to undertake?"

Before I answered that question, I needed to ask a few of my own.

"Can you tell me, Mrs. Von Wassenburg, about the nature of the documents?" Then it struck me that there was no reason to continue our conversation standing by the open door. I gestured for her to follow me to my desk and she sat down there in the straight-backed oak chair.

"Well," she said, putting her black beaded purse on my desk, "these will be copies of a brief prospectus that I wish to distribute among potential investors, in the form of a personal letter. May I tell you something in complete confidence?"

I nodded and said she could. The expression on her still-pretty face was one of satisfaction at her cleverness.

"I wish to create the impression that my husband and I are approaching each person purely as an individual. Each needs to think that he, or she, alone is being presented with this very fine opportunity. People like to think themselves special, you know, and this is a means of making that impression."

It sounded like a good tactic to me. "So folks will be more inclined to make an investment in your business, thinking they are the first to come aboard?"

She nodded. "That is the effect one hopes for."

"May I ask about the nature of your enterprise?"

She leaned toward me, as if she feared someone eavesdropping on us—though we were quite alone.

"Even as we speak, my husband is up in Alaska, where he has staked two claims a day's hike up off the Yukon River, a few dozen miles east of St. Michael. I hope you understand, Mrs. Harrison, that I cannot tell you the exact locations."

"Of course," I said. Though why she thought I might

have the means to dispatch claim-jumpers to Alaska in short order baffled me.

"We have resources of our own, Johann and I. But the cost in men, mules, and materiel to fully exploit these claims far exceeds what we can handle. So, while Johann is living rough up in Alaska, keeping an eye on things, I am visiting people I know in St. Louis, as well as in Chicago and Seattle. I am partway to getting the funds we need. Several more investors here would put us over the top."

"Well," I said, "good news indeed. I was under the impression, though, that the gold rush up north had waned."

She chuckled. "Mrs. Harrison, as my husband discovered, the gold does not know that. The gold keeps no schedule. It waits patiently in the ground until someone with grit and perseverance comes along with a shovel and a mule. Here, look."

She took her purse from the desk and reached into some pocket inside, searching. Withdrawing her clenched fist, she opened it, revealing a luminous yellow object about the size and shape of two peanut shells mashed together. She laid the object in my open palm.

I took a sharp intake of breath, realizing that the gold nugget in my hand represented many months of rent and food and clothing and books. It almost seemed to radiate warmth into my palm, like a little sun. The thing mesmerized me.

Mrs. Von Wassenburg beamed at me. "Beautiful, is it not?" And she was quite right. The gold nugget not only represented wealth and freedom, but was lovely to look at and to touch. I had never in my life held anything like it. Feeling a strange little pang of reluctance, I handed the lump of precious metal back to her.

"Yes, it is," I said. "Now, can you tell me how long the document is that needs typing?"

"I can do better than that," she answered, replacing the gold into its cavity in her purse. She pulled out a folded piece of foolscap and gave it to me.

Her gold-mining prospectus was written out in a loose, looping hand on the entire front side of the paper and part of the back. I estimated about eleven hundred words. There was some technical language in there, as well, that would require special care.

"How many copies will you need?"

"Six, to start with, Mrs. Harrison. To be delivered to me at the Planter's Hotel. I will pay you in cash when you bring them."

I told her how much her cost would be and she agreed instantly, handing me another, smaller sheet of paper with names and addresses on it. I recognized some of them as leading figures in St. Louis society; names I had seen many a time in the newspaper. Mrs. Von Wassenburg was nothing if not ambitious.

"I will send over the letterhead you are to use by courier," she said, rising to her feet. "Well, this has been a pleasure. I will see you in...?"

"Day after tomorrow, I should say. At two o'clock, if you'll be there."

She said she would and we went out into the hallway. I could feel the day's waxing heat coming deeper into the building. The thing most urgently needed for the office was an electric fan, but my partner was stubbornly resisting the extra expense.

"Let me walk you downstairs," I said.

She shot me a glowing smile. "How kind of you, Mrs. Harrison."

We started down, laughing and joking—quite pleased with ourselves. I jabbered away, making small talk about this and that, but my thoughts were with the nugget of gold and how wonderful it had felt in my hand.

If I had known at that moment what was to come, I would have taken the woman by her shoulders, shoved hard, and sent her tumbling down. To her death, I should have hoped.

There, at the bottom of the stairs, I couldn't get my mind off the feel of the gold nugget warming the palm of my hand. It had intoxicated me. Feeling the need for a treat, I ambled around the corner and bought a small package of chocolate candy from the confectionary. The owner there knows me well, chocolate being the one indulgence I cannot live without.

The rest of my day and the morning of the next day were devoted to a business meeting at an association of brewers in a fancy office building downtown. I took shorthand dictation in a rather palatial boardroom, then rushed back to the office to type it up for delivery bright and early on Wednesday.

I began on Mrs. Von Wassenburg's prospectuses that afternoon, and had them done by mid-morning the day after, a Thursday. It made me proud that she would not be able to find the merest hint of an error in the six copies; each, of course, addressed to a different individual. There had been two or three mishaps, but she had provided plenty of stationery with which to begin anew. It was a rather sumptuous cotton rag paper of cream color, with "Von Wassenburg Mining" and a New York City address printed on top in an elegant script. Even the watermark said "Von Wassenburg."

By the time I finished, I had almost committed the details of the Von Wassenburgs' prospectus to memory. It quoted the assays carried out at the two mining sites, which seemed most encouraging. It listed the costs in men and materiel needed to fully exploit the finds. It laid out a schedule for operations, once complete funding was secured. And it proffered a purchase of ten shares at a minimum at a cost of one thousand dollars per share. The Von Wassenburgs estimated that any investor getting in on the ground floor of the mining venture would at least triple his investment in a matter of two or three years.

The very idea of making so much money so quickly practically made my head spin. Stupidly, I began to wonder if I could raise ten thousand dollars to put into the enterprise—that is, if Mrs. Von Wassenburg would have me. The gold nugget still held me in its thrall and I felt eager to try my hand at making a small fortune. I hate to admit it, but I had become a little feverish, a little greedy.

I had just about finished the last prospectus, addressed to a leading philanthropist of the city, when I stood to stretch—sitting too long causes my left knee to stiffen sometimes. I went over to the window.

"Are you almost done with those letters, then, Jeanette?"

I turned around and saw my business partner, Mrs. Ruth Gardiner, standing just inside the door, putting her hat atop the coat rack. She was a tall, thin woman with a narrow face that looked rather severe in repose. But, in fact, she laughed a lot and very much enjoyed a good joke. We had both done typing from our homes and were introduced to each other by our Underwood dealer.

"Almost, Ruthie," I answered, stretching my arms up in the air. "I'm taking them to the client's hotel just after lunch. I promised them to her by two."

"What's the job about?" She came over to my desk and peeked down at the little pile of Von Wassenburg stationery.

"A kind of prospectus for investing in a gold mine up in Alaska."

"My goodness," she said, bending down for a closer look at the letterhead. "Does this have something to do with the Baroness Von Wassenburg?"

I gave her a surprised look. "Well, I just know her as Mrs. Von Wassenburg. Is she some sort of nobility?"

Ruthie put her hands on her hips and gazed at me rather sternly. "You don't read the society pages, do you? The baroness has been written up several times during her visit to St. Louis. She's quite the thing, apparently."

"If you'd like, you can tag along when I deliver the prospectuses."

"May I?" Ruthie asked, sounding a little giddy. "I've never met a baroness before."

"Until the other day," I confessed, "neither had I."

Ruthie and I arrived at the Planter's Hotel on North Pine a bit before two and made our way through the grand lobby to the elevator, and up to the sixth floor. We were greeted at the door of the baroness's suite by a slender, dark-haired young man who introduced himself as her son, Kurt Von Wassenburg.

Whether he was the heir to the title, I had no idea. I only know that he had dancing brown eyes and a very friendly manner. He asked us to seat ourselves and wondered if we would like to have some tea and chocolate while we waited for his mother, who was in another room with one of her potential investors.

Of course, I could not turn down the offer and helped myself to the most delicious chocolate creams I had ever tasted, imported, I was told, from Switzerland.

Mr. Von Wassenburg was perfectly delightful, an amiable conversationalist who managed to make two somewhat older ladies feel like the center of the world. He asked about our business and where we were from and about our families. He seemed especially interested to know that I was related to John MacDougall. I'm afraid I was guilty of name-dropping of the most shameless kind. I hadn't seen John in some time, but I so wanted to impress our host with the fact that I, too, had connections to the exalted world of high finance.

"The mining magnate John MacDougall is your relative?" he asked, sounding very impressed.

"Oh, yes," I replied. "John was married to my lovely cousin Alice, who unfortunately passed away several years ago. But I regularly correspond with his daughter, Mary, who is of course my first cousin, once removed."

You could almost see the glint in the young man's eyes. "I imagine Mr. MacDougall has more money than he knows what to do with," he said, in a German accent that seemed oddly thicker than his mother's. "If you are so inclined, please let him know about the Von Wassenburg mines. A sure way to turn ten thousand or twenty thousand into sixty or eighty thousand. You might even consider investing yourself, Mrs. Harrison. It takes only ten thousand."

Even though I *had* thought about it, when he said it, it sounded absurd. "If only I had that sort of money to gamble."

"Ah, but it is no gamble, Mrs. Harrison," the handsome aristocrat declared. "It is practically a sure thing. My father is staking the family honor on it."

Just then Ruthie leaned toward me—we were sitting next to each other on a fancy maroon velvet sofa—and whispered in my ear. "Perhaps we could go in together.

That way neither of us would have to risk as much."

Ten thousand dollars is an awful lot of money. Still, Ruthie's idea suddenly sounded feasible. My little house was paid for, but I supposed I could take a mortgage on it and extract some money. I had a tidy amount in the bank, as well.

I see now what a chuckleheaded fool I was. Having fallen in thrall to the Von Wassenburgs' charm, I began to think it quite reasonable to cash in my assets for this wonderful investment.

It was so intoxicating, being there in an opulent suite with a handsome young man who was plying us with chocolates and compliments. It was a milieu that seemed somehow within reach, once I had bought shares in the Von Wassenburg mines and tripled my investment. I suddenly could envision myself as a woman of independent means, booking grand accommodations at the Palmer House the next time I visited Chicago.

In the midst of my daydream, a door across the room swung open and out came the baroness and her visitor, an older gentleman. When she introduced him, I sucked in my breath. His name was immediately recognizable. He was a retired banker and one of the city's most noted philanthropists. It was exciting just to be in the man's presence. The baroness certainly had impressive connections. I had no doubt the banker would be one of the larger shareholders in her husband's mining venture.

"Ah, Mrs. Harrison," the baroness said, after she had shown the gentleman out. "Right on time. You have my letters?"

I said that I did, and handed her the folder. She flipped it open and leafed through the pages.

"It all looks in order." She turned to her son. "Kurt, will you give Mrs. Harrison her money. Twelve dollars, I believe it was?"

While Kurt, as he insisted we call him, went for my payment, I introduced Ruthie to the baroness. When her son returned, he handed me the money, then whispered in his mother's ear. She looked at us and her face brightened.

"My son tells me, ladies, that you yourselves might have some interest in taking part in our little enterprise. Is that right?"

I felt a bit intoxicated, and so, apparently, did Ruthie. We nodded and said that we did, but that it might take a little time to gather our finances.

"Well, we have sold about half of the shares that we are prepared to offer," the baroness said with a satisfied smile. "And I expect the rest will go quickly, once we distribute these beautifully typed prospectuses. So if you really mean to invest, my dear ladies, you must not dally."

And so began what would eventually become the train wreck of my brief career as a financial speculator.

After Ruthie and I left the baroness's suite, we immediately began to make our plans. She would need to discuss the investment with her husband over the weekend and hoped to put together perhaps two or three thousand dollars.

I, on the other hand, was free to do whatever I wished with my money. That, at least, is an advantage of being a widow.

I spent Saturday morning with pencil and paper, calculating what I might do with the money we would make from our investment. I intended to earmark some for our business, with the hope of expanding the number of customers we could service by hiring full-time help. And of course I would use some of the money to travel. I had been to Chicago several times, but never to New York. I wondered how much a journey to London and Paris would cost.

My head was still in the clouds when the doorbell rang and a messenger handed me a letter. It was an invitation from Kurt Von Wassenburg to join him that evening for dinner. His mother was otherwise occupied so we would be dining alone in the fine restaurant at the Planter's Hotel. Naturally, I sent the messenger back with a positive reply. How excited I felt!

I spent the afternoon deciding what to wear. I did not have many party costumes, but I did find a dress that I had worn occasionally when Daniel was still alive. He always said it highlighted my best attributes. He very much appreciated my figure, which needs no corset to achieve the desired shape. Looking in the mirror at myself, I was pleased to see that it still fit me perfectly. I might even have hoped to turn a few heads as I came into the dining room.

Kurt evidently agreed with my assessment, as he greeted me with an intake of breath and an admiring look up and down. "Jeanette," he said, "I barely recognized you. You light up the room in that dress."

The evening continued on in that vein. Courses and drinks mixed in with conversation and flirtation. I was very flattered by Kurt's attention. Caught up in the gaiety of the evening, I'm afraid I drank a wee bit too much. That's why I was so free with the information I gave him about John MacDougall and his daughter. I am ashamed to admit that I even told him exactly what street they lived on up in Duluth, and where their apartment was in St. Paul, Minnesota.

"I expect that a young woman with Mary's wealth has to fight off potential suitors," he observed.

"I should imagine so," I remember saying over my third or fourth glass of wine. "She is quite lovely, although I don't think she realizes it. There's something of the tomboy about her."

From there the conversation went on to travel and theater, of which the man was quite a connoisseur. While he certainly could have taken advantage of me later that evening, Kurt acted the perfect gentleman, sending me home in a hansom cab and vowing to see me again soon. When I woke up the next morning, my head was aching. It wasn't until afternoon and a few cups of good strong coffee that I was again able to go over the figures I had come up with regarding my shares of the gold mine venture. I was anxious to hear what Ruthie thought she could scrape together.

But Monday morning, as soon as I returned to the office from a meeting for which I had taken shorthand notes, Ruthie took me aside, so that our two part-time girls couldn't overhear us. She looked crestfallen.

"I'm so sorry, Jeanette, but Philip says no. He is quite sure that the baroness is on the up and up, keeping company with…" And she said the name of the retired banker whom we had seen in the baroness's suite. "But two or three thousand is an awful lot of money to risk on a gold mine venture in far-away Alaska. It took us a lot of sweat and quite a few years to get comfortable again after the last depression. Philip doesn't want to speculate with our hard-earned money. I'm sorry, Jeanette. So sorry."

I had calculated what I could bring to the table. A new mortgage on my house in the amount of four thousand dollars might be possible and my savings account of two thousand would bring the amount up to six thousand—still four thousand short. There was my equity in the typing agency. But I was reluctant to draw upon that—even if Ruthie was willing to buy some or all of it.

It so happened over the next few days I was able to secure commitments for three thousand dollars from several of my friends. But, of course, that still left me a thousand short. My dream of making a killing in Alaskan gold was not to be. That was when I received a message from Baroness Von Wassenburg that she needed more copies of her prospectus letter, and could I please do them quickly?

When I delivered them, I found her having tea by herself. I was disappointed Kurt wasn't there. I had rather hoped to see him again, and would not have said no if he had asked me to dinner a second time. I confess that I had so enjoyed spending those hours in the company of such a handsome young man.

The baroness took the newly typed letters and paged through them, examining each sheet carefully. "Your work is quite excellent, Mrs. Harrison. You would not believe the trouble we have had from typists in other cities. I am so much in your debt."

Startled by her generous praise, I thanked her profusely and wondered if, perhaps, she might write a brief testimonial on behalf of the Summit Typing Bureau. She said she would be happy to and would mail it to me.

I thanked her one more time, and started to leave.

And, oh, how agreeable my life would have been if I had just kept walking!

But I turned back. "I had hoped to raise the ten thousand you require, Baroness. But I am afraid I haven't been able to do so."

From her chair, she gave me a look of what almost seemed motherly concern. "I am so sorry to hear it, Mrs. Harrison. We are almost entirely subscribed and another two or three investors is all that we need."

I mustered up the happiest smile I could. "I hope your husband strikes a very rich vein, and that all your investors reap handsome benefits. Please give my regards to your son." I then turned to leave.

"Just a moment."

I faced the woman again, wondering what she wanted.

"How much can you invest, then?"

"I don't have it in hand, but I'm certain I could raise nine thousand."

She motioned me to sit in the chair opposite hers. Putting her hand to her chin, she regarded me in an almost affectionate way. I could tell that in her younger days, she must have been quite a beauty.

"Now this is just between the two of us," she said, practically in a whisper. "I have made no exceptions for anyone else. But in your case, because you have been so helpful to us, I would be happy to take an investment of nine thousand dollars. That will get you nine shares in Von Wassenburg Mining."

For a second, I almost felt the room spin. My delight at her acceptance was suddenly overshadowed by the realization of what I was agreeing to. I would be committing every cent of cash I had to this enterprise—and the hard-earned money of my friends. I told her it would take me a few days to get the money and bring it to her in the form of a cashier's check. Then I steeled myself for what I needed to do.

"Nine thousand dollars is an awful lot of money," I said with a certain timorousness.

"Indeed, it is," the baroness agreed.

"Before I collect the funds, may I ask if you possess any references that I might review?" I was almost afraid she would call me an ungrateful wretch and throw me out.

"Very sensible of you to ask," she said. "And we have such documentation for our investors. If you will wait here, I shall fetch the material."

The portfolio she handed me contained letters from bankers in New York, Chicago, Philadelphia, London, Berlin, and Munich that confirmed the probity and credit-worthiness of the baron and baroness—though, of course, I could not read what the German bankers said. There were testimonials from earlier business partners. There were clippings from newspapers about the couple's mining venture. Several letters recounted how pleased their authors had been to invest in an earlier enterprise involving a railroad. There was a document in German describing the noble lineage of the Von Wassenburgs, with an English translation.

It was all very impressive and reassuring. And I remembered having met the prominent retired banker in this very room just a few short days ago. More than anything, his involvement convinced me to take the plunge and invest in the gold mines. For if such a distinguished gentleman was doing business with the baroness, was that not a ringing endorsement of the investment's safety?

Convinced of her trustworthiness, I handed the portfolio back to her. Then I asked her a little favor.

"May I see the gold nugget again, Baroness?"

She smiled and laughed. "Of course."

Like a damned fool, I stood there wearing a stupid grin, fondling in my hand the very instrument of my own destruction. But the little thing was so lovely, so smooth, so warm, so seductive, that I held no thought in my head of doing anything but moving forward.

When I presented the baroness with the cashier's check the next week, she sent Kurt down to the hotel offices to fetch the bookkeeper, who happened to also be a notary. While we waited, she took a blank certificate of stock ownership for Von Wassenburg Mining and filled in my name, my address, and the number of shares that I had purchased. She signed and dated the form, and when the bookkeeper arrived, he notarized it.

"Now before you go," the baroness said, "I am going to provide you with the information that you will need in exercising your ownership of this investment. How to contact Von Wassenburg Mining. As well as our own personal addresses in New York, London, and Munich. In the event that you wish to sell your shares, instructions are provided. We, meaning Von Wassenburg Mining, ask only that we be provided with the right of first refusal."

"Meaning," I said, "that I first offer to sell the shares back to you?"

"Correct. You will receive quarterly reports on the progress of the mines and, God willing, in two or so years you will begin to receive annual dividend checks. And that is not counting the appreciation of the value of your shares."

On a blank sheet of the same letterhead that she had given me to type her prospectuses, she wrote down her various addresses and brief instructions for selling the stock. She also asked for the addresses of my business and my home.

I shook the woman's hand and started to leave. But before I was out the door, Kurt took me aside and asked if I would again do him the honor of dining with him some evening next week. I said of course, it sounded wonderful. He said he would send a note with the date and place.

I can tell you, I left the hotel walking on a cloud. Confident in the knowledge that I was quite the canny investor to have hitched my wagon to the Von Wassenburgs, and giddy at the prospect of another evening with Kurt. It was not until the weekend that I realized I had forgotten another, far smaller financial transaction involving the baroness: I had neglected to collect the twelve dollars that she owed me for the second batch of letters.

My work the following Monday required me to be a few blocks from the Planter's Hotel, so I decided to stop and collect my small debt. The hotel elevator was not in operation, due to a mechanical fault. So, huffing and puffing, I mounted the six flights of stairs and found myself at the door to the baroness's suite. It was open and a maid's cart, full of its linens and supplies, was parked in the hallway. I rapped lightly on the doorframe and the maid appeared. She was a young black woman.

"Yes, ma'am?" she said. "How can I help you?"

"I just came to call on the Baroness Von Wassenburg. I

have some business I need to conduct with her. If she isn't here, perhaps her son could help me."

Thinking back on it, the maid's reaction was almost comical. Her expression gyrated between amusement and discomfort, in equal measure; as if she didn't know quite what to say.

"Is there a problem?" I asked.

She raised her eyebrows. "Guess you could say that, ma'am."

"What is it? Has the baroness taken ill?"

She looked up and down the hallway. "You won't tell anyone I told you, will you?"

I shook my head. "Of course not."

"Well, yesterday a gentleman comes here with a policeman…"

I could feel my blood beginning to go cold.

"But the room was empty. Everyone had skedaddled."

"Why did the police want to talk to the Von Wassenburgs?" I asked apprehensively.

"They found out the son and mother—only she isn't his mother—are some kind of swindlers getting thousands of dollars off of rich white folks."

Then she saw my ashen face and looked embarrassed, as though she sensed my situation.

"Sorry, ma'am, I didn't mean any offense."

"No offense taken," I mumbled. "You say the baroness is not Kurt's mother?"

She shook her head. "No. They say he's her lover. And she's sure not royalty. She's from New York City."

My knees nearly buckled.

"And has anyone seen the baroness…the woman?"

"Not since yesterday morning," the maid said, shaking her head. "She still owes the hotel for two weeks of accommodation."

As you can imagine, I left the place in a daze. For several minutes, I leaned against a light pole, shaking my head and repeating, "Stupid woman, stupid woman."

I finally remembered the banker I had seen in the hotel room. The one whose involvement had clinched the deal for me. Surely he could offer some advice on what to do. He probably already had his lawyers working on getting his money back.

The financial institution he founded was five blocks away. I ran as fast as I could down the street, no doubt alarming several other pedestrians along the way. I was panting by the time I climbed the steps. I immediately went to the first desk I saw and asked if the banker perhaps still kept an office there. "Why, yes he does," the skinny, bespectacled clerk said. "But I'm afraid he spends his summers up at his lake cottage in Wisconsin." He then nodded up at a portrait hanging on the wall.

A gold plate attached to the frame identified the subject as the founder of the bank. He was a very distinguished gentleman, but in no way did he resemble the man to whom the baroness had introduced me. I almost laughed out loud. Jeanette Harrison was living proof of that famous P.T. Barnum dictum—there is a sucker born every minute. And I certainly was one of them.

Instead of taking the streetcar back to the office, I simply wandered on foot. For hours and hours. Along the way, I stopped at a tavern and fortified myself with two brandies. When I finally walked into the office at about five that afternoon, Ruthie and the two girls rushed to me, wondering where I had been. I was far too mortified to speak in front of the young women, but I took my partner aside and told her.

She had the look of someone who had just felt a bullet whiz by her left ear, and hit the person right behind. That would, of course, be me.

I went to the police, who took down my information, but could do nothing more than to promise to keep me informed. The detective I spoke with said they hoped to recover the tens of thousands taken by the "Von Wassenburgs." But he did not sound encouraging.

Bit by bit, the facts of the swindle came out in a series of newspaper articles. The baroness was known by several aliases—Jane Smithson, Serena Kotlikoff, Hilda Potter. Her so-called "son" Kurt was revealed to be an actor from Baltimore, Richard Prudhomme. The real Baron and Baroness Von Wassenburg did live in Munich, but neither of them had ever set foot on the North American continent. And there was no one up in Alaska wresting gold from the earth on behalf of them or the criminals who impersonated them.

With the enormity of the debacle spread out before me, I realized that the first thing I needed to do was pay back the good friends who had gone in for the last three thousand dollars. Since I had only a few hundred left in my bank account, I offered to sell my part of the bureau to Ruthie, and she accepted. Suddenly, I was an employee at the business I had co-founded and the owner of a house with a full mortgage. I went to work, aiming to climb up out of the hole I'd dug for myself.

What bothered me almost as much as losing my entire fortune, such as it was, was the thought that I had divulged so much information about John and Mary MacDougall to the shady man I thought was Kurt Von Wassenburg. Fortunately, John MacDougall was a canny man of business—I didn't for a second think that he could be drawn into any dubious scheme.

But Mary was but a child, not yet twenty years old. She always struck me as a levelheaded girl. But in the presence of an attractive, suave older gentleman, I don't know how susceptible she might be. I wrote to the MacDougalls regularly, as I always had done. But I did not have the courage to reveal what had happened, even though they ought to be warned. I was too big a coward.

So the days went on. Every night, as I sat alone in my little house, I would have a glass of brandy or gin. It had been my refuge after Daniel died and I believed I could control it. Later on it was two or three glasses. Sometimes I would run dry and walk to the tavern a block away.

The months dragged by. I began to get to work late, as

I slept off my liquor. Eventually I stopped going and rather quickly lost the house to the bank. I stayed in cheap boarding houses for a while, and spent many a night sitting in a train station to save money. I nearly froze my hands and feet some of those cold winter evenings and days. It was only good luck that saved me from harm on two or three occasions.

I was fortunate to talk to a man in a tavern who lived at a boarding house in a rough part of town, run by his sister. They needed someone to cook and clean and would offer room, board, and a few dollars a week. I agreed and ended up working harder than I ever have in my entire life. But I have managed to stop drinking, though it's still awfully tempting, I can tell you, to disappear into a bottle of brandy. Apart from death, it is the ultimate escape.

My friends no doubt wonder where I have gone, and why. I just cannot face them. I haven't written to the MacDougalls in quite some time now. Occasionally on my one evening off a week, I walk down to my old business, the one now owned by Ruthie Gardiner. I look up at those windows high above the street. I never see Ruthie—I always make sure it's well past closing time. And I let memories of better days flood over me.

I am content with my lot in life, which is of my own making. I am strong and I will survive. Sleep may be elusive, with old Gertie snoring the night away. But when I do fall asleep, I can still dream. And one thing I dream about is getting my hands around the throat of the "baroness." And squeezing. Squeezing. Squeezing.

Postscript

June 1902

I started writing this account some months ago to explain what had happened to me, in the event I died without giving witness. But it seems the tale is not quite over.

I had made another of my evening visits to my old business a month ago, on a beautiful May day. I had started the long walk home, pausing to look in a window that displayed lovely ladies' dresses, when I noticed someone across the street.

He was a slouching, shifty fellow standing in a store entrance, watching me. Clearly watching me. I had never seen him before. And as I started walking, he started walking, too. When I stopped, he stopped. Why was he stalking me?

I made my way home, using side streets and back alleys, assured that I had given him the slip. But a few mornings later, as I set out to run some errands for the landlady, I saw him again. He clung to me like a shadow as I went from store to store, then dropped out of sight as I came back home.

It troubled me a bit. But I figured that if he were going to attack me, he would have found better circumstances. And if he was intending to perpetrate some kind of scam on me—well, good luck to him. I had nothing to lose, as I already had lost it all.

I didn't see him again for several weeks. But just this morning, as I was helping to clean up the breakfast dishes, a knock came on the door. After a few moments, my employer came out to the kitchen. "Mrs. Harrison," she said in a disapproving tone, "you have a visitor. Whatever he wants, be quick. We have all the bedding to wash this morning."

I went into the parlor where my slouching, shifty shadow was waiting. By now I was more curious than afraid. What on earth did the man want of me?

"Mrs. Harrison?" he asked, giving me a thorough examination from top to bottom. He stood before me, hat in hand.

"Yes," I replied.

"Mrs. Jeanette Harrison?"

"That's me. What do you want?"

He looked a little amused at my irritation. "I am here on behalf of John MacDougall. He hired the detective agency that employs me to track you down, seeing as how you vanished, for all practical purposes."

"Oh," was all I could manage to say.

"I have notified Mr. MacDougall about your troubles and present situation, and he would like to help."

"He would?"

"Mr. MacDougall has authorized me to offer you the job of personal secretary to his daughter." The slouching detective thrust a white envelope at me. "This here is an open train ticket to Duluth and cash money to cover your expenses on the trip. The letter in the envelope explains the terms of your employment and your wages. He says you are to notify him of your decision as soon as is practicable."

The look on his face said I would be a damned fool to say no.

And so I will begin anew. Duluth is a charming town, as I recall from my earlier visits. After the turmoil of these last few years, handling social correspondence and appointments for my sweet young cousin Mary will seem quite refreshing.

Mary has a good head on her shoulders and all kinds of interests, one of which, by now, will no doubt be finding a suitable husband and starting her family. I can well picture myself as the sedate companion who will help her along that path. What a quiet, tranquil life it will be.

Acknowledgements

This book was made much better by the valuable insights and suggestions that came from my team of editors, beta readers, and proofreaders. Once again, I want to thank Marlo Garnsworthy, Kate Collins, Jeri Smith, Marie Joseph, and Sue Wichmann.

About the Author

Richard Audry is the pen name of D. R. Martin. As Richard Audry, he is the author of the Mary MacDougall historical mystery series and the King Harald Canine Cozy mystery series. Under his own name, he has written the Johnny Graphic middle-grade ghost adventure series, the Marta Hjelm mystery *Smoking Ruin*, and two books of literary commentary: *Travis McGee & Me* and *Four Science Fiction Masters*. You can follow D. R. at drmartinbooks.com.

If you enjoyed *A Daughter's Doubt*, be sure to read these mysteries by Richard Audry…

A Mary MacDougall Mystery Duet

by Richard Audry

The year is 1901 and young Mary MacDougall has a rather improbable ambition—to become a consulting detective. *A Mary MacDougall Mystery Duet* features the two cases that establish her as a force to be reckoned with.

In the first novella, *A Pretty Little Plot*, Mary's painting instructor is charged with kidnapping two of his students. And it's up to Mary to save him or condemn him. The second novella, *The Stolen Star*, follows Mary as she unpeels layers of deceit and duplicity during a snowy Christmas season, in the hunt for a purloined and very valuable sapphire.

In addition to the paperback and Kindle edition of Duet, *both* A Pretty Little Plot *and* The Stolen Star *are available separately as e-books.*

The Karma of King Harald

by Richard Audry

When springtime arrives in picturesque New Bergen, so too do the tourists and antiquers. This year, though, there are some unwelcome visitors. Extortion. Arson. And murder.

Join Andy Skyberg and his crime-sniffing mutt King Harald as they embark on their very first mystery adventure.

Available as a paperback and in various e-book editions.

King Harald's Heist
by Richard Audry

As the leaves begin to change color in New Bergen, Andy Skyberg wants to turn his full attention to his sister's new restaurant—and to the beautiful Finnish architect who's managing the project.

But Andy's big ol' mutt King Harald has a kennel full of trouble in store for him, beginning with a pilfered thousand-dollar bill and a naughty garden gnome. Before long, the crime-sniffing pooch finds even more deep doo-doo to toss his boss into.

Available as a paperback and in various e-book editions.

Smoking Ruin
by D. R. Martin

Minneapolis P.I. Marta Hjelm failed to prevent a murder that was waiting to happen. Her guilt has brought her right to the edge of burnout and dropout. But a prize specimen from her ancient past—her cheating ex-husband—appears out of nowhere with a gig too good to turn down. One last job, Marta figures, can't hurt. But hurt it does, as Marta tries to make sense of a terrorist plot at a major ad agency.

Available as a paperback and in various e-book editions.

27302367R00176

Made in the USA
Columbia, SC
24 September 2018